TAKE
ME
OUT
THE
BACK

Carolyn Geduld

Black Rose Writing — Texas

ISBN: 978-1-68433-509-1
PUBLISHED BY BLACK ROSE WRITING
www.blackrosewriting.com

Printed in the United States of America
Suggested Retail Price (SRP) $18.95

Take Me Out the Back is printed in Baskerville

*As a planet-friendly publisher, Black Rose Writing does its best to eliminate unnecessary waste to reduce paper usage and energy costs, while never compromising the reading experience. As a result, the final word count vs. page count may not meet common expectations.

Grateful acknowledgement is made to the following for previously published chapters:

Not Your Mother's Breastmilk: "The Coroner" published under the title "The Pink Envelop," April 26, 2019

Otherwise Engaged: A Literature and Arts Journal, Volume 3, Summer 2019: "The Administrator" under the title "Mother's Instinct," May 22, 2019

Pennsylvania Literary Journal: An Avalanche of Reviews, Poetry and Stories: Volume XI, Issue 1, Spring 2019: A different version of "The Mayor" was published under the title "The Timid Mayor," June 3, 2019

Dime Show Review: "The Obsessed" under the title "Eternal Love Forever," June 12, 2019

Dual Coast (Prolific Press): "The Visitor" published under the title "The Compliment," June 19, 2019

The Writing Disorder: "The Receptionist" under the title "Sore Throat," June 21, 2019

Scarlet Leaf: "The Records Keeper" under the title "The Rash," September 5, 2019

Persimmon Tree: "The Wife" under the title "The Bad Thing," September 17th, 2019

Children, Churches, and Daddies: "The Political Advisor," February 1, 2020

ACKNOWLEDGEMENTS

To Rabbi Leon Olenick, for starting me on my writing journey.

To Christina Ryan, whose love and encouragement is the pillar that has held me up.

To Michael Taft, for the patience to read every word as soon as it was written.

To my writing group for their constant support: Richard Balaban, Julie Bloom, Jackie and Leon Olenick, and Audrey Heller.

To my readers: Rich Balaban, Sue Swartz, Pat Medland, Paula Gordon, Jo Baum.

To those who cheered me on, including Sarah Frommer, John Woodcock, Doreen Cole, Ryan Cole, George Stern, Carl Stern, Renate Peters, and the Bloomington Writers' Guild.

To Ryan Cole, for publishing advice.

To my sons, Daniel and Marcus Geduld and my granddaughter Violet Geduld, for giving me a reason to write.

To my husband, Harry, who is remembered.

To David King and the Black Rose Writing team.

For my brother, Michael Taft

and

In Memory of those who died tragically and unnecessarily
in the course of a mass shooting

TAKE
ME
OUT
THE
BACK

CONTENTS

I. THE SHOOTING

1. THE MAINTENANCE MAN

"I promise. I'll never put you in a nursing home."

The Maintenance Man was on his knees in front of his mother, who was seated in her recliner. He held both her tremulous hands. Her fingers fluttered like moths against his palms. She stared straight ahead, towards him. Her lips quivered, as if she were about to say a tearful endearment.

He worked at one of the top-rated dementia nursing homes in the state, yet he could not afford the fee for his own mother, herself a victim of Alzheimer's, to be placed there. Not that he would put her there or in any nursing home, even if he could afford it. You took care of your own. Some people just dump their elderly parents anywhere, as long as they do not have to take care of them themselves. As if a fancy place made it okay when it was just plain wrong.

He and his sister, Flo, disagreed about that. She would put their mother into a more affordable facility and even thrust brochures from nursing homes into his hands. But he had Power of Attorney, not her, so it was his decision. Mom lived at home with him. Flo came over during the day to change Mom's Depends and cook her burgers and chicken noodle soup. He took over as soon as he returned from work, washing the dishes and getting Mom ready for bed.

"Wake up. Mom doesn't know either of us. She doesn't know where she is or that Dad is dead. *She's not there anymore.*" His sister pointed her finger at him, scolding.

"How do you know that, Flo. Can you prove Mom doesn't know us? Just because she can't speak doesn't mean she can't hear, doesn't mean she can't understand."

"She has a blank stare."

"I don't think so. When I talk to her about things, like how my boss gets on me at work, she looks me in the eye and frowns, sometimes. I think she's in there. She just has trouble letting us know."

"She always frowns. You're in denial. She belongs in a nursing home."

"Oh, you'd like that! Then you could stay at home and watch Judge Judy all day instead of taking care of the woman who raised you."

After Flo grabbed her car keys and left in a huff, he talked to Mom.

"Don't worry, Mom." He curled his hand around hers. "I'll never leave you. We're both going to stay right here, at home. Both of us."

She was a frail slip of herself, over ninety years old, in her blue cardigan and darker blue stretch pants, looking at him—or in his direction, Flo would say.

He never married or lived anywhere but with his parents, and then with his mother after his father passed away, a good twenty years ago. Unlike Flo, who moved out when she was less than eighteen, unable to wait a minute longer to get away. She did not know Mom nearly as well as he did. He had been with Mom every day for close to sixty-five years.

He knew in his bones that Mom understood him. They always had a special relationship. When Dad was alive, he complained that they were too close, that he should get out of the house, meet women, get married, have a life. Sometimes Dad banged his fist on the table.

The Maintenance Man was good with his hands. That was his excuse.

"I'll look for an apartment as soon as I finish the bathroom remodel" or "Let me just tile the kitchen, and then I'll investigate rentals." There was also dry walling the basement, insulating the attic, and re-staining the deck, not to mention resurfacing the driveway and putting new sod on the lawn's bald spots.

After Dad suddenly died in his sleep, the Maintenance Man was not about to leave Mom alone. As the years went by, she slowly became forgetful. Sometimes she confused him with his father and Flo with her sister. There came a time when she stopped saying their names. It was possible she did not remember their names. And she was growing quieter. By her late eighties, she was no longer speaking or doing much of anything. She needed round-the-clock care.

He wondered if he would have to retire early when Flo stepped up to the plate. She was older than him and already collecting her pension.

"I can just as well do nothing with Mom as I can at my own house. That's not to say I agree Mom should still be at home, but as long as you insist on it, I'll do my share."

He knew his mother so well that even after she stopped speaking, he could tell what she was likely to be thinking, what she would likely say if she still had a voice. Often, when they were alone, he had conversations with her in which he spoke for her. As best he could, he imitated her manner of speaking.

"Don't listen to Flo, Mom. You know I'll never put you in a nursing home."

"You're such a good boy, Sidney." He raised his voice an octave when speaking as her.

"Even if I could afford the place where I work, I'd still keep you at home with me."

"I'll stay right here until you decide what's best."

That brought a twinkle to Mom's eyes. They both knew she was not going anywhere.

Years ago, whenever Mom and Dad learned someone they knew had dementia, they both said, "If I ever get like that, take me out the back and shoot me." They joked with each other about which one should shoot the other first. If, for instance, one of them forgot someone's name or the title of a movie, they said the same joking things.

"Now, what was the name of that Hitchcock movie about the hotel?" Dad said. "It's on the tip of my tongue. If this keeps up, you'll just have to take me out back and shoot me."

"I can't believe I lost my purse again," Mom said. "Next time you'll just have to take me out back and shoot me."

After Dad died, Mom continued to joke the same way. But it did not seem as funny.

When Mom became forgetful, a neurologist tested her. It turned out that Mom had a Mild Cognitive Disorder. It was likely to progress to a full-blown dementia, probably Alzheimer's, in time. When she heard that, she said the familiar words.

"Just take me out back and shoot me."

Was this still a joke? He discussed it with Mom several times over the years.

Before and even after she lost her speech, she always said the same thing.

"When the time comes, you'll know what to do, Sidney. I won't have to tell you."

He knew there would come a day when Mom's dignity declined. He saw it at work. The residents who no longer looked presentable, who were skeletal or catatonic, who could not get out of bed, who were on their last legs, were shuffled to the back rooms. The casual visitor did not see them.

With this in mind but without any clear plan, he decided to buy a handgun online. He was surprised to discover this was legal in Indiana. All he had to do was cough up three or four hundred dollars. He would easily pass a background check. He had never had so much as a speeding ticket. Choosing a weapon from an online store, he put it with the appropriate ammunition in the cart, and clicked on "buy." A package would come in the mail in a week or so.

"When the time comes, you'll know what to do, Sidney. I won't have to tell you."

When the gun arrived in a plain unmarked box, Flo was there to accept the delivery.

"What's this?"

"Books."

"Since when do you read books?"

"I'm thinking Mom might like me to read to her."

"Nonsense," Flo guffawed.

After she left, he put the package on the top shelf of his closet knowing that, even if Flo searched, she was too short to reach it.

The next day, one of the residents at work had a seizure in the cafeteria, and there was general unrest. The staff had their hands full. He noticed the nurses' station was unattended. No one was paying attention to him. He slipped behind the desk and snatched a container of Haldol. This was a medication he had heard of. Many of the residents were given a dose of it if they needed sedation.

Later, at home, he placed the Haldol on the same shelf as the package containing the gun. After dinner, he talked to Mom about what had happened that day, omitting the part about the medication he had stolen.

"The resident who had a seizure has no dignity left, Mom. He used to be a famous scientist, but he isn't himself anymore. What do you think, Mom?"

"You know what I think, Sidney."

"The Bible says we are all worthwhile. We are all created in God's image. But what if some people are no longer in that image? What if they're so far from who they once were that they're not even human?"

"That's a thought, son."

"What if they don't recognize anyone anymore, and they aren't recognizable to anyone either?"

"What to do in that case is obvious. You know it is."

He put his large head in his hands.

"I'm not sure."

"Soon you'll be sure. You'll do the right thing."

"Mom, you know I wouldn't want to hurt you."

"You'll figure out a way not to hurt me. Soon. Soon."

He had some vacation days to use before the end of the year.

"You should get out of town when I take time off," he told Flo. He himself wanted nothing more than to spend his days at home. He did not want to leave Mom.

Flo reluctantly agreed and leafed through cruise brochures.

"Soon," Mom was saying whenever it was just the two of them. "Soon."

If he were to do it, it would be during the week Flo was gone. There might not be another chance for a very long time.

But how could he live without Mom? The idea made him panic. Maybe it was better to have a little bit of the person Mom used to be—and maybe still was, hidden deep inside of herself—than no Mom at all.

He was so stricken by the thought of not having any Mom at all that he openly wept.

"I'll always be with you. You're still my baby boy. You know what you have to do."

Finally, the day arrived when Flo was to take her trip. She had given him her itinerary and contact information. Then she had the taxi stop off at the house on the way to the airport.

"Are you absolutely sure you can manage without me?"

"I'm sure."

"It's not too late for me to cancel if you have any doubts."

"Just go. Have a good time. You deserve it, Sis." He patted her on the back to reassure her.

Flo returned to the taxi and went. He was alone with Mom.

The next day, he brought the package down from the closet shelf and opened it. As soon as he saw the gun, something dropped in his chest. Quickly, he re-wrapped the package and put it back. He lay face up on the bed, staring at the overhead light fixture.

"Soon. Soon," he heard Mom saying, even though she was in another part of the house, in her bedroom. It seemed, however, she was right next to him, whispering in his ear.

"Be my good boy. You know what to do."

He had a strange sensation, as if there were deep cuts on his body, and the blood was pouring out. It was like an emptying, a hollowing. In this state, he got up and took the package down again. Because he was good with his hands, he unpacked the gun and loaded it without reading the instructions. He did not think. All he did was listen to Mom. She told him what to do.

"Take the pills into the kitchen and put them in the coffee grinder, son. All of them. Then get the hot cocoa mix from the pantry and follow the directions on the package. When the cocoa is ready, stir in the ground pills."

He took the Haldol into the kitchen and dumped the pills into the coffee grinder. Then he got the cocoa mix and wiped his streaming eyes on his sleeve so he could read the directions. If Mom's voice had not been right next to his ear, urging him on, he might have passed out.

Then he went to get Mom.

"It's time, Mom."

"You're my good brave boy."

"Let's button your cardigan so you won't be cold."

"You know what to do."

He lifted Mom and carried her out to the back yard, setting her down on a lawn chair.

"I better get you a shawl. It's cooling off."

He went back into the house for a shawl and the cocoa. Back outside, he gently wrapped the shawl around Mom's shoulders.

"Thank you, son."

But then a spell of weeping came over him, and he stood there, holding the mug.

"Be careful, Sidney. You don't want to spill the cocoa." Mom was a bit sharp.

"Okay." He sniffled. "I'm okay now."

He held the cocoa to her lips, and she slowly drank it. He heard her singing while she drank. An old song she sang to him when he was a boy.

You are my sunshine, my only sunshine.

You make me happy when skies are gray....

Several minutes later, Mom closed her eyes. It was close to sundown. He still heard Mom's voice.

"You have to wait until it's dark, son, so the neighbors won't see. "

He sat on a lawn chair next to Mom. He held her tiny hand. The fluttering was slowing. Her fingers relaxed. He closed his eyes. Maybe he dozed off because when he opened them, it was dark. The neighboring houses were invisible. He assumed no one could see into the yard since there were no lights.

Mom's head was tilted back. Her jaw had dropped. Her raspy breath paused for several seconds, then resumed. He rose and took the mug into the house. In the kitchen, he washed and dried it and put it away. He put the cocoa box back in the pantry. Then he went to his room to get the gun and a pillow.

He hoped what he had seen in the movies—a pillow used to muffle the sound of a gun—was correct. But he did not much care. If he had to lose Mom, it did not matter to him if anyone heard the shot.

"Just take me out back and shoot me."

Without turning on any light, he went back to the yard. With Mom's words of encouragement in his ear, he braced the pillow against the back of her head with the gun and pulled the trigger. Then he went back in the house and waited. He did not hear anything. Maybe the gun did not go off. He could not remember if it did, or it didn't. He had to find out. He could not allow Mom to remain outside without being sure.

Hunting through the kitchen cabinet draws, he found the flashlight. He was surprised to see the gun was still in his hand. Should it be? Back outside, he turned the flashlight beam in the direction of Mom and approached. Something was very wrong with her face. Immediately, he turned off the beam. He stood for a moment listening. There was no sound of raspy breathing.

"You're my good boy. My very good boy."

He went back in the house and put the flashlight away.

"What should I do now, Mom?"

"You know what to do, son."

He went out to the carport and got into his Ford. All those poor people where he worked, lying in the back rooms without any dignity, with no one to do what needed to be done. He drove the familiar route on automatic pilot. It would be lightly staffed at night. He parked, keyed himself in, and walked down the corridor as he so often did. When he passed the nurses' station, he waved at the night nurse, who had seen him whenever there was an after hours need for maintenance.

Making his way to the back of the building, he checked the ammunition. He figured he needed ten bullets. Or was it called "rounds." When he reached the back units, he went from room to room. Without bothering to use a pillow, he shot each resident once in the back of the head. He closed his eyes each time to avoid seeing the result.

When he was finished, he walked out the back door. The gun was still in his hand. He sat on one of the benches designed for residents. The faint wail of a siren blared in the distance. He was calmer now, more alert. Never had he felt—he had difficulty finding the words to describe it—more like his true self.

As the sirens grew louder, he knew what he had to do. Raising his now unloaded gun and pointing it toward the back door, he said:

"Take me out the back and shoot me."

II. DURING

2. THE WITNESS

Cat waited in the Camaro, reapplying mascara, in the nursing home's tiny visitors' parking lot. It was close to ten at night, and hers was the only car there. It had been parked near the entrance so her husband, Buddy, could run in to make a late delivery. The flowers for some old person's birthday were already wilted from being left out of water for so long. Buddy had been promised two bottles of Jim Beam by his cousin, who was too wasted to do his job himself.

Another car pulled into the spot to her right. A man stepped out wearing the type of brown overalls maintenance workers or janitors wear. He held something in his left hand. Cat gasped. It was a gun, perhaps a Glock, the kind her father owned, although she could not tell for sure. But it surely was a handgun. She was able to get a closer look at it while the man closed his car door. He never looked her way. As he walked to the entrance and keyed himself in, he dangled the gun loosely at this side, not bothering to conceal it.

Immediately, she sent a text to Buddy, who was still inside.

9:40 p.m. Just saw a guy enter the building with a gun. Maybe a Glock. Get to safety. Fast.

Delivered. Read. The fuck!

She dialed 911 and told the dispatcher what she had seen. Cat was advised to stay on the line, but she hung up in order to try to reach Buddy. Several minutes went by. Everything was quiet. Cat sat in the car, clutching her make-up bag, listening. Then she heard it. *Pop. Pop. Pop.* She knew what the sound was right away.

"Buddy!" She called out. Then she began texting.

9:45 p.m. R U ok?????

Delivered.

There were more pops. Then silence. Cat exhaled in short, audible bursts. She slid onto the floorboard, scrunching herself up to fit. Hopefully, if there was any gunfire in the parking lot, she would be protected. She kept texting, but Buddy was not answering. Her phone rang. It was the dispatcher's number, not Buddy, so Cat did not accept it. She thought she counted ten pops. She tried to remember. Did Glocks take ten rounds or fifteen?

After the tenth pop, there was a strange quietness. In the distance, sounds of sirens were coming closer. Others inside must have also called 911. Cat kept expecting to hear screams. She was trembling. What would she do if Buddy were dead, or worse, lying in there dying, whispering her name?

Just then, she heard running. Raising herself just enough to peek out the passenger window, she saw several people rushing out the door. A couple wore the white button down dresses nurses wear. All were much younger than nursing home residents. She assumed they were staff. Buddy was not among them.

Cat was not big on religion even though she was raised in church. She needed to get right with God before expecting any miracles. Nevertheless, she began praying with her head on her knees.

Please, God, let Buddy be okay. We'll both be good from now on.

A police car screeched into the parking lot. The thudding of feet hurried toward the entrance. She saw the head of a deputy passing by the Camaro. Once he was inside, there was silence again for a tense two or three minutes. Then she heard a single shout, followed by a barrage of pops. Cat's teeth chattered.

She peeked again, just in time to see the front door flung open. Buddy came dashing out. He bounded to the car, got in the driver's seat, and peeled away. Luckily, the cop was still in the building. No one tried to stop him.

"Oh, my God! Oh, my God! I got it all, Cat!" Ragged panting punctuated his words.

As he drove away from the nursing home, a caravan of emergency vehicles going in the other direction forced him to slow down as they passed. That is when he took notice of Cat, who still sat on the floorboard.

"What are you doing down there?"

"Trying not to get killed, asshole." She was sobbing. "I was scared you were dead in there."

He pulled into a dark residential street and turned off the motor.

"C'mon, Babe. Get up. I'm okay. It's all okay."

Cat struggled up onto the seat. She looked at Buddy with a mascara-streaked face, checking him out. Then she threw herself on him, weeping. He held her close.

"Babe, it's not only okay. It's better than okay."

Better than okay? Cat pulled away, pushing her damp red curls out of her eyes.

"What did you do, Buddy?"

"I got the whole thing on my phone. The whole fucking thing!"

"What do you mean?"

"I videoed it, Babe. I had just done the delivery, and as I was stepping out the door of the room, this guy passes me carrying a gun. He doesn't even look at me. He's like in a daze or high or something. His eyes were real funny, like devil eyes. He just kept walking down the hall, not even fast."

"Oh, my God."

"I knew something bad was coming down. And I saw your text. I turned on the video on my phone and followed him. He never even turned around. It was like he didn't fucking care."

Buddy passed his phone to Cat. She turned on the recording. There was the back of the guy with the Glock slowly walking down a hall. He went into a room. The video turned toward him but only recorded darkness. The first *pop* was heard.

"That's not...he didn't..."

"Yeah, he fucking shot someone in there."

The video continued. The guy went into several more rooms, with the *pop* sound following. By the fifth room, Buddy decided to chance going into the doorway. For the next five rooms, the video captured the victims being shot in the head at close range. Their bodies jerked and spasmed after the blast, then lay still in their beds. The shooter passed right by Buddy without stopping, as if Buddy were not even there.

"Holy shit," Cat whispered.

"Wait. There's more."

The video followed the shooter outside the back door. He sat on a bench, waiting, still holding the weapon, still not appearing to notice Buddy. This continued for several minutes. Then, suddenly, the image turned toward the ground. The tips of Buddy's old beat-up sneakers could be seen as the view moved.

"You can see where I went to crouch behind this big fucking bush. I was hiding there when this cop burst in."

The video continued, showing the back of the deputy moving toward the shooter. He could be heard ordering him to drop his weapon. The video swerved until the shooter could be seen in front of the deputy. The shooter raised his Glock. There were a series of more *pops.* Then the image turned to the ground again.

"That's when I ran the hell out of there. I was scared I'd get my ass shot off."

"You idiot. You could've gotten yourself killed." She sobbed on Buddy's chest again.

Taking her chin in his fingers, he raised her head.

"Babe. See this?" He took his phone from her and held it up. "You know what this is?"

"Your phone?"

"This ain't just no phone, Babe. This is our ticket to Chicago."

"What do you mean?"

"This is like…like…fucking gold."

Cat sat up straight, staring at him. In the dim light, she could not read his expression. Was he messing with her or what?

"You said you wanted us to move to Chicago, didn't you? Huh? Well, I have the video of that guy shooting old people. And of him getting his ass killed by the cop. I'm going to sell this to the TV people, Babe."

"What? Are you crazy? You're asking for trouble, going to the news."

"No, Babe. The TV stations buy videos that regular people take. You know, like of tornadoes and stuff. I'm going to sell the footage of the guy killing those zombies in the nursing home."

He planted a kiss on the phone.

"How much you wanna bet we get a thousand for the video. Maybe five, ten thousand. That's dollars, Babe. I mean, guys have shot up schools and clubs, but this is the first time in a nursing home. I always knew I'd get lucky someday."

Cat turned in her seat and faced the windshield. Was Buddy onto something? Would they really be able to move to Chicago? Or was he going to do another stupid ass thing that would land him in trouble. And what about those people. They were dead. Murdered. There was something all wrong with Buddy's plan.

"So, like, how're you going to sell it?"

"The trouble with you is you don't watch TV enough, Babe. I've seen how in reality crime shows. You call the stations and ask for the news desks. You tell them what you have and send them, maybe, ten seconds of it. You know, like a preview in the movies. Then you negotiate. You name a price, they name a price. Just like scoring drugs."

Cat did not know what to say. She wanted to believe him. But there were so many times he had some scheme he was so sure of. Then it all went south, and he wound up doing time. If you added it all up, he had been inside more years than he had been outside. She could not figure out if this video thing was legit or not. Buddy made it sound good, but he always did. Cat decided her best bet was to wait and see.

"You gotta act fast with the media. The shooting will be in the next news cycle. I'll drop you off, Babe, then go get our thousands."

He let her off at the trailer they shared with her mother.

"Mom?" Cat called.

Her mother was already passed out on her LaZyBoy. Cat finished off the quarter inch of whiskey her mother left in a mason jar on the side table. She wished they had stopped and picked up the Jim Beam before Buddy went off to make his sale. Now she had nothing to do but watch TV. Searching under her mother, she found the remote. She clicked through to the news station. The anchor was talking about the shooting. There was video of the chaos in the parking lot that occurred after they left. The emergency vehicles they passed while speeding away were seen in the background, while those staff people who had not fled were being interviewed.

"I was never so scared…"

Buddy was right about one thing. There was no footage of the killings or of the shooter being killed by the cop. Nervously, she sat in the second

LaZyBoy, next to her mother, and waited. Her mother's purse was on the coffee table. She fished inside for a cigarette and lit up. Even though she was trying to quit, she figured this time would not count. She was way too stressed and did not want to go crazy. It would wake her mother.

The phone rang. It was the dispatcher again. Cat would have to get rid of her phone or the cops would find her. Maybe it was a mistake to call 911.

Several hours later, Buddy came back. He had a bottle of Jim Beam, but from the way he looked, Cat immediately knew he traded the second bottle to his cousin for a hit.

"What happened? Did you sell the video?"

"Get packed. We're leaving for Chicago right away. Hurry!"

"Buddy!"

He reached into his pocket, pulled out a few crisp bills, and held them out to her. She counted. Fifty dollars. Meanwhile, he was acting paranoid, turning off the lights, dashing from window to widow, and peeking out. She had seen him like this before, but never this bad.

"They said most of the footage was too graphic. They only took twenty seconds. They paid on the spot, so I gave them what they wanted. It's gas money for Chicago. Babe! Don't just stand there. We've got to go."

"Now? Let's get some sleep first. We can go in the morning."

Buddy opened the Jim Beam and took a long swallow.

"The thing is, Babe…you see…the fucking news desk. There was this guy there besides the news desk guy. I think he was FBI. He heard about the police shooting footage, and now he's after me to get it. He knows how much it's worth—probably fucking millions—and he wants it for the FBI."

"Buddy. You're paranoid from the hit. You aren't making any sense!"

"Don't argue, Babe. We've got to leave. Get in the car."

"We don't have enough money."

Seeing Cat's mother's purse on the coffee table, Buddy dumped out the contents and took the money.

"That's her Social Security!"

"She can get more cash from your brother. Let's go."

Cat knew that things would get worse if she resisted. She did not want him to slug her.

"Okay. Okay. But I'll drive. You're too high to drive."

Cautiously, looking out the door in all directions and not seeing the FBI, he sprinted to the car. After grabbing a few items of clothing and the rest of her mother's cigarettes, Cat followed.

It was almost daylight when Cat took the ramp to the Interstate heading north. Buddy was scanning the highway, twisting to see the road behind the Camaro. A green Ford passed them on the left.

"There. That one. It's the FBI. I saw the driver. He's the one who was at the news desk. The one who didn't say anything. He wants the phone, Cat."

Buddy began panting. A sickly smell arising from him spread through the car.

"Calm down. Put the phone in the glove compartment if you're worried."

"He's going to slow down until he is alongside us, and then he'll shoot me." His voice was a panicky higher pitch than usual.

"No, Buddy. He won't. It's an ordinary Ford. It's not the FBI."

But Buddy was not listening. He was folded over, with his head down as low as he could get it, sobbing out loud.

"It's all over. *Sob.* I didn't do fucking nothing. *Sob.* He's going to shoot me in the head. *Sob.*"

They were on route to Chicago. Cat knew Buddy would be out of his mind the whole way. But it was only paranoia. He would be fine by the next day. Their new life in the city would begin. It was what they had dreamed of. As long as they were together, the rest did not matter to Cat.

"Buddy will find a way to make it work."

That was the thought that kept her from losing it while the dispatcher's calls chased her all the way to the border of Illinois.

3. THE VISITOR

The Visitor fell into a light doze while spending time with her friend, the Russian Professor, in the Hospice section of the nursing home. This was not unusual. Her habit was to arrive after dinner and sit in the corner chair of the Professor's tiny room for two or three hours. Often, an aide shook her shoulder gently to see if she wanted to leave. Her friend would be asleep. He was seldom awake anymore.

On the last night she would ever see the Professor, a large man entered the room. Through half-opened eyes, she recognized the Maintenance Man. Perhaps the thermostat needed an adjustment. Without even glancing at her, he went directly to the Professor's bedside. A loud bang brought her to alertness. Briefly, there was jerking movement under the Professor's blankets. The Maintenance Man turned and walked out. A few seconds later, there was a bang from the next room.

The Visitor did not move. Her brain seemed frozen and unable to process what was happening. But then, she heard the Professor's accented voice, as it was before Alzheimers robbed him of speech.

"Leave right now. Go out the back door."

When the next bang occurred, she quickly rose and ran down to the enclosed garden out back. It was very dark outside. If there was an exit to the parking lot, she could not see it, even with her phone flashlight.

"Find the darkest bench and wait there."

She followed the Professor's instructions. Something frightening was happening in the building, but it was peaceful in the garden. It was the first time in a long time that the Professor spoke to her in whole sentences.

After several more bangs, the back door opened. She saw the silhouette of the Maintenance Man. He sat on the bench nearest the door. Several minutes went by without incident. Then he raised his arm. An object was in his hand that looked like a gun. The door opened again, and someone who might have been a police officer yelled.

"Drop your weapon!"

The Visitor saw that the Maintenance Man was not obeying. He did not drop anything. Another bang followed. The Maintenance Man fell off the bench and lay sprawled on the ground.

Then the Professor spoke once more to the Visitor.

"Clever."

It was a voice close to her ear. She patted the bench in case the Professor was sitting beside her, so close had the voice seemed. There was no one.

She heard that word the first time over twenty years before at the house of her former Russian Literature professor. She had never been to a professor's house before. It was a small gathering for his students. The Professor had singled out the Visitor by name and called her "clever." She was tempted to think there might be another young woman with the same name in the room. She actually looked around. But she was the only one.

No one had ever told her she was smart or clever or intelligent. She plodded along in her classes diligently, rarely being noticed. In fact, she could not recall ever having been complimented. Her mother was the stern sort, not given to affection and quick to criticize. She never knew her father.

"Clever." The word repeated in her mind over the years like a catchy tune. Had the Professor really called her "clever?" He had been talking about politics. She said something, she did not remember what, and he gave her the compliment. He looked straight at her. Not like most people, who looked over her shoulder or above her head when they spoke to her. With the Professor, she had the sense of being really seen. This made all the others look her way, at the quiet one who never spoke. She blushed.

The Professor was an old-fashioned gentleman. He bowed slightly when she rose to leave the gathering, causing a strand of his dyed black hair to fall forward onto thick eyebrows. Then he, who no doubt surrounded himself with people of the highest caliber, smiled at her. She, who was just an ordinary student, up until then nothing special.

She heard the word before. It was her mother who said, "You're getting to be too clever for your own good." If she tried to talk to her mother about something she learned in high school—the Civil War, the meaning of light years, algebra—or that she heard on the news, her mother responded with that expression.

That is why the Professor's opinion mattered so much. If he were just an ordinary person, like her mother, he could not decide she was clever. But he lived in a house filled with books in the part of town where all the professors lived. There was a grand piano in the front room, and a working fireplace. Real paintings hung on the walls, mostly portraits of people who might have been the Professor's relatives. Clearly, the Professor was an important educated man.

The morning after the gathering, the Visitor decided to drive by the Professor's house before going to class. She went around his block at normal speed, just to see what his house looked like in the daytime. It was an older two story brick residence with a tidy front yard. A wrought-iron fence surrounded the property. Although it was daylight, the curtains were still drawn. A newspaper lay across the front steps, not yet picked up.

She was satisfied. She had seen the house, inside and out. Secretly, she hoped the Professor would step outside in an elegant maroon robe. As he was bending to pick up the paper, he would see her. A smile of recognition would cross his face. Delightedly, he would wave at her, then beckon. She would park the car and get out.

"So pleased to see you. Will you please to join me for *coo*p coffee?"

She would ascend the stairs. He would hold the door open for her. Then he would gently take her by the elbow and guide her into a sitting room. He would excuse himself. A few minutes later, he would reappear with a coffee service.

"Now please to tell how you *coo*me to do clever remark *oo*ther evenin*k*."

But even though she returned for several mornings in a row, she did not see him. Each day, a fresh newspaper lay on the steps, suggesting that it was being picked up at a later time. On the third morning, she distinctly heard that word "clever" again just as she was driving past his front door. Surely, it was her imagination or perhaps a street noise she interpreted as the sound of the word. She stepped on the brake and looked around. The Professor was not outside. If he were peeking at her through the curtains and saying the word inside the house, it would not have been possible for her to have heard.

On succeeding days, there were times she heard the word and times she did not. It became part of her routine to detour to the Professor's street every day. Always, the curtains were drawn. Always, a fresh newspaper had been tossed on the front steps. The Professor did not appear, although she heard his voice. "Clever."

There came a time when the unexpected happened. As her car approached the house, she saw the door open. There was a pounding in her chest. For a moment, no one appeared. Then an orange-haired woman, about the Professor's age, came out and hurried down the stairs. Without pause, she got into the smart red Toyota at the curb, adjusted her long camel coat beneath her, closed the door, and maneuvered out of the parking space.

The Visitor gasped. She braked the car hard. Could this woman possibly be the Professor's lover? Was she the one who picked up the newspapers? She had to follow her and find out who she was. While driving, she sobbed out loud, wiping her face on her sleeve. That was *her* professor. The orange-haired woman had no right to be there.

Thoughts she knew to be ridiculous boiled up into her mind. She was no longer the Professor's student. He might not even remember her. She was blowing up his compliment into something it probably was not. A single word, said a single time. Yet, out of the Professor's presence, she heard him say it to her many times. That meant something, didn't it?

She drove right behind the orange-haired woman, not caring if it was nerve-wracking to tailgate. After ten minutes, the car pulled into the elementary school. The Visitor pulled in, too, and idled her car. The red Toyota parked in a space reserved for staff. The woman got out, her hair shining in the sunlight as she walked to the school and entered. The Visitor sat there without turning off the motor. The engine chugged, as if impatient. Digging her phone out of her purse, she googled the staff of the school. The orange-haired woman was a first grade teacher. Her photograph was posted in the directory. Her name was Irena Petrov. Petrov. What kind of name was that? Russian?

The Visitor guessed the Professor and Irena Petrov spoke to each other in their incomprehensible language. Even if she were with them, she would not be able to understand. She would be left out. Irena Petrov would be the one making clever remarks. The Visitor imagined the two of them sitting in the Professor's parlor, relaxed, smoking, the Professor laughing at the orange-haired woman's witticisms.

She had to get to the campus. Gunning the motor while thinking about Irena Petrov, she pulled out onto the road. She accelerated. Speed was the only thing that gratified her, the feel of the car barreling along the blackened pavement, pulling away from the school fast. Her teeth clenched as if biting. Her nostrils flared with forced exhalations.

During her classes, she could not concentrate. All she could think of was of Irena Petrov. It was no doubt because of her that she had not heard the Professor's compliment that day. What if she prevented the Professor from ever saying the compliment again? The Visitor was horrified by this thought. Maybe the Professor would want to say it, except then Irena Petrov would get angry. She might make a sarcastic comment about the Visitor that would be wounding to the Professor. She would deny the Visitor what was rightfully hers.

This was intolerable. Just before the elementary school's closing time, she drove back and parked again. The red Toyota was in sight. As soon as Irena Petrov appeared and started driving, the Visitor followed her to a house that was apparently her home. Now that she knew where Irena Petrov lived, the Visitor no longer went to the Professor's house each morning. Instead, she went to Irena Petrov's. Whenever she did not see the orange-haired woman emerge in time for school, the Visitor assumed she was at the Professor's house.

The Visitor understood it did not matter how often the Professor and Irena Petrov were together. Yet, she could not stop herself from needing to know whatever details were available to her. Which nights they spent together. Who brought in the newspaper. What happened on the weekends, when the Visitor parked near Irena Petrov's house and watched for activity. On Saturdays and Sundays, she might see her leave and come back with groceries, tend to her garden, sweep her front stoop, or—even worse—drive to the Professor's house.

Sometimes, she followed Irena Petrov to the supermarket. It was of interest to her to see what items were put in her cart. Celery. Spices. Wheat bread. The Visitor put the same items into her own cart. She followed her out, squinting to see in the harsh sunlight, and watched her drive away in her late model Toyota. Maybe it was a gift from the Professor, a gift that should have been hers. Irena Petrov was a thief. She had stolen what really belonged to another. She could not be permitted to get away with what amounted to a crime.

Acting on impulse, the Visitor drove to the hardware store and bought a can of black spray paint. When it was very late, she drove to Irena Petrov's house, parking a short distance away. Shaking the can, she walked to the red Toyota, which was parked in the street. Starting at the back end and moving forward to the front, she sprayed "B-I-T-C" in huge letters. She added the "H" to the hood. Then she tossed the can into Irena Petrov's front yard and left.

On the way to her apartment, she had a fit of giggles. Soon, she was laughing out loud at the thought of Irena Petrov opening her door the next morning, then turning to lock it. She would hurry down the stairs and take quick steps toward the car. She would not want to be late for school. Suddenly, she would see and stop in her tracks. She would drop her purse, her books. As if to prevent a screech, she would cover her mouth with her hand. Slowly walking around the car, taking in the offensive word, she would realize it was meant for her.

That one word, "bitch," would stay in her head all day. She would wonder who had painted it on her car. Perhaps, as the day wore on, she would figure out that she was indeed a "bitch," someone who took what did not belong to her. She might guess that the Professor belonged to someone else, and she was a "bitch" for stealing him. When she saw her reflection or looked in the mirror, she might find herself whispering the word "bitch" repeatedly. That word, so descriptive of what she was, would never leave her consciousness from that day on.

It pleased the Visitor greatly to imagine the low state to which Irena Petrov might sink as the word burrowed into her mind, like a brain-eating worm. The woman who had appeared to be so full of pride, with her ostentatious orange hair and boorish red Toyota, would be humbled. As time went by and the word continued to plague her, she might age, gain weight, take to drink. The Professor would lose interest as she became slovenly. No longer would she be invited to his house.

How delighted the Visitor was. With renewed confidence, she stopped following Irena Petrov and returned to the Professor's house each morning, sure he would soon come out as she was passing and invite her in. Everything was the same. The curtains were still drawn. A fresh newspaper lay on the steps. All she had to do was to be patient and make the daily trip.

But on the fourth morning, she was appalled to see Irena Petrov emerge from the Professor's house again. The Toyota, which had been parked further down the road, was unmarked. Apparently, the word "bitch" had been erased, somehow. The color of the car seemed an even brighter red. It must have been polished after being cleaned.

The Visitor slowed down. A car behind her beeped. Irena Petrov turned to look. Their eyes met. Irena's glance was mocking, the Visitor thought. There may have been a slight smile on her face. She had triumphed. The Professor was still hers. Her car was unblemished. She had stopped the compliment, which the Visitor did not hear anymore.

She drove on but had to stop on a quiet street a few blocks away. Sitting in her car, she wept. She wanted to die. She wanted to kill herself. She wanted to kill Irena Petrov. The words of her mother came back to her. "You're too clever for your own good." This made her cry harder as she realized the truth of those words.

What of her own good had she accomplished? She had become infatuated with an older man who might not remember her. Yet this did not matter. She still wanted him for herself. As shameful as it was to admit, her heart could not be controlled. She might be sitting several blocks away, but she was still waiting for him to walk by, see her, and greet her. She was waiting to hear him call to her as she drove by his house, as she would continue to do for years.

It was another two decades before the Visitor's wish was granted in part. She had stayed in the college town after graduation to remain near the Professor. During this time, he had aged considerably. In later years, she had seen him emerge from his house using a cane, then a walker. At some point, Irena Petrov disappeared. Then, one day during her drive-by, there was an ambulance parked outside of his house.

The Visitor discovered that the Professor had been admitted to the nursing home for people with dementia. After careful observation, she determined he had no visitors. Claiming she was an old friend, the Visitor began spending time with him after dinner, every evening. The facility had an open door policy for visitation. None of the staff ever questioned her right to be there. The Professor may not have recognized her, but he smiled benignly in her direction when she entered his room. Frequently, she heard him call her "clever" again, both when she was in his room, always when her back was turned, and when she was in her own residence.

It was she, not Irena Petrov, who would be with him until the end. It was she who would hear his last word, addressed to her. She would continue to hear the compliment long after that night, long after the investigations, the FBI interviews, the newspaper articles, the sparse funeral. When everyone had forgotten him, she would remember.

The Professor was hers.

4. THE NURSE

The Nursing Home

The Nurse was frozen by the sound.

Pop! Pop! Pop!

She was about to head out the door of the nursing home when she heard it. It was coming from the Hospice section in the rear of the building.

Someone yelled: "Get out! He's got a gun!"

Oh my God

She crammed herself under the desk of the nurses' station. She heard footsteps running out the front entrance. It had to be some of the staff. The residents would not have the mental capacity to understand the danger.

She knew it was plain wrong to abandon the residents.

God help me. I should be protecting them.

But she was operating on instinct now, and instinct told her to save herself.

Pop! Pop! Pop!

Taking a deep, terrified breath, she got up just long enough to grab her cell phone, then ducked down again. Calling 911, she whispered to the dispatcher, hardly able to get the words out.

"I'm...I'm in the dementia nursing home...There's shooting. Please hurry!"

She hung up before the dispatcher could ask her name. Ed would not like her to give her name. He did not trust civilian authorities.

As frightened as she was, she still worried that Ed would not believe her reason for not leaving work on time. He was sure to check her odometer.

She counted—ten shots. Then silence. She did not stir. Was the shooter reloading? Should she run for it? She was scared to move, but also scared to be late for Ed. Why was she worried about Ed when her life was at stake? What was wrong with her?

The Marriage

They were still newlyweds. After a whirlwind two month courtship, Ed proposed. Because he did not believe in God or religion, they were married in the courthouse, with just her parents in attendance. Ed was estranged from his own family and would not speak about them. She should not expect to meet his parents or siblings.

Ed was to be her third husband. A simple courthouse ceremony was fine with her. It was embarrassing to have had two failed marriages. Better to keep things low key this time.

Actually, she knew very little about her new husband.

"I have a top secret job at the Crane military base. I can't discuss any of the details with you. I could lose my security clearance if I did." He held her in his arms while explaining.

"That's good enough for me. I love you too much to care if you can't tell me."

She pulled back to gaze deeply into his eyes—so beautiful and mysterious. She was thrilled that such an appealing and unusual man would love an ordinary woman like herself. She was going to make sure this marriage succeeded.

It was decided that instead of a honeymoon, they would spend the first night of their marriage in Ed's rural house, where she would be living from now on. She was not surprised that a man who was so concerned about details would live in a small neat house, just three rooms. Ed had few possessions beyond bare necessities.

"I learned to live a minimalist lifestyle when I spent time in Japan," he said. "Discipline of mind and body. That's what the monks taught me."

He showed her the few boxes of rice, noodles, and nori in the single kitchen cabinet.

"I want us both to live as I've learned to do."

She saw the sense in his request, in a way. But it meant giving up everything that made life pleasant and comfortable—television, pets, comfy chairs. Nevertheless, she would give Ed's lifestyle a try. Later, she might slowly introduce changes.

The Nursing Home

Residents were beginning to react to the shooting. At first, there was wailing coming from the rear of the building. The Nurse thought it was the victims of the shooting or, more likely since it was not agonized, those who were unharmed but nearby. This was followed by a sense of alarm spreading through the facility. Residents were crying and howling. Those who could still speak were sobbing about going home or wanting their mothers.

The Nurse held her hands over her ears.

I will not listen. I will not listen.

But nothing drowned out the sounds of such distress. The Nurse felt the urge to start screaming herself, which was only suppressed by the greater terror of attracting the shooter to her hiding place.

The Marriage

The morning after their marriage ceremony, Ed brought a breakfast tray to bed. While she ate the spare vegan food, he asked her—for the first time—to tell him about her previous marriages. This was bewildering because during their courtship he had repeatedly said that the present was all that counted. They were not to ask about each other's pasts.

"There isn't much to tell." She chewed on the dry rice crackers. Ed did not eat until noon. "My first marriage was to my high school boyfriend. We were both eighteen. Within two weeks, we were both back with our parents. Our marriage was annulled six months later."

Ed listened silently. She took a sip from the tiny cup of green tea.

"My second marriage only lasted a year. It was to a graduate student on the rebound from his ex-girlfriend. Later, he told me he could not make love to me unless he imagined I was his ex."

She pushed the tray aside and put her arms around Ed, drawing him to her.

"Neither of those marriages counted. There was no real love. Not like there is now, between us."

Ed pushed himself away, asking her for the names of her ex-husbands. Then, he secluded himself in the den for several hours. She supposed he was working. He mostly worked remotely, from home. She occupied herself tidying up the already tidy rooms and hanging the few items of clothing she brought in her side of the small closet, already emptied for her by Ed. She arranged her toiletries on the limited space Ed created for her on a shelf above the sink in the tiny bathroom.

Later, when Ed came out of the den, he astonished her by handing her print-outs of an internet search he had done on her previous husbands. There was information about the work and relationship histories of both men since the annulment and divorce, none of it known to her.

That night, the second night of their marriage, Ed surprised her by the roughness of his love-making, so unlike the gentleness and consideration he had shown before. Although she found it painful, she did not ask him to stop. Later, she wondered why. All she could come up with was that she did not want to ruin a one-day old marriage.

The Nursing Home
From her hiding place under the desk, the Nurse was startled when she heard the entrance being smashed open. Did the shooter make his way around to the front of the building and enter again? Or was it the police or even another shooter? She was dry-mouth panting. She knew the residents were crowding around her station by the closeness of their terrified vocalizations. Would they all be shot? Would the shooter come around the desk, looking for her? Her teeth chattered.

The Marriage
On the second day of her marriage, she and Ed both returned to work. He did not believe in personal days or vacations days. While they were apart, she received many loving texts from Ed, some at ten-minute intervals.

"What are you doing right this second?"

And "Can you leave work early? I'm home now, and I can't be without you a moment more. You should quit your job."

She did the best she could to reply to each one, but had to skip some while dealing with residents. She smiled at his little jokes when she had to keep him waiting.

"Tired of me already?" And "Are you forgetting about me so soon?"

She arrived home on the second night of her marriage to discover that Ed was locked in his den. When she knocked, he said "Later."

Surely, he was working. But when he came out after three hours, saying nothing, and going straight to bed without pausing, she realized he was not speaking to her. When she joined him in bed, he kept his back to her.

"Ed? Are you angry at me? Did I do something wrong?"

When he did not answer, she wept.

"I'm so sorry. Whatever it is, I'm so sorry I hurt you."

He reached for her. She wept in his arms. He, too, had tears on his face.

"I can't lose you. When you don't answer my texts, I imagine you have stopped loving me. You must answer me right away. Just one word is enough. You must promise never to scare me like that again."

"I promise."

That night, his love making was tender, gentler than it had ever been. She spent the rest of the night asleep in his arms.

The next day, no matter what she was doing, she replied to his texts immediately. She even tried to match his word count so he would not think she was too busy for him, even though she was. She skipped all her breaks in order not to fall behind with the medications.

The Nurse knew what her women friends would say. She was starting off her marriage on the wrong foot, allowing her husband to make the rules. If she did not assert herself, she would lose her identity. Yet, if she simply responded to Ed's texts as soon as they were delivered, he might soon be reassured enough to be reasonable. He just needed some time to settle into the marriage. He was still proving his love to her by wanting her constant attention.

The Nursing Home

The Nurse heard the footsteps move stealthily past the station and down the hall toward the back. There was a tense silence, then another *pop*. She waited for more shots. There were none. Residents were in a state of hysteria. She hated herself for being such a coward—in the nursing home and at home, too.

The Marriage

On the third night of their marriage, Ed greeted her with a candle-lit dinner. The vegan menu was exotic and must have taken hours to prepare. She knew better than to ask him how he had spared the time from his job. A spicy stew with organic roasted root vegetables. A coconut mango tart for dessert. Wine without sulfite.

After dinner, he said he had something serious to discuss with her. At this, she felt a shiver of alarm.

"Have I done something wrong? Aren't I answering your texts fast enough?"

Ed smiled, as if she had asked a childish question. "Your replies are just fine," he said, dismissively. "What I want to discuss is far more important than texts."

The Nurse frowned. If answering the texts was so vital the day before, why wasn't it just as vital a day later?

Ed reached across the table for her hand.

"You know that during the marriage ceremony we promised to love and honor each other."

"Yes," she said, gazing at his exquisitely sculptured face. He was by far the handsomest man she ever met. Her shoulders relaxed, and with it, her suspicions eased.

"There is one more vow we must make to keep our marriage strong."

"Okay." She wondered where this was going.

"We must each promise to be one-hundred percent honest with each other. No matter what. Even if honesty would be hurtful."

She stared at Ed. His intense blue eyes. Looking straight into hers. As if seeing into her soul. As if allowing her to see into his.

"Of course. I'll do anything to make us closer." She meant it.

"Promise me," he insisted. "Promise you will never lie to me. "

"I promise.".

"Say the rest. What do you promise?"

"I promise never to lie to you."

Ed began to cry. Suddenly, he seemed very young. "No one has ever made me that promise."

She rose from her chair and went around the table to him. "Oh, Ed. I love you so much. I will never lie to you. I promise."

He held her tightly against him. She stroked and soothed him.

Everything is going to be alright, she told herself.

The Nursing Home

The entrance door of the nursing home was opening and closing at rapid intervals.

"Police. Is anyone up here hurt?"

Cautiously, the Nurse peeked over the desk. Several police officers were mingling with the still hysterical residents in front of the station. Relief washed over her. Soon after, she started to tremble violently, now that help had arrived.

The Marriage

On the fourth day of her marriage, her mother phoned. Ed was in the kitchen area washing dishes—the few they owned. He had a precise way of soaping and rinsing them. She wandered to the other end of the room while talking.

When she hung up, Ed was wringing out the dish cloth with hard twists. "You must never do that again."

"Do what again?"

"Walk away from me when you're on the phone. So I can't hear what you're saying."

"It was just my mother." She laughed. He was being absurd.

Ed glared at her, then went swiftly into the den and closed the door. This time, he did not come out, and she was forced to go to bed alone feeling sick to her stomach. She did not see him again until she came home from work the next day. When she pulled the car up, he was standing in the doorway, waiting for her. She stood at the bottom of the steps, looking up at him.

"What do you want me to do?" She was annoyed. All she had done was to speak on the phone to her mother. What did Ed expect?

"Come in, and I'll tell you." His expression was stern.

Once inside, Ed demanded she give him all of her passwords. And she had to turn all devices over to him each evening before dinner for inspection. This shocked her. Her annoyance grew.

"Yes, but what do you think you'll find?"

"Whether you have been lying to me"

"But I promised I wouldn't lie. And I have nothing to lie about."

"How else will I know." She should not expect him to be able to give her his passwords, since his devices were classified top secret by the government.

The next time she came home from work, she handed over her phone. She had talked herself into it while she was at work, reasoning that giving Ed what he wanted was harmless, since she had nothing to hide. He took it into his den and returned a half-hour later.

"What's this number?"

"That one? That's my mother."

"What did she want?"

"She wants to see us. She wants us over for dinner tomorrow."

Ed looked at her. "Don't you understand? We don't need anyone but each other. We don't need friends or parents. I love you too much to share you with *anyone.* Call your mother right now and tell her we're not coming."

As she dialed the number with Ed watching, she realized she was obeying him as if she were a servant, and they hadn't been married for even a week. She was becoming just like her mother. Giving in to a man.

During the next week, Ed alternated between silent brooding, often in his den, and tearful clinging with abundant texts and Japanese-style meals. It seemed he had two distinct sides, and she never knew which she would find when she returned from work or when she woke in the morning.

The Nursing Home

The Nurse realized she might be the only staff people in the building. She also knew she should leave right away, before the police stopped her. The residents were anything but calmed by the array of strangers rushing into the facility—more police officers, EMTs, a few relatives who had somehow found out, and the distracted administrator with her cell phone on her ear. Even though it was callous, the Nurse slipped out the front door. She went right to her car and made her way around the haphazardly parked emergency vehicles to the road.

She would rather sneak out, leaving the residents, than make Ed suspicious. The woman who was independent enough to earn a nursing degree was turning into something she did not recognize.

The Marriage

In their third week together, Ed revealed that his depression was caused by the lies she had told him about her former marriages.

"What lies?" She asked, confused, wracking her brain to think of anything dishonest she might have said in her short account of her brief marriages.

"That's for you to confess to me. You know I work for the government. I have access to ways of discovery the ordinary citizen doesn't have. You can't hide anything from me. You might as well confess."

"I don't know what you mean. There was nothing more to those relationships than what I already told you."

"You promised to be a hundred percent honest with me. I will never trust you if you break your promise. I cannot love you if you lie."

They went back and forth for nearly an hour. He kept insisting she confess to what he knew anyway. She protested that she was being honest. She could not imagine what "secrets" he discovered about her marriages. They were both so innocuous.

Finally, he retreated to his den, as he had done before, promising to do more research. First, he delivered a warning.

"It would be better for our marriage if you confessed before I uncover even more of your lies. I won't be angry if you tell the truth. But I can't say how I would feel if you continue to be dishonest. I can't say what I would do."

She went to the bedroom and crept under the covers, still in her nurse's uniform, with her white shoes on. Thoughts pin-wheeled in her head.

Would the government have secretly tracked me, recorded me, for the past fifteen years? Was that even possible? Was there something, some indiscretion, I don't remember that is stored in a government file, somewhere? That Ed could pull up? It's plausible, isn't it? Who knew what satellites and drones were capable of? What internet hackers could find?

She thought of the nursing home medical records, now computerized, and possible for someone in Russia or China to breach, with the histories of the elderly patients available for who-knows-what purpose. Blackmail. Exposure. Even arrest for old crimes.

Sometimes, erroneous information was entered into medical records by mistake. Perhaps there was a mistake in her file, something transposed from someone else's file to hers. The more she considered, the more that seemed the most logical explanation for whatever Ed was finding. She wished she could see the file so she would know what the mistake might be.

If there was a mistake, all she had to do is point it out to Ed. She would make him believe her.

The Nursing Home

The Nurse drove as fast as the speed limit allowed. A number of media vans from the affiliates of the national networks were going in the other direction. What happened at work was similar to the mass shootings that occurred in schools and malls. This would be the first in a nursing home. She gripped the steering wheel tightly. She wondered if it was illegal for a witness to leave the scene of a crime, especially a crime with many victims. She had no excuse—unless trying to save a marriage was an excuse.

The Marriage

Ed was cold to her for several days. On the one-month anniversary of their wedding, she came home to a simple prepared meal of beans and rice. Ed was not there. There was an unsigned note taped to his empty plate.

"I'm going away on an assignment. If you decide to be honest with me, our loving relationship can continue. If you decide to keep lying, I would prefer that you leave before I get back."

Distraught, she paced around the tiny house. If she left, it would be her third short marriage. Another black mark. Besides, Ed was the love of her life. Even if the marriage was difficult and Ed was unreasonable, even if he were crazy, she could not bear to see their love end. She was approaching her mid-thirties, and this might be her only chance to have true love. Not to mention a family.

She would have to lie to Ed to convince him she was telling the truth. The lie had to be about how one of her former marriages ended. That was what Ed harped on. If what she told him was not in her file, she would pretend to be perplexed, to not know how that could be. She would take her chances.

When Ed finally returned several days later, she said she had a confession to make. Ed seemed pleased. He held her hands after they were both seated.

"I'm ready to hear your confession."

She was very nervous. Would he know she was lying?

"Well, the truth is that I cheated on my second husband. He found out. That is why my second marriage ended."

Ed smiled. "Who was the affair with?"

She anticipated this question and chose one of the staff at work to be her supposed lover. She guessed that if she made up a name, Ed would quickly discover it with whatever government research tools were available to him.

"It was Sid Stone, the Maintenance Man at the nursing home."

Ed looked at her with moist eyes. "When you are honest with me, I know you really do love me. I don't care what you tell me, as long as you are completely honest."

This time, Ed went into the den only for an hour. She heard the sound of the printer grinding. She guessed correctly that he was researching the Maintenance Man on the internet. As before, he came out with a number of pages of material on him, from his birth announcement to a recent photo of the nursing home staff.

The next day, after dinner, he asked her for details about her affair. How had they met, how did the affair start, how often did they get together? She invented answers. Her "honesty" pleased him. He would disappear into the den for a while for the "verification process," known only to government agents working in the Secret Service or the NSA. Once her answers had been "verified," there was another set of questions. Where did she and her lover have sex? What kind of sex? Did they "sext" between meetings? And another trip to the den after she fumbled through her answers.

After a lovingly intimate night and loving texts from Ed the next day, which she did not hesitate to reply to in an equally loving way, she came home to more questions from Ed.

Which sex acts had she performed? How often had she performed each one? Who initiated each act?

She asked for time to check her memory before answering in order to be sure she was accurate. Ed graciously consented to an hour. She went into the bedroom to think. She knew she could not keep up the lies.

I can't keep inventing answers. I don't know what to say. How is Ed verifying my lies, anyway? Since they are lies. How could so many errors be in my file? Is there even a file?

Once again, she began by being chagrined by the predicament Ed maneuvered her into, and ending by telling herself that she was smart enough to fix the relationship.

Biting her lip, she came to a decision. She had to stop lying to Ed. She had to confess to him that she only lied to please him. She had to promise again to be a hundred percent honest. Apprehensively, she came out of the bedroom and told Ed she had something to confess. Clearly, Ed was anticipating answers to his latest set of questions.

"I need to tell you that everything I said about the Maintenance Man was a lie."

"What do you mean?" He was holding her hands, as was his custom during her confessions. His grip tightened painfully.

"I only lied to you because you did not believe the truth. I thought if I lied, if I made up a story about a lover, you'd love me again." She tried to sound sensible.

For a moment, Ed took this in without expression. Then his beautiful face distorted with fury. He bared his teeth. His grip tightened more until her fingers seemed about to break.

Suddenly releasing her hands, he stood up and turned his back to her.

"I'll need time to think. I'm going into the den. Don't disturb me."

Just before he closed the door, he said, "I never thought I would be married to a liar. You fooled me."

Then the door slammed shut, leaving her panting, with bruised fingers, wretched and unnerved.

When Ed finally emerged, she begged and pleaded for forgiveness. She would never lie again. She would never hurt him again. She promised. She wept. She groveled. If only he would not leave her. She was acting exactly as her mother had with her husbands. She knew it, but could not stop herself.

After several days of coldness and begging, Ed finally forgave her, conditionally. Forgiving was not the same as trusting. He would have to step up his surveillance. Besides checking emails and texts daily, he would be checking her odometer. Cameras would be installed in the house she would never be able to find or detect. He would use government resources to spy on her every move.

"Don't think that you can even have thoughts I won't know about. Don't think you will always know all I know about you. Whether it is about your past or the present, assume I know much more than you think I know. Never again will you be able to fool me, to keep a secret from me."

After this severe warning, Ed went to the bedroom, curled up in the bed, and wept loudly.

"I thought you loved me. I thought I had at last found someone I could really, really trust. Your lies have stabbed me in the heart."

She sat on the bed, saying "I'm sorry. I'm sorry." Over and over again until he grew calm and turned to her.

"I love you so much." He was holding her now. "Promise me. Promise you will never ever lie again."

"I promise I will never lie to you again about anything."

That night, their love making was intense, clutching, grasping. It was as if their very skin was a barrier they had to cross.

The Nursing Home

The Nurse had a few miles to go when she thought to turn on the car radio. She tuned to a local station. There was a live report from the nursing home. She was amazed by the details she had not been able to see while she was hiding there. Indeed, it was a mass shooting. The alleged perpetrator was killed by a heroic police officer. The area was being cordoned off and a search was proceeding for any additional shooters. The public in surrounding areas was urged to stay in their homes and report anything unusual to the police.

The Marriage

Several days passed without incident. She answered all of Ed's texts immediately. She did not care if he checked the odometer and her devices. He once again prepared the sparse meals. The closeness of their relationship was at least a possibility.

But when a missed call appeared on her cell phone, Ed spotted the unknown number right away. He demanded to know who had called her.

"I don't know, unless it's someone from work."

Ed was instantly suspicious. He redialed the number. It was disconnected.

"I'm thinking it's from the Maintenance Man, trying to reach you on a cheap throwaway phone so he won't be caught."

"It's not possible! It might be a Robocall. But not from the Maintenance Man."

Ed took a step toward her.

"Is the Maintenance Man your lover after all? Is that the truth you have been covering up?"

"What?" She was incredulous that this was starting up again.

"I said 'Is he your lover?'"

"No. Of course not."

Ed took another step. He was quite close to her now.

"Will you submit to a polygraph?"

"What?" Was he serious?

He went into the den. Moments later, he returned with a metal box. Three large dials were arranged across its top. Wires—electrodes?—emerged from an opening on one side.

"This is a portable polygraph." He placed it on the table. "Sit here," he instructed, pointing to one of the two chairs, "and hold out your arms."

"Don't you have to be an expert to administer a polygraph?"

"I am an expert."

"It doesn't look like the kind of machine I've seen on TV."

"It's for interrogations in the field. That's all I am permitted to say."

Never had she been more confused. Suddenly, she was exhausted. It was so tiring to defend herself from the man she loved. It was easier to give in.

Dabbing some gel on the ends of the electrodes, he placed two on each arm. He plugged in the machine and turned it on. It did not make any sound.

"Are you ready?"

"I don't know. I'm nervous."

"The polygraph takes anxiety into account. We will start with a few neutral questions to get a baseline."

He asked her for her name, address, and where she worked. Her heart was beating fast.

Then he asked, "Was the phone call from the Maintenance Man?"

"No!"

Ed took some seconds reading and adjusting knobs under the three dials.

"Do you know the person who phoned you?"

"No."

After a few more seconds of reading and adjusting, "Are you having an affair with the Maintenance Man?"

"No."

Ed appeared to be reading something complicated. He brow furrowed and his glance shifted from one dial to another. Then he turned the machine off and ripped the electrodes off her arm. He sat down and stared at her.

"Well?"

Taking his time, he finally answered: "The polygraph indicates deception about your answers."

She was astounded. "How can that be?"

"I'm going into the den to think." He picked up the box. He did not seem angry, just distant, as if she had been one of the people under suspicion he had probably dealt with many times before for the government.

He was still in the den when she had to leave for the evening shift at work. In an agitated state, she drove to the nursing home and took her position behind the nurses' station.

How could a polygraph have indicated she was lying when she was telling the truth? Was the machine broken? How could she get Ed to believe her? Where would she get the energy?

The Nursing Home

Her hand shook when she held the medication spreadsheet. The letters and numbers blurred. She needed something to be able to work, like Valium, which was one of the drugs the nursing home had on hand, prescribed for several patients. While no one was looking, she took a Valium from its pill container and popped it into her mouth. She never stole medication from patients before.

Only this once, she told herself.

Ten minutes later, just as she began to feel the Valium kick in, her phone vibrated. It was a text from Ed. He was waiting for her at home. He had recordings of her phone conversations with her lover, the Maintenance Man. They would talk about it when she returned.

She would finish dispensing the medications and ask an aide to distribute them to the patients. She would leave work early to clear things up with Ed.

Just then, she saw the Maintenance Man enter the building. He passed her without a word. How ridiculous for Ed to believe she would have an affair with a bald, aging man. If only she had a photo of him to show Ed.

It was while having these thoughts that the Nurse heard the sounds.

Pop! Pop! Pop!

The Marriage

As she was pulling into her driveway, she made the connection.

The Maintenance Man. My God! He must have been the shooter!

Rushing in the door, she breathlessly told her husband that there had been shots fired at the nursing home. She had hidden under her desk the whole time. It was on the news—it was one of those mass shootings. She thought she had narrowly escaped with her life.

He listened passively, then turned his back on her, while saying:

"You lied."

III. BEFORE DAWN

5. THE MAYOR

Philippa was sorting the Mayor's medication when the text came. She filled the seven day pill box. Colorful tablets—yellow, blue, orange, and white—crowded each section. The amount of medication the Mayor took was unknown to the public. The Opposition, if it found out, would use his medical history against him. Thankfully, their good friend Dr. Conrad had pronounced the Mayor "healthy for a man his age and fit for office."

He took the yellow pill, the one for anxiety and insomnia, before getting into bed. Philippa noticed he was already dozing, slack-jawed, with partially shut eyes exposing a thin white crescent above his bottom lid. How old he looked! The handsome politician she married a decade earlier, so energetic she ran to keep up with him on campaign tours, was approaching eighty. He was slowing down. Now she took his arm and pulled him along when they walked together.

The text was from Maxine, his political advisor.

Today 10:38 p.m. Just heard on the police scanner. A massacre at the Alzheimer's nursing home a few minutes ago. Many shot. Come ASAP. Fran will be here to handle media. HURRY!

Before she put the phone down, the Police Chief called.

"I'm setting up a command center at the nursing home. This one's going national. At least ten residents were shot in the head. They're probably all dead. We got the perpetrator. He's dead, too. The Coroner's coming to do the pronouncements. Better bring the Old Man over here. You've got a half-hour, I'd say, before the media arrives."

She listened in shock. Why on earth would anyone kill people with Alzheimer's? What for?

With difficulty, she roused the Mayor, shaking him by the shoulder. Sedation caused confusion. This was another thing the public did not know. Increasingly, she was taking over as his grasp of situations diminished.

"What? What?" His voice slurred.

"You have to wake up. There's been a shooting. Sit on the edge of the bed for a few minutes until your blood pressure levels out while I dress." She helped him swing his legs out from under the blankets.

She pulled one of several red outfits from her closet. Since their marriage, she always dressed in bright red. This was to distinguish herself from his three former wives, older dowdy women who only wore black or beige. She had been an actress and was considered a beauty. Now that she was in her fifties, still a quarter century younger than her husband, she worked at keeping up her appearance.

"What happened?" He sounded more alert.

"A shooting in the nursing home. We've got to get over there. Here. Put on this pair of pants and this jacket. No tie. You need that rushed-right-over look. Where's your shoes?"

In the car, she kept poking him to keep him awake. He had a thermos of instant coffee she found time to make. Hopefully, the caffeine would counteract the sleeping pill. She answered a number of calls while driving, first from Thomas, the Emergency Management Coordinator. He would probably get into control issues with the Police Chief. That was an old story. Maxine called to ask how long it would be before they arrived. Ten minutes. The Publisher of The Herald asked what she knew about the shooting. Nothing.

She drove through the Indiana college town. It was a small enough municipality to take less than a half hour to drive from the city limits on one side to the other. The biggest issues the Mayor's office dealt with concerned zoning and traffic patterns, and they caused enough voter stir. A mass shooting would attract statewide and even national interest. It would be the first media frenzy in the Mayor's six consecutive terms.

CNN and the other affiliates would be driving down from the state capital. She figured they would arrive at the nursing home in twenty minutes. The Mayor had to gear up for them. He would be good when the caffeine kicked in. As usual, he repeated his old memories when they were by themselves.

"When America's Mayor—that was Rudy Giuliani—stood on the ruins of the twin towers, he said *We're going to rebuild, and we're going to be stronger than we were before...terrorism can't stop us.* It was a perfect thing to say at the time. I should say something like that."

Philippa suppressed an urge to snap at him. Was he crazy? Guiliani? Fortunately, she trained herself to maintain an even tone.

"Let's wait and see. Maxine can tell you the best way to play this."

In 2001, the Mayor was still under the thumb of his father, who had been Mayor for many years before dying in his mid-eighties. Voters thought his son would be another steely politician, intimidating the City Council. Instead, they got his third wife, Claudette, and then Philippa, the powers behind the throne. They were no match for the Mayor's father, who even bullied the state legislature into passing bills beneficial to the town.

Finally, they were nearing the nursing home. Up ahead, the blinking red lights of emergency vehicles were visible. Pulling to the side, she put the car into neutral and turned to him, straightening his collar, then having second thoughts and shifting it off center again.

"You can do this. I'll be right beside you. Maxine and Fran will help."

"I know."

"Just watch out for Thomas. You know how he is."

"I know."

Back on the road, Philippa had a lump in the pit of her stomach. Who knew what carnage they would see? And how would she get her husband through the chaos in one piece? She drove around the police barrier that straddled the lanes and into the nursing home parking lot, weaving around the emergency vehicles—ambulances, fire trucks, sheriff cars—until she found a spot to park. Maxine rushed toward them as they were getting out of the car. She had her phone to her ear. The three stood together. Fran had not arrived yet.

"What do you know?" Philippa asked.

"The shooter was the Maintenance Man on the staff here. He entered the building with his passkey around ten. No one thought anything of it. He walked right past the nurses' station to the Hospice section. The victims were all in Hospice."

"He murdered people who were already dying?" The Mayor asked.

"Merciful God!" Philippa said.

"The shooter is dead out back. A Deputy took him out. It was a suicide-by-cop thing. He raised his weapon, but it was out of bullets."

"Does anyone know why he did it?" Philippa asked.

Maxine shrugged. "Media should be here in a few minutes. It's going to be a circus."

"Maybe he didn't like his job," the Mayor said.

"Look," Maxine said, putting her hand on the Mayor's arm, "I know what happened is awful, but you have a job to do. Comfort families. Support the first responders. Show leadership—and here's the important part—as much as possible do everything in front of the cameras. You might as well get some good PR out of this."

"Right."

"As soon as Fran gets herself here, she can arrange interviews for you with the affiliates. Remember: 'This is a sad day for our town. We will come together to support the grieving families because that's the kind of town this is'."

"Yes. Right."

"And Philippa, get Fran to put some make-up on the Mayor. He looks too green. A little green is okay, though."

"We'll talk to the Police Chief while we're waiting."

They walked to the command central, an array of microphones and a lectern near the entrance. The Chief was conferring with a sound technician who was testing the mics.

"Do you have what you need?" The Mayor asked. Philippa noted that the sedative had worn off. He was no longer slurring words.

"I think so. But there are staff and residents inside who have been terrorized. They might feel better if you went in there and do what you do best—meet, greet, and comfort."

"Testing. Testing."

"Gotta warn you, though. Nothing's been cleaned up yet. We're waiting for the Coroner. Can't touch anything until she gets here. Oh. The Administrator. Her name is Jill Wilson. She was destroyed when I saw her."

"I'll look for her."

The lump in Philippa's stomach grew as they entered the facility. She held her husband's arm, under the illusion he might still be capable of protecting her. Although the shooter was dead, it felt risky to enter the premises after so many killings had occurred a mere hour before.

Just then, a voice called to them.

"Wait!"

It was Thomas, the Emergency Management Coordinator, right behind them.

"It's Tommy," Philippa said.

"I just got here. What a crazy thing. In a nursing home, for God's sake. For people with Alzheimer's. At least they probably didn't know what was happening."

"Right."

"Are you coming with us, Tommy? My stomach's already turning."

Inside, the staff, all women, were huddled behind the nurses' station. A couple were crying. Residents were grouped in front of the station, some in wheel chairs, some just standing with vacant expressions. A sharp smell of urine as well as other unidentifiable odors greeted them. Philippa took shallow breaths through her mouth. Tommy got a handkerchief from his pocket and held it to his nose. The Mayor, who had little sense of smell, seemed unaffected.

Lately, she had seen him "turn off"—she didn't know how else to describe it—when something unpleasant happened. His face became rigid, like a block. There was no sign that he felt anything. Now it came to her. His vacant expression resembled that of some of the residents. She hated to think what that meant.

A Deputy appeared and asked if the three wished to see the Hospice area. He led them down a long hallway to an area cordoned off by yellow crime scene tape.

"This is just temporary. The Coroner will probably rearrange the tape. It's part of her job. Just don't touch anything. If you can look in the doorways without entering the rooms, it would be best," the Deputy said as they ducked under the tape.

He turned on the light at the entrance to the first room. Inside was a shocking sight. A nearly skeletal figure was hanging off the side of the bed in a hospital gown. Its fingers and the edges of its hair touched a large puddle of blood on the floor. The bed linens and the wall were blood splattered. Lumps of gray matter were scattered on the blanket. Brain tissue? Even more disturbing was the back of the victim's head, a shapeless bloody mass of bone, hair, and gore.

Philippa vomited into a nearby wastebasket. Tommy buoyed himself up with one outstretched palm on the wall outside the room, while holding his handkerchief to his mouth with his free hand. The Mayor continued to stare blankly, swallowing repeatedly.

The Deputy led the Mayor to each of the other nine rooms. Philippa and Tommy stayed behind. The Coroner came rushing in, but stopped when she saw them.

"Are you okay? Do you need a wipe?"

"I lost my lunch."

The Coroner felt around in a large satchel she had brought until she found a packet of wipes, handing them to Philippa.

"I'm guessing you looked at the victims."

"Just one." Philippa vigorously wiped the front of her red jacket.

"The sight of mutilated corpses takes getting used to. Most people instinctively react to the sight of blood. Do you need to sit down?"

Philippa was lightheaded and perspiring.

"I'll be okay in a minute. I've got to guide my husband through a 'good Mayor' act. Heaven knows if he'll be up to it. I had to wake him to get him here. He's not at his best this late. What time is it?"

"Apple Watch says eleven-thirty-two. I've got to get started. There's lots to do before I can declare all ten dead. There's a slim chance that one or two survived, but the Deputies are good at telling. They say all are dead. I've just got to make it official."

"Okay. Don't let me keep you." She noticed Tommy talking to a woman in a suit and walked over. The Mayor, having completed his gruesome tour, joined her without saying anything.

"You okay?"

He nodded.

Tommy introduced them to Ms. Wilson, the nursing home Administrator.

"Call me Jill." She was as pale as Philippa imagined she must look—shiny with sweat, ashen, tremulous. Her voice shook when she spoke.

"We have a situation here. Most of the Housekeepers and Aides ran off. A couple of Nurses are still here. But I don't have the coverage to give residents the care they need. Many are frightened. Some are on oxygen. All need help toileting. They can't take care of themselves. And in a few hours, breakfast preparation should start. I don't know if any of my kitchen staff will show up."

Philippa, the Mayor, and Tommy looked somberly at Jill. The horror in the Hospice section was not the only dreadfulness. It was sinking in. The shooting was a calamity for the survivors, too.

"I've been communicating with Corporate. They suggested transferring residents to the hospital or other facilities. Believe me, that's the first thing I tried. There's not more than half a dozen beds available in the whole town."

"Geez. Can it get any worse?" Tommy said.

"We may have more fatalities if the residents aren't cared for properly. They can easily get pneumonia or urinary track infections. They can fall and break bones if they try to do some things for themselves. And they must have their medications."

With moist eyes, Jill addressed the Mayor directly. "I do have an idea, Mayor. It's not strictly legal and it is certainly a violation of our accreditation, so I will need your written approval."

"Right."

"We're here to help," Philippa said.

"I've already called the families of the victims. Now I have to contact the families of survivors to let them know their loved ones are okay. Once they know the situation, I'll ask for one or two relatives to come and help out. Just overnight. Corporate is flying in extra staff tomorrow."

There was silence as Jill's idea was absorbed. The media would be there at any moment. There was no time to consider.

"I've prepared a permission letter, Mayor. I have it right here with a pen. All you have to do is sign it." She took a piece of paper out of a folder she had been carrying and held it out.

The Mayor looked at his wife. She nodded. He scribbled his signature.

"Thank you, Mayor. I don't know what else to do."

Philippa embraced Jill. "Tell us what you need, and we will move heaven and earth to get it for you."

"Thank you, Mrs. Mayor."

"I'll have the emergency vehicles relocate to the back so the families can park in the front. And I'll round up some grief counselors," Tommy said, glad to have something useful to do.

The Mayor remembered his role. He put his arm around Jill. "How are you holding up?"

"As well as can be expected." She suppressed a sob.

"I'll need you to stay strong. We all have to stay strong."

"Yes, Sir."

"Can I depend on you?"

"Yes, Sir."

He gave her shoulder a squeeze. She turned to go.

"I think I should sit down. Just for a minute," he said. He stumbled to a chair.

So he had been affected after all. Philippa was almost relieved. He was having a normal reaction. He held his balding head in his hands. His once thick brown mane had thinned considerably and grayed over the years.

"Are you okay, honey?"

"It was the pudding on the trays that got me. I don't know why. More than the stuffed animals and photographs from their younger days. And the thick yellow toenails sticking out from the bedding. Terrible." She rubbed his back.

"It reminded me of my father in the open casket. He still looked robust—not like those people. I still miss him."

"I know you do." He did not appear to remember his father's cruelty and lack of approval. How he had said his son was not going to be up to the Mayor's job.

The Deputy who had been standing discreetly in the background, stepped forward.

"Sir, do you wish to see the shooter out back?"

The Mayor looked at his wife again. It had to be done. She nodded.

"Give me a minute."

"The media's probably here. Fran will be waiting. Let's get it over with. I'll go with you."

He stood up, and she took his arm. She wondered if she could bear the sight of another corpse. With the Deputy leading the way, they went out the back door. All three froze at the sight of the Maintenance Man, lying face-down, with an exit wound visible on his back. Blood had seeped from under him onto the concrete patio. His gun was still clutched in his hand.

Philippa had a coughing fit and doubled over. To her relief, she did not vomit again. The Mayor looked awful. Nothing was said. There was nothing to say. They made their way back down the hall to the entrance just as Maxine was running in to get them.

"Is Fran here?" Philippa asked.

"In the kitchen making coffee. Mayor, I want you on camera giving out cups of coffee to whoever. The media's outside setting up now. They're all here. CNN, NBC, ABC, and even the BBC. Are you ready, Mayor?"

"Yes."

"Middle ground. Upset, but not too upset. In charge. Get it?"

"Got it."

Philippa wished they could go home. How she yearned to crawl into bed and sleep. Or watch silly game shows on TV. Anything mindless. Anything other than being here. However, she knew what she had to do. Keep the Mayor on track.

The Deputy keyed them out. In contrast to the relative silence inside the building, there was chaos outside. Tommy was directing emergency vehicles to the back of the building. Sirens blared as more police cars arrived. Media trucks parked helter-skelter on the grass or wherever there was room. Wide-eyed relatives pulled into the front lot. Camera and sound technicians set up interviews with whomever they could. There was a media truck from the Herald present as well. The print reporters jockeyed with the video technicians for the best coverage. The Police Chief called out instructions on a megaphone.

Maxine told the Mayor to remain near the front door. Fran handed him styrofoam cups of coffee to hand to relatives and first responders. He was in his role now, giving hugs, coffee, and comforting words, to all who permitted it. Cameras were recording him. Maxine nodded affirmatively to Philippa.

She knew her husband. If he wasn't watched carefully, he might sink to the ground at the first kind word. He might lay there sobbing, calling for his father or even Rudy Giuliani, America's Mayor, who would never let terrorism win.

6. THE JOURNALIST

The text said *"URGENT."*

Sylvia lay in bed, unable to sleep. It was one-thirty a.m. She re-read the text. It was from Barry, the Executive Editor of The Herald. Everyone come to the newsroom. There had been a mass shooting. That is all it said.

Immediately, she got up and searched for clean clothing that would not look baggy, now that she was no longer a "solid-looking woman." She rushed to the meeting. When she reached the office, Barry had already started.

"The shooter entered the nursing home between nine-thirty and ten." He rubbed his puffy eyes.

The entire staff crammed into the conference room. The remarkable thing was, since the lay-offs, they all thirty fit in. That would not have been the case in the old days.

"The shooter was the Maintenance Man. I'm told he walked straight to the Hospice section and killed all the patients. Ten of them."

"Hospice—isn't that where they put the patients who are already dying?" Maggie, the receptionist, asked.

Barry nodded 'yes.' "Then, the shooter went out the back door and raised his gun, unloaded as it turned out, just as the police got there. He was shot dead."

The room was unusually silent. The percolator on the coffee cart dripped. The fluorescent lights above the conference table buzzed. Someone passed a flask around. It was a no-smoking building, but several lit up.

"The shooters name was Sid Stone. Spelled like it sounds. S-T-O-N-E."

Sylvia tried to take it in. Here? A mass shooting in the area covered by their paper—a small university town in southern Indiana? Their town had always been so lucky. Tornadoes swept around it, pummeling the rest of the county. When the reservoir overran its banks, the town's streets escaped flooding. Murder was rare, so rare that the Police Beat column often consisted only of misdemeanors.

"I've already had a call from the Associated Press asking about our coverage. I told them we have a team on it," Barry said.

This made everyone laugh. A team. At the time of the lay-offs, the paper edition was downsized from twelve pages to six. The digital edition was all that held the circulation constant. There were only two reporters left, Sylvia and Peter, who was part-time. Since there was a last hire/first fire policy, everyone in the room was gray-haired. Sylvia was in her sixties. The century-old daily was on its last legs. Most of the staff were in bed asleep or watching Seinfeld reruns on TV at the time the murders were occurring.

"Okay, okay. Look! We're just going to have to make this happen. There are days of coverage for something like this. Sylvia," he said, addressing her as the senior reporter, "You are the team head. I'm putting Peter, Alice, and Roy under you."

"What?" Sylvia said. "Boss, Alice and Roy are in *Marketing*."

"I've never even done an interview," Alice said.

Roy began pouring coffee into white Styrofoam cups and passing them around. "I guess this is my chance to move into reporting like I've always said I wanted. Now I better look in the mirror and ask myself if I was telling the truth."

"The rest of you aren't off the hook. If I need more feet on the ground, I'll call on any of you. I don't care if you're in Circulation—I'm looking at you, Don."

The sleepy-looking man he named opened his alarmed eyes.

"Look, folks, this could increase subscriptions. Lord knows we need that. If you don't want this paper to fold, get busy! I know you're tired. Push through it. You can sleep next week. Meeting adjourned." Barry rose abruptly.

Sylvia accepted a cup from Roy, knowing it was a bad idea. Coffee on an empty stomach was sure to bring on another spell of indigestion. But she needed the caffeine. She turned to the pudgy overnight editor of the digital edition, who was sitting next to her. He chain-smoked and was already on his second cigarette since the start of the short meeting.

"Fill me in on anything you know."

"Not much more than you already heard. I did a 'breaking' for the overnight. There's supposed to be a press briefing around nine a.m."

"Have the relatives been informed?"

"You won't believe this. Most of the staff did the chicken-shit thing and ran off. The spouses and children have been called in to care for the residents. "

"You're kidding, right?"

"It's ironic. A nut-case kills dying old folks, and the kids who dumped their moms and dads into a nursing home in the first place, have to take care of them anyway."

On the way out of the conference room, Sylvia called Peter, Alice and Roy over to her cubicle for a planning meeting. The four squeezed in. Sylvia sank heavily onto her desk chair.

"There's going to be a lot to cover—press conferences, updates, memorials, funerals. And interviews with the staff, who I guarantee will say the shooter was quiet, kept to himself, and never caused any trouble. Interviews with family members of the victims—those will be hard. Peter and I will take those. And the corporate people who own the nursing home chain."

"I'll research the corporation," said Alice, "No interviews."

"Okay—Peter, Roy, the three of us should attend the update in the morning and fan out to interview whoever we can. Peter, can you chase down the Police Chief?"

"On it."

"And bring along a couple of the video people for the digital edition."

A few minutes after the last sip of coffee, the pain was already starting, just below Sylvia's diaphragm. She tried not to squirm.

"You okay?" Alice asked.

"Yeah. Fine. Just coffee blowing a hole in my stomach. I'll be okay."

They spent the next fifteen minutes planning in more detail. Then the conversation took a turn.

"I'm just sick about this," Alice said. "Shooting old people who can't defend themselves. It's...It's...horrendous." She bit back tears. Up until this point, they were treating the shooting as they would any other news story, divvying up tasks, accepting assignments.

"I can't wrap my head around it," Roy said softly, as if pleading. "Who would do something like that? Kill people in Hospice?"

Just then Barry appeared at the cubicle entrance. He drew a folded white handkerchief from his pocket and wiped his perspiring face.

"I just had a call from a source. The shooter killed his mother before going to the nursing home." He pocketed the handkerchief.

"What?" Roy shouted.

"Shot in the back of the head, like the others."

"Oh, my God," Sylvia said. The pain was worsening. The throbbing in her throat began again. She hadn't felt it for several hours.

Alice was openly weeping now. "His mother? He killed his own mother?"

Sylvia thought of her father, dead at forty-eight of a heart attack, and of her mother, heartbroken at the loss of her husband, soon descending into early Alzheimer's. Her mother had been a resident of the same nursing home the shooter targeted. She died years ago of pneumonia in the same Hospice area.

Sylvia said she would go right to the main crime scene, but the others should go home until the press conference. With all the caffeine in her system, she did not think she could sleep anyway.

She walked Barry to his office. He was still perspiring.

"You okay, Boss?"

"Yes…No…I doubt any of us are going to be okay."

The pain shooting up Sylvia's back was more intense than usual. She winced.

"What's the matter, Sylvia? You look so washed out. Are you okay?"

"Just my back, Boss. Arthritis. An aging person's friend."

"Well, you be careful."

"Yeah…"

In her car, Sylvia had a weird mixture of emotions—hopeless and agitated. She wanted to lay her head on the steering wheel and weep but also hit her head on it. Those poor old people.

It was odd to have both feelings at once. Separately, however, they were familiar. Losing her parents made her very sad. But she was also ashamed of how little she had done for them while selfishly living her own sorry life—chasing after men who did not want her, raising a forty-year-old drug addicted daughter, drinking too much herself, working for a newspaper that would probably fold before she could retire without a penny saved.

At the nursing home, she showed the Deputy guarding the parking lot entrance her press card, and he motioned her in. She found a spot around back with the emergency vehicles and media vans. The affiliate TV people would be stepping all over her—the local print reporter. At the same time, the Mayor and Police Chief would be pushing her aside to gain national attention. She would have to muscle her way up from the lowest rung on the ladder, even though she was on first-name basis with the town's power elite.

She walked around to the front of the building. The small visitor parking lot was filled. The chaotic scene playing out reminded her of the aftermath of the school shootings she had seen on TV. Family members were assembling. Relatives of victims who were just informed had rushed over. They were easy to distinguish by the strength of their emotions. Clustered in small groups, they cried and held each other. A few collapsed in hysteria.

Another, stunned-looking part of the assemblage were the family members of the residents who survived. They were quieter and more composed.

"There but for the grace of God…," one was saying.

These relatives were waiting for clearance to go inside and care for their family members. Sylvia approached a man who was standing near the others, but slightly apart. She asked if he was there because of a connection to a resident.

"Yes. My father's in there. Someone called me to come over and stay with him," he said. Then, he glared at her, thrusting his finger in her face. "Are you a journalist? This is the fault of people like you. If you didn't report all these shootings, you wouldn't be giving lunatics ideas. The guy who did this was a copy-cat. He probably read about another shooting in your newspaper or heard about it on TV. He just picked a unique setting."

"Thank you, sir." She moved away, abashed.

The throbbing in her throat grew worse. She understood where the man was coming from. It was a classic dilemma—the public's right to know versus the public interest. A journalism school debate brought to life.

It was like her choice to her put her mother in a nursing home, knowing it might hasten her death, rather than care for her herself. Somehow it was related.

Just then, there was a text from her daughter.

4:12 a.m. Hi, Mom. How's it going?

That kind of friendly opening could only mean one thing. Her daughter wanted a favor. But Sylvia knew from long experience that any favor was likely related to drugs.

Delivered. Read. Can't talk now. I'm working overtime.

Read. I'm waiting at home for U. Need to borrow gas money to get to work. Let me know when U R off.

Her daughter did have a job. She needed gas to get to work. That much was true. But giving her the money was called "enabling" because it allowed her to spend her salary on drugs, sure that her mother would bail her out. If Sylvia refused, her daughter could lose her job. Then she would have to let her daughter live with her again. Or allow her to die on the streets.

Sylvia felt a headache starting. It was more pressure than pain. Perhaps someone had made coffee for the relatives and emergency workers. Another cup would ruin her stomach, but it might stop the headache. On her way around to the back of the building again, she phoned Peter.

"I'm sorry to wake you. I'm at the nursing home. There's a lot going on. I'm afraid I need you here as soon as possible. Oh—can you bring some Advil? My head is killing me."

In the rear parking lot, Sylvia interviewed an ambulance driver, who was sitting in the cab. She leaned against the door.

"It's hours since the shooting. Why the delay?"

"It's a crime scene. And there are ten victims. The police photographers took a half hour on each one. They all had to be ID'd. The Coroner had to declare each one dead—she didn't get here right away. Then they had to be bagged. It takes a while."

"Where will you take them?"

"The morgue. The Coroner's already back there. Each one will have an autopsy. That's what the guys tell me." He meant the Emergency Medical Technicians—the EMTs.

4:25 a.m. I have to be at work at 5. Where R U?

"Have you seen any coffee around here? I think I have a migraine," she said to the driver.

"No, but I have vodka in my thermos. Doesn't make your breath smell."

He passed it to her, and she took a big gulp, then screwed the top back on.

"Thanks. I owe you one."

She wandered around looking for someone else to interview. Badly, she wanted to go to her car and lie across the front seat. Just for five minutes. Her car was very close. The headache and the back pain were still there. No one was watching. She slipped into the car and lay down. Instantly, she was asleep.

It seemed like less than a minute later that her phone rang. It was Peter.

"I'm here, in the front. I can't see you."

It seemed difficult to breathe. What was it she wanted Peter to do? She answered him without sitting up.

"Don't worry about me. Start interviewing whoever will talk to you. We're racing with the affiliates."

"You sound funny. Do you want the Advil I brought?"

"Later. I'm onto something right now."

"Okay."

The vodka must be what was keeping her from being alert. She struggled to sit up. Mustn't go back to sleep.

4:40. Mom. I have to be at work in twenty minutes. And stop for gas. I need U. Now.

Sylvia was confused. Her daughter was asking for something. What?

There was a noise at the back entrance of the nursing home. The door opened, and two EMTs pushed a gurney with a body bag to the ambulance and loaded it in the cargo area. The ambulance drove off, probably with the last of the victims. Now, only the police vehicles and the affiliate vans were left, except for a few random sedans like hers.

Sylvia opened the glove compartment and fished around. In the back was her emergency cigarette. She had given up smoking a few months back, but with so much pressure, she needed to smoke. She lit up.

Her mother was also taken out the back door on a gurney when she died. There wasn't a body bag. Just a sheet placed tastefully over her, covering her face. She was loaded into a hearse from the funeral home.

Sylvia watched while the mortician, wearing a black suit and tie, directed the proceedings.

Before she moved to the nursing home, her mother pleaded to be allowed to stay with Sylvia. She promised to be no trouble. But her mother was trouble, forgetting to turn off the stove, wandering out of the house and getting lost, not able to attend to her own hygiene. She could not be left alone.

All Sylvia could do was harden her heart and sign the admission papers. A week later, her mother stopped asking to go home. She may have no longer remembered her home. By the time her mother died, Sylvia numbly accepted it as inevitable.

That had been emotional numbness. Now a physical numbness was creeping up her left arm. Was it a pinched nerve? She drew on the cigarette. How good it felt to have smoke in her lungs again. Suddenly, she was fully alert, no longer sleepy. In fact, she was feeling good, more than good, even wonderful. She stared at the brickwork that sided the back of the building. Never before had she been aware of how beautiful bricks and mortar were. They were astonishing. How could they be laid so precisely? Why had she never noticed before?

The cigarette was fantastic, although she was inhaling with difficulty. There was a heavy feeling in her chest, but the back pain and headache had disappeared. She thought of the ten hospice victims, who had suffered but were out of their misery now, like her mother. How happy she felt for them all. Happy, happy.

The heaviness in her chest was worse. She wanted to finish the cigarette, but all she could take were short, shallow puffs. The sunrise, appearing out the passenger side window, caught her eye. Such glory! A bright glaring fireball was growing, rising upward, covering the entire sky. The sun, the sky, the bricks, the cigarette—all spectacular.

She was so joyous when the familiar man in the black suit and tie, who might have been Barry, placed her ever so gently on the gurney, in her own body bag.

4:55. Fuck U, Mom.

7. THE POLITICAL ADVISOR

"How many more mass killings will there be in America before something stops them?" Maxine moaned to Ann over morning coffee in their kitchen.

She was telling Ann about the shooting in the nursing home the night before. The Maintenance Man on the staff had murdered ten residents before a Deputy killed him. Thank God it was not a school. She accompanied the Mayor to the crime scene a half hour after the killings occurred and stayed past dawn.

"I'm still wired. It was chaos! There were emergency responders, grieving relatives, traumatized staff, the media, and the usual attention-grabbing bullshit from the usual suspects."

She specifically meant Thomas, the Emergency Management Coordinator, who angled to be the next Mayor. The President of the City Council was another one, always trying to wheedle his way into more power. The Police Chief, a classic scene stealer, tried to hog the cameras. And the Mayor might have let them, if Maxine had not been there to supply the necessary back bone.

"You'd think politics would take a back seat during a tragedy like this. But behind the scenes, it was the same old idiocies."

"You've been up all night," Ann said. "Can you get some sleep?"

"I'll grab a couple of hours. I asked Philippa to call me when the Mayor wakes up. Fran is arranging a press conference—probably at noon. I bet the Mayor will have to barf five times before I can get him in front of a mic."

"Good God!"

"Yeah."

Two hours later, Ann was shaking Maxine awake in their bedroom, holding out the phone.

"It's Philippa."

"Okay." She blinked, taking it from Ann, ready to speak to the Mayor's wife.

"Well?" Ann asked when Maxine hung up.

"Philippa is preparing him. I'm meeting them both at eleven-forty-five for the press conference. I better take a shower while I have a chance."

Maxine, who had lost her mother at an early age and had been raised by her ambitious father, had won an internship with the Mayor's office while in college. After graduation, she started working for the Mayor's campaign organization. He was the ideal candidate. The problems were not apparent until he took office and actually had to govern. Then he froze up when a decision was needed. In truth, he was a follower, not a leader. Maxine was chosen as his advisor in part because he was more comfortable with women than men and in part because, like his wife Philippa, she was willing to take control.

"There's a fax coming in," Ann shouted from her basement home-office. Ann was a freelance event planner, working remotely. She brought the fax up to Sally.

"Oh! Thank God. Someone from Party headquarters in Indianapolis sent a speech. I was worried about him ad-libbing. Okay. Let's see. Yes. This is good. It's a 'we all stand together in the face of tragedy' speech. Perfect."

She grabbed clothing from her political outfits closet. She chose a black blazer, black pants, and charcoal blouse that suited her tall, angular frame. The first funerals for the four Jewish victims, whose tradition it was to be interred no more than forty-eight hours after death, started right after the news conference, two today and two tomorrow morning. The remaining six Christian funerals were spread through the following days. The Mayor was obligated to attend each one. It would be bad PR for him to miss any.

While she was gelling her hair into dark spikes, she realized that Ann was hanging around. This was unlike Ann, who was always, like Maxine, on the phone, doing something on her laptop, or running to a meeting. They often talked about needing to slow down and spend more time together. And Ann was still in her bathrobe, another oddity. She was an early riser and almost always dressed right after breakfast.

But now, she was just standing there, biting one of the blond strands of hair that hung limply over her face.

"Annie? Is something up?"

"No. No. Well, yes. We'll have to talk later."

Not good, Maxine thought, turning to face her.

"Annie. You're not breaking up with me, are you?"

Maxine always brought the worst possibility out into the open as fast as she could. If it was bad news, she needed to know right away.

"It's not that. I'm not breaking up with you. It's something else. It can wait."

"Right." Anything else could be discussed when she came home that night. First, she had to get herself and the Mayor through the next ten hours.

The Command Center had been relocated from the nursing home to the town hall, and the press conference would be held on the front steps. Fran, the Communications Officer, was organizing the speakers—first the Hospital Chaplain, who would get things going with a prayer, then the Police Chief followed by the nursing home Administrator. After that, the Mayor.

When Maxine arrived, Fran was dabbing make-up on him in an attempt to reduce the puffiness of his eyes and ashen complexion.

"I'm going for the 'stayed-up-all-night-to-ensure-the-safety-of-us-all' look," Fran smirked to Maxine.

The media people were milling about, adjusting their equipment. Right behind them, sixty to seventy members of the public stood waiting. Precisely at noon, the Chaplain walked up to the microphones and bowed his head.

"Heavenly Father, we ask You to transform the evil that has visited our community into love for one another….."

Next, the Police Chief stepped forward to give his update. The shooter had acted alone. His motive was unknown. The FBI would be conducting its own investigation. Meanwhile, an eleventh victim had been discovered. It was the shooter's mother, age eighty-five, who was found dead in her backyard, shot in the head.

What! Maxine thought. Son of a bitch! The Chief didn't tell us about the mother!

Disgusted by the Chief's underhandedness, she decided to take a break inside the town hall during the nursing home Administrator's report. It was fortunate that the speech from headquarters was generic enough not to give away the lack of coordination between the Chief and the Mayor's staff. She knew what the Chief's excuse would be—he did not want to disturb her or the Mayor when they might have fallen asleep. As if.

She needed to vent to Ann. That would make her feel better. Then she remembered their conversation that morning.

Oh my God, she thought. She wants to break up with me. She said "No," but what if that was just to spare my feelings until the day is over?

She and Ann had only been together for four months. It was the longest Maxine had ever been with anyone. Before Ann, her life had been one long string of hook-ups, mostly with others in political circles. She met Ann when the regular party event planner had the flu, and a local substitute had to be hired. They had been together since that day. She was sure that Ann was the love of her life. She began texting.

Today. 12:20. You're not leaving me, right?

Delivered. Read. I'm not leaving you.

Read. Freaking out here. Just tell me what the subject is that you want to talk about.

Read. Don't freak out. It's about Sandy.

Read. Sandy! Your Ex? Are you going back to Sandy?

Read. No. I'm not. No.

Still unsure, Maxine reluctantly went back outside to hear the end of the Mayor's speech.

"Our hearts may be filled with sorrow today, but we stand strong and we stand together. United, we say 'no' to those who spread hatred." He looked up at the audience. "Now I will take a few questions."

Maxine was anticipating what would happen when she went home.

"What did you want to talk about?" She imagined asking.

"I'm so, so sorry. I've made a mistake. It's not about you. It's about me. I didn't know myself. But I've been talking to Sandy again, and now I know that it is her I love."

A pain shot through Maxine's head. If the nursing home shooter were not dead, she might have thought she was his next victim. She actually put her hand through her hair, feeling for the wetness of blood. There was none. It was just a headache.

"What's the matter?" Fran whispered.

"Nothing. How's he been doing with the questions?"

"Fine. I've signaled him to wind it up. The first funeral is in forty-five, and we've got to get some food into him."

"Philippa can take him to a drive-thru. I'm going to run home for a few minutes. Meet you at the cemetery. Can you locate a yarmulke and a Jewish prayer shawl for him?"

"Will do. I'll run by the synagogue."

Maxine's head continued to throb. She drove home, went inside, and called to Ann.

"I only have a few minutes. Please, Annie, don't make me wait. Tell me if you are leaving me for Sandy."

"I already told you it wasn't anything like that," Ann said, coming down the stairs and standing in the foyer with Maxine. "Look. The mass killing last night? That's not the only thing that happened. There was a fire in Sandy's apartment. Everything Sandy owns was either consumed by fire or smoke-polluted. The Fire Marshal won't let anyone return, even to look for things that might still be undamaged. The building will have to be demolished. Sandy has nowhere to go."

"That happened last night? Why didn't anyone tell me?"

"The thing is, you know how guilty I feel about Sandy. She's a good, sweet person who never did anything wrong. I left her for you. It wasn't her fault that I fell in love with you."

"And?"

"And she can't go live with her family. They disowned her when she came out—and I'm the one who urged that. She has no place she can afford to go."

"Not true, Annie. She can rent something else."

"It's not so easy. She can't do stairs, which eliminates ninety percent of the rentals. And her disability check is too small for anything around here. She can't afford a motel, either."

"It's not our problem."

"It's my problem. If she and I had been married, I'd be paying her maintenance."

"But you weren't even engaged."

Ann turned to walk into the kitchen. Maxine followed. At the sink, Ann filled a glass with water. The clock on the wall ticked. The refrigerator hummed.

With her back to Maxine, she said "There's something else."

Maxine's stomach knotted. "What?"

"Don't get mad."

"What is it?"

"You won't get mad, will you?"

"Christ, just tell me."

"She's upstairs."

"Who."

"Sandy."

"What?"

"She's in the spare bedroom."

"No, Annie! No! Don't do this to me!" Maxine dropped onto a kitchen chair.

Ann banged down the glass and faced Maxine. "There was nothing else I could do."

"Without talking to me first? That's fucked."

"I told you not to get mad."

"Oh my God—what time is it?" She looked at her phone. "I've got to go. I can't do this now."

"We'll work it out. You'll see."

Just before slamming out the door, Maxine said, "I thought you said she can't do stairs."

"She can't."

"Well, somehow she got herself upstairs, didn't she?"

Maxine ran out to her car and sped to the cemetery. When she arrived, the funeral was underway. There was chanting in Hebrew. The casket was lowered, and everyone lined up in front of a large pile of loose soil next to the grave. The Rabbi handed the shovel to the first person, an elderly woman who was likely the widow of the victim. She scooped a bit of soil onto the tip of the shovel and threw it on top of the casket. For a moment, she stood there looking down. Then, she moved away, dabbing her eyes with a handkerchief. Meanwhile, the second person in line picked up the shovel. Philippa and the Mayor stood in the back, waiting their turns.

A small group of people standing around the apparent widow caught Maxine's eye. The older woman and two younger women were weeping, hanging onto each other. Two men hovered over them, wiping their eyes on their sleeves. The Rabbi had given shovel duty to one of the elders. He went to the widow and folded her in his arms.

For the first time, it hit Maxine. Real people were really suffering. The shooter had shed real blood. He even killed his own mother. That really appalled Maxine. His mother! She had been so caught up in her job of making the Mayor look good that she had done what she always did—not looked beyond her own nose. And now this situation with Ann's Ex. Maxine wondered if she was about to weep, too.

Ann had been coming down the stairs earlier, when Maxine came in the door. Of course! She had been upstairs with Sandy. They had been planning how to tell Maxine—in stages. First, Ann would say that Sandy had nowhere to go because of a fire. Was that even true? Did the Police Chief not mention it because it never happened? Then, she would be told that Sandy had already moved in upstairs. Even though she not supposed to be able to climb stairs. Next, when Maxine went home after the second funeral, in the later afternoon, Ann would tell her she was back together with Sandy. In Maxine's own house!

Maxine paced back and forth in the cemetery parking lot. Most of the crowd was returning to the synagogue for the start of the second funeral, then accompanying the second casket back out to the cemetery. Philippa and the Mayor waited for them in their car. Maxine guessed the Mayor would use the time to nap. She knocked on Philippa's side. Philippa rolled down the window.

"You guys need anything?"

"No, we're fine. Hey! Are you okay? You look like you've been crying."

Maxine looked over at the Mayor. He was already dozing.

"Ann is being weird. I don't know."

"Weird how?"

"She's let Sandy move into our spare bedroom."

"What!" Philippa rolled the window down further and grabbed Sally's forearm.

"Yeah. She says she's not breaking up with me, but I don't know."

"Her Ex? In your house?"

"I don't know what to do, Philippa."

"Just don't do anything hasty. Talk to them. Get some clarity. Okay?"

"Yeah. You're right. I may be freaking out over nothing."

Maxine resumed her pacing, trying to work off her anxiety. Eventually, the line of vehicles returned to the cemetery, with two limousines in the lead. The casket was borne to the gravesite on the shoulders of six people. This time, it was a man—probably the son of the deceased—who seemed to be the principal mourner. He was openly weeping. But what got to Maxine was a girl of about seven who had her arms around him and was burying her face in his jacket. Maxine sniffled into a tissue, then quickly shook her head.

While the crowd was lining up to shovel dirt onto the second casket, she ducked into her car to text Ann.

3:32. If Sandy can't do stairs, how did you get her up there?

Delivered. Read. It took forever. She had to stop every second step to catch her breath.

Read. How are you thinking this will work, if I ever agree to it.

Read. Sandy will stay upstairs. I'll bring her what she needs. You never have to see her, if you don't want to.

Read. But Annie! I'll know she's there. I won't be able to get it out of my mind. It won't be the same. It won't be just the two of us.

Read. If you don't let her stay, I'll wind up feeling even guiltier and resent you.

Read. You're saying either way it won't be the same. That's just great!

Read. Don't be mad.

Media trucks were pulling up. Fran's car was among them. Maxine went to meet her.

"Show time," Fran said. "If you get His Highness up here, he may get to say a few words on camera about the funerals."

Maxine walked over to Philippa and whispered to her. Philippa took the Mayor's arm and guided him to the road. Maxine figured there was nothing more she could do. As long as Fran was on media duty, she could slip away. She was anxious to get home.

While driving, she reflected. The shooter had changed everything. The mass killing was putting the town in the national spotlight. The FBI investigation would instigate rumors of second shooters funded by outside organizations. The Mayor would be propped up and re-elected, while those behind the scenes and his wife held him together with twine.

During the funerals, Maxine had moments of empathy for the victims and their families. But then a much deeper sorrow, secretly present since her mother's death when she was a young child, frightened her into covering it up again with chilly ambition.

What Maxine feared was that she, Ann, and Sandy would be living together in a shifting pattern of couplings and uncouplings. That, and the Mayor's upcoming campaign, would keep her from dwelling on the personal tragedy that happened to her twenty years before. That terrible loss had shaped her into her the kind of cynical opportunist who, having gradually forsaken every shred of idealism, even used a calamity like the murder of eleven people as a stepping stone to political success.

8. THE CORONER

The Coroner's work phone beeped just as she settled down in her bathrobe, with a glass of merlot, her calico curled up next to her, prepared to watch a rerun of "Miss Marple" on PBS. It was a text from the Police Chief.

"Ten shot, probable fatalities, in dementia nursing home. Alleged perp shot, also probably dead. Come ASAP."

Without shutting off the TV, she put on her work clothes, white lab jacket, and rushed off. When she arrived, the scene was mayhem—police, media people, relatives of victims—all running around in a state of shock. The ten victims were in the Hospice section of the nursing home. That was good news. It was a self-contained area. She easily isolated it with yellow crime-scene tape. The alleged perp was out in the back garden, another easily taped area.

After she re-taped what had been hastily put up by the deputies, she was about to enter the room of the first victim when she noticed a photograph of a young woman in the frame beneath the nameplate. It must have been the victim at a much younger age. The Coroner was startled. The face in the photograph looked familiar. Yet, since the victim was in her nineties, it had to be taken before the Coroner was born. It stuck in her mind as she began the next phase of her work.

Going from victim to victim, she declared each one dead. Once the homicide lab people finished their dusting, photographing, and gathering evidence, the bodies could be ID'd, bagged, and sent to the morgue for autopsies, as required under Indiana law. This had to be started immediately out of respect for the surviving families, who would be waiting to receive the bodies in order to conduct funerals. There would be no sleep for her that night.

Back in the exam room at the morgue, it was almost morning when the first cadaver arrived. Her assistant was not there yet, so the EMT helped her remove the bag before taking off to collect the others. The autopsy would not be difficult. The medical records had been faxed, so she knew the cause of the cadaver's last illness. She had to locate the entrance, trajectory, and exit of the bullet in the head.

The photograph was still nagging at her. All at once, she knew. The woman in the photo looked like a slightly older version of a girl the Coroner had been obsessed with for decades. Neither the opening of the skull, the removal of the brain, nor the inspection of the surrounding facial area would stop the cascade of obsessive thoughts. They were a constant presence anyway, no matter what she was doing. Her mind insisted on drifting back to events that happened thirty years earlier, when she was fifteen.

It would have cost the popular girl nothing to say 'Hi' to me. What did she know of the courage it took a person like me to say 'Hello' to a person like her. She turned away from me so she would not have to answer. Was that a flicker of revulsion on her face? If so, it was an instant for her, not even committed to memory. Or just the kind of memory swept from the brain during deep sleep. Like it never existed. While for me, it was carved into the amygdala, like a trauma, startled into lucid being again by any of a hundred triggers.

Amygdala. A little almond-shaped part of the brain. There are two of them. Amygdalae. The parts that never forget. It will never forget how I felt. Not now, thirty years later, not ever. That's how deeply she hurt me. My amygdalae will remember, always.

Once the first autopsy was completed, the Coroner went to the sink area to wash up before writing her report. This area of the exam room reminded her of the kitchen area of the high school cafeteria. The whole room came back to her intact. The mustard-colored walls, the strong smell of fried potatoes, the din, kids laughing (maybe at her), sitting by herself at an unoccupied table. She always sat where she had the best view of the popular girl. Every day, she promised herself she would say something that would cause the popular girl to look at her. Every day she lost her nerve. The popular girl never looked her way.

Because I am ugly. Ugly.

Obsessively, she squeezed and pinched the pimples on her forehead and cheeks. Her hair, which she cut herself, lay in uneven slabs around her head. She squinted through smudged eyeglasses she seldom thought to clean.

So ugly.

The Coroner's memory was interrupted when, at last, her young assistant arrived. Now things moved more quickly. They transferred the first cadaver to a trolley, wheeled it into the cold room, and placed it in a drawer. Then they took the second of the eleven cadavers to the exam room and started the next autopsy.

Even during the procedure, the Coroner was obsessing about the past.

In desperation, back then, she made a plan. She would either say "hello" to the popular girl or she would kill herself. She would swallow a bottle of aspirin. The choice would force her to act. The next morning, still not knowing what she would do, she rose an hour early. The school bus would not come for two hours. In the shower, she used water that was nearly scalding and scrubbed herself hard with a loofa. She lathered her hair with a harsh-smelling shampoo, then briskly towel dried herself. Carefully, she ironed a shirt of pure white cotton and checked her outfit for stains. All the while, there was a tingling in her limbs and a hard thumping in her chest.

Today is the day. I say 'hello' to her or I die.

She did not remember the school bus ride or her morning classes. What she did remember was sitting in her usual seat in the cafeteria with the popular girl in view. A steaming tray lay before her. Nausea stopped her from eating. All the while, a voice in her head spoke.

Now. Now. Do it now or die!

Suddenly, she felt herself rising to her feet. It was as if something else yanked her up and lifted her feet, one step at a time. The cerebrum, which controls walking, took over. The cerebrum walked her, foot by foot, nearer to the popular girl's table. Then it caused her to stop a few inches from the popular girl. All the other kids at the table stopped talking and looked at her. Some had jeering smiles, some just looked perplexed. What was *she* doing there? Her cerebrum caused her to look straight at the popular girl.

"Hello," she said, softly.

The popular girl stared at her briefly, then returned to her lunch. She looked away from the one who had the effrontery to approach her unbidden. There was an awkward silence. Her cerebrum kept her frozen in place, unacceptably, as if she was too dumb to know she was not wanted.

Then her cerebrum jerked into action and made her run from the cafeteria, down the cinder block hallway, and out the school door. The secretary or a teacher called after her.

"Hey! Stop! Come back here right now!"

Her cerebrum did not listen. It caused her to run fast and far, red-faced, panting, so very embarrassed. Why had she made the choice to greet the popular girl instead of dying? She deserved to die. Because she said 'hello,' she was condemned to live with her shame. Never did she go into the high school cafeteria again. Instead, she hid in a stall in the girls' bathroom during the lunch period, quietly pulling her hair out strand by strand, until she created a bald spot for others to stare at and ridicule.

"Do you want to finish all the autopsies today?" It was her assistant. "We will have to miss a second night of sleep to do it. I don't know if I can be on my feet that long."

"We'll see how it goes."

Her assistant was how old? Twenty-five? And tired already? Here she was, a woman of forty-five, never married, never having gone on a single date. The popular girl had also become a woman of forty-five. The Coroner had kept track of her from afar for all these years. Their families were acquainted enough for the Coroner to overhear information about the popular girl, not that she would ever show interest or ask. Over time, she learned where the popular girl had gone to college, about her marriage and subsequent divorce, the jobs she had taken in Chicago and Birmingham, and more recently, that she had returned to their home town in southern Indiana to take care of her ailing mother. The popular girl was living with her mother a few blocks away from the Coroner.

Back in their high school days, the Coroner often took refuge in the library when she wanted a quiet place to be alone. She seldom read. The words in books fell away from her mind as soon as she read them. But she did like pictures. One time, she found a book left on a library table titled "Know Your Brain." In large print on the first page was a paragraph she could retain. It said the brain was an organ, one of a number of organs in the body, like the liver, the spleen, and even the skin. It was part of her, but it was not "her." It controlled her with its own parts—the cerebellum, the cerebrum, the frontal lobe. Yet, if she was not her brain, who was she? Where was she? Was she even in her body, or was that an illusion?

It was her brain that made her fearful of running into the popular girl, now that she lived nearby. And it was her brain that also made her hope to see the popular girl, who she still hated and still loved. Unless that was what *she*, the real *she*, felt and not just the organ in her head. In any case, she guessed it would not do any harm to just have a peek at the popular girl, to see what she was like thirty years later and to find out if she still felt the same way about her.

The Coroner began driving by the popular girl's house whenever she needed to go to the supermarket or on her way to work. Many times, she circled the popular girl's house before the day came that the door opened, and there she was, hurrying down the steps with a watering can in her hand. The popular girl was older, heavier, and with cropped hair. But she was recognizable to the Coroner—and still beautiful. How stunning it was to see her in person, to be near her for a moment as she drove by, craning her neck, her hands tightly gripping the steering wheel. That was all she wanted—a look.

During the tedium of writing the reports, while her assistant took a break, the Coroner daydreamed. The popular girl would show up at her apartment. She had heard that the Coroner was living there, and she wanted to visit her. She would bring a bouquet from her garden. The Coroner would invite her in. She and her guest would sit in the front room. The popular girl would apologize for her rude behavior when they were in high school. She had remembered it with shame all these years. She hoped that the Coroner could forgive her. She hoped they could be friends.

The Coroner was not fool enough to believe her daydream had any chance of happening. The popular girl did not even know she existed, if she ever knew. Having her so nearby made the Coroner as desperate as she had been in high school. When she thought she could not stand the desperation one moment longer, a plan came to her from her cerebellum. It was similar to the command from the cerebellum she received thirty years before. She should either contact the popular girl or kill herself.

She did not disagree with her cerebellum. What was there to live for if she could not have a friendship, or even an acquaintanceship, with the popular girl? She had waited thirty years for this opportunity. It was time.

Now! Now! Do it now or die!

The assistant was back from her break. They began the fourth autopsy. The Coroner showed the assistant the different parts of the brain. The assistant was able to locate the trajectory of the bullet on her own. It was a rare opportunity for her, as there were few murders of this type in their town.

Later, the Coroner took a break while the assistant cleaned up. Once again, her thoughts turned to the popular girl. She would not risk seeking her out in person. She could not bear that sort of embarrassment again. She would write her a letter. A real letter on real paper. That way the popular girl would understand the special effort she had made, so unlike a dashed off email or text. Not that she knew the popular girl's email address or phone number.

She kept a box of pink stationary given to her during her childhood by one of her mother's boyfriends. Faintly, she remembered that he had wanted a gift in return. She did not recall what it was. It was hidden in her amygdala. Her mother threw out the boyfriend, but allowed her to keep the stationary. It was quality. The paper was linen. The envelop flaps had scalloped edges. She thought it too pretty to use.

It was time for a more substantial break in order to eat, change clothes, and get some sleep. The assistant showed signs of emotional fatigue. A mass shooting with so many victims was not what medical school prepared her for. They decided when to resume work. Both went home.

Before she even took her coat off, the Coroner went to her desk and found the stationary. She took out a single sheet. She did not write a salutation to the popular girl. She just began writing.

Every day, for the past thirty years, I have been in pain because of what you did to me in high school. You probably don't know what this is about. I will remind you. On May 28th, 1989, just after noon, I approached you in the high school cafeteria to say hello. You would not even look at me. You humiliated me in front of the whole school. I have never been able to forget the pain you caused me.

The Coroner's cerebellum decided she should tell the popular girl what she wanted from her.

I have a forgiving heart. If you want my forgiveness, you must write me a real letter, apologizing and confessing in detail to what you did to me and why you did it. I will give you a week to think it over and to figure out who I am. Then I will write you again and tell where to leave your written reply.

She did not sign her name. After sealing the pink letter in the pink envelope, she put it in the mailbox. The popular girl would get the letter the next day. It would be a long week of anxious thoughts.

Instead of using the time to sleep, the Coroner went to the library. She needed to know if the book that inspired her to go to medical school and that shaped so much of her thinking was still available. "Know your Brain." There it was, still in its familiar place in the Non-Fiction section. Flipping the pages of colorful illustrations, she stopped at the section on the amygdala. It was accompanied by a short paragraph:

"The amygdala is the emotional/irrational part of the brain. When an individual perceives a threat, the amygdala can take over the whole brain."

Was that what was happening to her?

She went back to the exam room early and started on the fifth autopsy. It was an elderly female. Not that it made a difference. Male. Female. Adult. Child. Ten victims or a hundred. Unlike her assistant, she didn't care. It was evident something was emerging in "her" that had been hidden by her brain. It was as if a snake was uncoiling and a clear, calculating self was coming into being. This *she* had given her the strength to mail the letter. No longer did she want to kill herself. Soon, she would write to the popular girl again, a short note on the same pink paper telling her where to leave her reply to the first letter.

The popular girl had been told to apologize and confess. If she did, she would be forgiven. But if she did not reply or if she failed to apologize in the way she had been instructed, she would have to be punished.

The Coroner knew about punishment. Her whole life since the incident in the high school cafeteria had been one long punishment. Now it might be the popular girl's turn. Time would tell. Once back in her apartment at the end of the autopsies, the Coroner took another pink sheet of stationary and began making a list of the punishments only a cerebrum with medical knowledge would know how to inflict without getting caught.

9. THE CHAPLAIN

The Hospice Chaplain was at home in his slippers, finishing his case notes at ten p.m., after a long day of ministering to those who were dying. A glass of whiskey waited on the side table, and the muted TV was tuned to CNN. His phone sounded. It was the Administrator of the dementia nursing home. That was odd. He was usually summoned by a nurse or the Hospice director.

"Frank. Are you sitting down?"

Her tone was urgent.

"I need you here immediately. Our Maintenance Man—you know him? He murdered the Hospice residents. All ten of them. He shot them in the head one-by-one, Frank."

"What!" He was instantly lightheaded. His blood pressure was spiking.

"All ten, Frank. A policeman finally shot the Maintenance Man. He's dead, too, Frank."

The whole Hospice unit? Ten of his clients murdered? Automatically, he placed two fingers on his wrist, feeling for his ragged pulse.

"Please…just come, Frank. We're going to need you."

"Okay. Right away."

Yet, he did not immediately get up. He sipped his whiskey while picturing his clients. Mr. Berg, ninety-seven years old. Expected to die within the week. Mrs. Chaney. Only seventy, but with a glioblastoma in her brain. Mr. Elliot, a stroke victim. Not expected to recover. His clients, murdered. It would be awful for the families, not to mention the staff. Cynthia. Mildred. And the volunteers, some quite young, college age.

He found a stray cigarette in the little drawer of the side table. He was planning to quit, but he needed a minute to get his blood pressure and pulse under control. Smoking would calm his nerves. His hands trembled as he snapped the lighter. He knew how to deal with those who were in an ordinary grieving process. Yes. But this time he would be handling the grief of a larger community reacting to deliberate murders.

A few spilled Xanax were in the same drawer. They had been shared with him by the family members of clients. He found two and downed them with the rest of the whiskey. He needed to urinate before he left. It was a slow and frequent process, now that his prostate was choking off his bladder. *God damn it!* One day he would need surgery, before the pencil thin stream was reduced to drips.

A banner appeared on CNN:

Mass murder in a nursing home in Indiana. Ten dead. Shooter killed by police.

Turning off the mute, he sat there, smoking and listening to the report. The video showed the blinking lights of emergency vehicles in the nursing home parking lot. People who were milling around at a distance were being interviewed. Some had heard the shots. All lived close by.

After stubbing out his cigarette, the Chaplain went to the bathroom. Several minutes later, he changed to fresher clothing. Finally, he was ready. He should be there in fifteen minutes.

The gas gauge was nearly on empty. He would have to stop at the Shell station. Gas was nearly three dollars per gallon there. But the Citgo station was a few cents cheaper and only a few blocks further on. He drove there. On his salary, every penny counted.

Before pulling back onto the road, he opened the thermos he filled with whiskey before leaving his apartment and shoved it between his legs. This was a violation of the open container law. But it was an emergency. Fortunately, the Xanax was kicking in. His breathing slowed. He drove the longer way to the nursing home. It was just a few minute's difference.

He passed the middle school and slowed. No one was there. The lights were off. He was reminded of Brenda, a dear child he met when she was twelve. Her grandfather died. She wept in his arms. He looked down at the mass of golden curls and felt a warm glow in the spot where her face was buried against his chest. Since that day, he often sat in his car across the street from the middle school, between visits to clients, hoping to catch a glimpse of her running down the school steps to catch the school bus. She was older, which might have lessened her appeal, except she still had the angelic golden curls ringing her head. As often happened, thoughts of Brenda caused him to stop in a darkened side-street, where he could take care of himself. No one saw, and no one was harmed.

Ten minutes later, he was back on the main road. He thought of what lay ahead. There was nothing to worry about. The prayers and words of comfort were very familiar to him. They were especially helpful with those who were unemotional. But the ones who sobbed openly were a challenge. There was usually a family member present who could help. A mass murder, on the other hand, was liable to draw fewer relatives who were calm themselves. He would make the emotional ones wait. They would have to learn to control themselves. He would not enable them. The calm ones would get his attention first.

The thermos was empty. How had that happened? He did not recall finishing the contents. It would not hurt, he told himself, to get a refill. There was a liquor store a bit further on. During the drive, he reminded himself that he was a master of his trade. No longer did he bother to attend mandatory continuing education classes, falsifying his list of course credits on his application for the annual license renewal instead.

What's the point? I'm already versed in the course contents. I could teach them myself.

At the liquor store, he purchased a bottle of Jack Daniel's, pouring all of it into the thermos. Now he had to urinate again. He used the liquor store restroom. Ten minutes later, he was back in his vehicle.

His phone rang. It was the nursing home. He did not risk answering while driving. In a short time, he would be there. He needed to U-turn, but the car insisted on going straight ahead. Soon he arrived at the city outskirts, heading into the county.

Did it really matter? His clients were dead. The families might not even be there yet. He had time to take a little drive. Even if some arrived before him, they would be too busy with the police and other officials to need spiritual guidance. Unfortunately, he forgot to take the stack of Hospice pamphlets on dealing with grief, always a good substitute if he ran out of things to say.

He did know comforting words and prayers. He memorized both during his training, twenty years ago. The assigned text book had the phrases he still used without variation. The three or four he knew by heart applied to just about any situation.

When there were complaints by those who claimed he lacked compassion and spontaneity, he reminded the Hospice director that the same words and prayers were used by clergy for hundreds of years. Millions benefitted from them. And if he were not the warmest or cleverest, if he sometimes forgot the memorized words of comfort or botched the prayers, the intent was what mattered.

And, no. He had never been drunk during funeral services. The families of clients who said that were probably put up to it by the popular Hospital Chaplin. How he hated the man. It was against his principles to sink to the Hospital Chaplin's level by giving cheap hugs or by listening to lengthy hysterical outbursts. These were the easy ways to gain a following.

He, on the other hand, bluntly told the dying they were facing judgment. They stared at him. He reminded families that death comes to us all. That was not the easy way. He was not trying to win friends. He was doing his job as the Holy One willed him to do it.

At the thought of the Hospital Chaplain, the Hospice Chaplain gripped the wheel until his knuckles turned white. How simple it was for a handsome clergyman to be trusted and admired. If they traded places for just a day, if the Hospital Chaplin had the severe overbite, the small chin, and the watery high tenor voice, while he had the good looks—just for a day—everyone would see who was the more in demand.

The Holy One willed him the more difficult path—the distressing investigations, the frequent job changes, the unfair evaluations, the near revocation of his license while he was forced to take unneeded classes in ethics. But he answered his calling as the Lord intended. All he had to do was trust in the Lord, who would be shown him the way.

But first, he needed to calm himself again. He could not show up at the nursing home with his heart beating against his chest like a caged bat. Without slowing, he reached over to the glove compartment and fished around for the bottle of Oxycontins. He took his hands off the steering wheel momentarily to open the container. It had been on the bedside of a deceased client, unnoticed by the distracted family. He put it in his pocket. After all, the client no longer needed pain killers.

Upending the container into his mouth, he swallowed a few. The two-lane road was winding into a rural area, without lights or signposts. He turned on his brights. Sooner or later he would reach the nursing home. Unless he continued on. He could just surrender to the Lord and let Him decide.

Ahead, he saw a vehicle coming toward him on the opposite side. He sped toward it. How bright its lights were, like two stars in the heavens, like a sign from the Lord.

Where Art Thou? He heard the Lord say.

"I'm coming," the Hospice Chaplain answered, weaving to the left.

10. THE WIFE

By the end of the second week after the shooting in the nursing home, the Wife was completely transformed. She would be unrecognizable to the people who knew her, both physically and mentally, and to herself as well. Only her husband, a resident of the nursing home, remained unaware of her change. But he was in an advanced stage of Alzheimers and slept much of the time.

She was floored by the disturbing phone call on the night of the shooting. If the man on the line gave his name, she did not remember it.

"Mrs. Gilbert?" He had a robotic voice. "I'm from the corporate headquarters of the nursing home. Your husband is fine. He is unhurt. There has been a crime at our facility in your town in Indiana. You may hear about it on the media. I wanted to contact you before you found out from that source and to reassure you that the crime did not involve your husband in any way."

"Crime?" Was there a robbery? Fraud?

"I'm afraid that a number of residents were shot. But not your husband."

There was some seconds of silence. Was he still on the line?

"We are told that the perpetrator was our Maintenance Man. Again, let me say—your husband was not one of those shot, and he did not observe the shooting. He was asleep in his room in the front of the building. The shootings were in the section located in the rear. Your husband was not awakened by the noise."

The Wife had a momentary vision of blood in the building, of stepping in it by mistake or somehow smearing it on herself. She shuddered.

"Mrs. Gilbert, may I go on? There is more, but I can call you back if you like."

"No. You may tell me."

"The perpetrator is deceased. He was shot by the police. It's possible there are other victims who weren't in the building. There is still an investigation going on."

"Should I go there?"

"Yes. I hope you will. Arrangements are being made for one or two visitors per resident to enter the building by the front door. As you can imagine, we are short-staffed, and it might be helpful for a family member or a spouse to be with each resident during this trying night. We should be fully operational in the morning."

He sounded as if he was reading from a script.

She stammered that she would go right away. But when she hung up, ridiculous fears began to plague her. She knew they were ridiculous because they had nothing to do with the awful thing that happened in her husband's nursing home. Instead, she was afraid of missing her self-care regimen. She could not miss a day without consequences. If she left now, she would have to skip her morning routine—yoga, meditation, skin exfoliation and moisturizing. Her low-calorie breakfast smoothy.

The Wife was seventy years old, but daily exercise, her attention to weight, hydration, detoxing, sufficient sleep, supplements, and a little Botox, helped her look younger, she believed. She said she was sixty-five when asked, and the usual response was a satisfying "No way! You don't look a day over fifty."

In her youth, she hunted for a man with the dark eyes and sculptured face of Peter Fonda, and she found him in the man who became her husband. Bob. Even at seventy-five, with a mind obliterated by Alzheimers, Bob was still erect and handsome with a head of thick white hair, although his facial expression was blank. The Wife took him to her own stylist rather than allow the nursing home barber to touch him, and she made sure he used the facility treadmill daily. Sometimes, she sneaked the dessert off of his dinner tray and threw it away.

During their long and she would say successful marriage, Bob had been an executive at a pharmaceutical company. Their affluence afforded them a good life with a large country home, condos in Florida and Colorado, and abundant travel. If Bob did not recognize her now, she joked that it was the secret to a good relationship—existing amicably without the irritating familiarity that could cause conflict. There was something to be said for superficiality.

After taking an hour to do the most crucial parts of her routine, the Wife drove to the home. It was still dark outside. She was surprised to find the road cordoned off. She had to identify herself to be allowed through. Perhaps a dozen police cars were parked at odd angles in front of the building, their red lights blinking. She parked in an empty space. An officer checked off her name when she entered the building. There was unusual activity in the hallways. EMTS, the police, and family members moved purposefully among the residents. But she found Bob in his room, still asleep. She closed his door and prepared to spend the remainder of the night sitting beside him.

The back of the building was where the Level Four's were housed. They were the ones in Hospice. She did not suppose any were still alive. She wanted to be sad, because it was sad when anyone was killed, even if it no longer mattered to them if they were alive or dead. But the murderer picked the right ones to kill, to be frank about it.

She was told, she now remembered, that the perpetrator—the killer— was the Maintenance Man. He was one of those people she barely noticed on the periphery of her life. He had been helpful lifting and carrying items when Bob moved in a year ago. But she did not recall having an interaction with him since. He was always there, somewhere, scurrying around the building with a belt of tools. That was all she noticed.

With a little prickle of fear, she wondered if he was the only shooter. Were the police looking for others? Were she and Bob in danger?

There was a knock on the door. A young police officer entered.

"Is everything okay in here, Ma'am?"

"Yes. My husband is asleep."

"Just checking, Ma'am. We're in the hallway if you need us."

The Wife wondered if this young man thought she was Bob's wife or if she looked young enough, attractive enough, to pass for Bob's daughter.

All of her life, she had been beautiful. As a baby, she won contests. She never knew what it was like not to be the most beautiful girl and, later, the most beautiful woman in the room. She always turned heads. Even in her advanced years, people seemed surprised to hear she was old enough to have a husband in a nursing home.

The Wife realized she only had a few years before she might wind up in a nursing home herself, looking as aged as all the women looked who lived at the facility. That is what it meant to look *bad* for one's age. Not just gray-haired, but unkempt, unstylish, incontinent, smelly. She would rather be dead.

But everyone said something like that. They would rather die before they lost something—their mind, their money, their spouse, their hair.

Yet, here was the Wife's chance, if there was a second killer. She could wander around, the building, making herself a target. She knew she would not. She was too scared to invite death. She only wished for it to happen quickly and painlessly in her sleep. But not just yet.

The day after the shootings, some residents were transferred to other facilities. The Wife decided to keep Bob where he was. It was not as if he knew or understood what had happened. His room had not changed. There was some staff turn over, but some from before remained, even if they were shell shocked. Besides, this was still the best such facility in town and the only one on the more fashionable east side. The others were across the tracks, so to speak. Very inconvenient.

The next day, the corporation that owned the nursing home sent an email listing supportive measures for the relatives and for the more cognizant residents. These included individual and group debriefings, grief counselors, information sessions with security experts, interviews with police officers, and discounts on the monthly fees for the remainder of the year.

During the next three days, reporters interviewed the relatives and spouses of the victims and of the surviving residents as well. Some were interviewed soon after they were told. Others—like the Wife—after it was discovered that the killer's mother was also a victim. Apparently, she had been shot first. The reporters wanted dramatic statements. They urged her to guess that the killer shot his mother as a demented act of euthanasia. Perhaps the residents were shot for the same reason before the killer provoked "suicide by cop" in the back of the building.

"Well, yes, possibly, euthanasia is a logical explanation, isn't it?" This response guaranteed her air time. "I never thought this could happen in a nursing home. And the Maintenance Man never seemed unhappy. He was always cheerful when I saw him," she said, repeatedly, in close-up, throughout the next forty-eight hours.

She was consistently identified as the "wife of seventy-five-year-old Bob Winston, a former executive in the pharmaceutical industry, now suffering from Alzheimer's Disease and unable to recognize family members."

The interviews were not only broadcast on the local TV news networks, but on CNN, Fox News, NBC, and all the major networks. The "Nursing Home Massacre" gripped the nation, as had the killing sprees in Orlando, Las Vegas, and most horrifically, in several schools.

She watched on the sixty-four inch television screen in her house, flipping from one channel to another. Each one showed her face in brutal detail, far more so than a magnifying mirror did, revealing a seventy-year-old woman who did look her age. She was shocked by the camera's blunt unkindness. Every wrinkle, every blemish, every pore was enlarged on screen. She was aware that media cameras made people look heavier and older than they were, but she never expected to look *this* old.

After the broadcasts, she had the worst migraine in her life. She could not get out of bed. Unable to bear any light, she lay in agony with the curtains closed and a clothe over her eyes. She stuffed cotton into her ears to avoid the torment of sound. She staggered to the bathroom to vomit and saw whirls and squiggles if she dared opened her eyes.

She did not visit Bob for several days. No one called. No one knocked on her door. If she had children, she could have asked them for help, but she had been too worried about ruining her figure to allow herself to get pregnant. She had no close friends—her beauty caused resentment in others, she imagined. Others could not be fully trusted.

When the pain finally subsided, she had no desire to go out. It was not as if Bob missed her. There was no one to miss her. The thought of her face on TV, in its dismaying oversized devastation—in bars, restaurants, gyms, hotel lobbies—shamed her terribly.

The word "faded beauty" kept running through her head. Her beauty was "fading." What did she have if she did not have her beauty? Nothing. She had no talent, no interests. She had never lived without beauty. Obsessively, she kept looking in the mirrors in the house. There were many. It used to please her to pass through rooms and see herself reflected wherever she went. Just as it pleased her—or reassured her—to see herself reflected in the admiring gaze of others.

But this was nonsense. She would shower, dress, and leave the house to shop, even though remnants of the migraine still lingered. Shopping therapy is what she needed. She would drive to the Keystone Mall in Indianapolis, more than an hour away. She would buy several new outfits at Nordstrom, Saks 5th Avenue, or Chicos.

On the drive up, she felt like herself again. But in the mall, she saw that the crowd, mostly a generation or two or three younger than her, looked at her with disinterest if they looked at her at all. Had they seen her ruined face on TV? Were they hiding disgust at her ugliness? In stores, she did not recall ever having been ignored by a salesperson. They always told her how good she looked in whatever she tried on. Not now.

She wound up slinking away without making a single purchase. She made the decision not to stop off to see Bob. She needed to go right home.

Her obsession with mirrors continued to grow. No longer was it a pleasure to glance at her reflection as she passed them. Still, she gazed at herself, searching for wrinkles, a sagging jaw line, a wattled neck, thinning hair. And with every gaze, she saw more evidence of decline. The memory of the close-ups on TV merged with what she saw reflected in mirrors.

There was a full-length mirror in her bedroom. Previously, she used it to admire her body, toned by hours spent at the gym. Now, she looked at herself with repulsion. How could she not have seen the sagging breasts, the soft belly, the weak underarm muscles, the mottled skin?

She was reluctant to leave the house. She phoned the supermarket to sign up for their delivery service as well as Amazon for subscription groceries and household goods. How she missed trips to the stores, the pharmacies, the bank, the dry cleaner, looking like a queen. And Bob at the facility—even though it had only been a week since she had seen him, he was already hazy, as if he were bleaching out. It was a relief that the nursing home was fully staffed again. She was not really needed there.

Frequent migraines began to confine her to bed more often. Or were they brain tumors, an aneurysm, cancer? One day, she awoke without pain, with new resolve. She would put on make-up, fix her hair, and drive to the Country Club for an afternoon of cards and drinks with the "regulars," women she had not seen much of since Bob had left home a year before.

But after parking her car, she had to pass big reflecting windows to get to the entrance. And she remembered the large tv monitor, always tuned to Fox News, that would have broadcast her aged face to the members. She changed her mind and drove back home. This happened three times before she gave up.

She was becoming a hermit for no good reason. What kind of values did she have if she allowed her aging appearance, her "fading beauty," to dominate her? What kind of person was she? So selfish. So narcissistic. So without character. She would fight this. She would go to an Alanon meeting. It was not just for those with alcoholics in their lives, she had been told. Anyone who wished to do 12-Step work was welcome. The meetings were held in a church basement.

When she entered, she saw that she was the grandmother, if not the great-grandmother, of the group. No one was within twenty years of her age. And she looked out of place in her silk lime-green suit. Everyone was wearing jeans and many wore oversized lumber-jack shirts. She turned and fled.

At home, she daydreamed. She remembered being crowned beauty queen at high school proms, the county fair, and the local and state Miss America, Mrs. America, and Miss Universe Beauty contests, in an era before feminist activism put a stop to such events. She remembered going to parties and functions with Bob. There were invitations to the Captain's table on cruise ships and upgrades at hotels.

When another week had gone by, she saw a half-inch of gray root growth in the part in her hair. And without Botox, the wrinkles around her eyes and across her brow were deepening. Her eyebrows were nearly absent and her lips were colorless without make-up. She avoided mirrors, taking down the ones she could manage by herself and shoving them in closets.

With nothing to do, she thought more deeply about the shooting. She pictured the killer shooting his mother, an older woman, maybe one who looked like her, a "faded beauty." Perhaps he hated his mother for becoming old and ugly. Perhaps that is why he killed the Level Fours. Ugliness offended him. Ugliness was offensive.

Her thoughts careened. On the one hand, everyone is told that beauty is skin deep, meaning it is a person's soul, their character, that defines their worth. On the other hand, it is important to keep up appearances, to have good hygiene, to get dental treatment and good haircuts to be socially acceptable.

These thoughts, in tension with one another, crippled her with headaches. Never had she thought so intensely and for so many hours at a time. Never had she thought much at all, except about things like the colors of upholstery. She wished she could talk her thoughts over with the killer, the Maintenance Man. He might be the only one who could have helped her understand. But he died for his ideals, whatever they were. What had her ideal been? A runway model? A movie actress? Jane Fonda? How stupid! That made her laugh, briefly.

Suddenly, she knew what to do. Throwing on a pair of sweat pants and an old shirt of Bob's, she drove to the nursing home. Bob was there, silent and unchanged, as if time had stopped, probably looking younger at this point than she did. She took a chair next to him. After sitting with Bob for hours without speaking, she felt her breath slow and her muscles relax. The pattern on the wallpaper put her in a trance, which was interrupted from time to time by calls for meals and the nurse coming to give Bob his medicine. The facility had returned to normal. It was the only place in the world she desired to be, where none of her acquaintances would see her.

From now on, she would be spending the whole day with Bob, going home at night only to sleep. Or she could learn to sleep sitting up in the chair next to Bob's bed, as she attempted to do the night the shooting happened.

She would wait there, until the second shooter arrived to kill her, even if it took years.

IV. THE NEXT MORNING

11. THE SHOOTER'S SISTER

Had someone fallen overboard?

This was Flo's first thought when she was awakened by voices murmuring outside her cruise cabin door. There was both a man's voice and a woman's voice. Their conversation seemed to be tense. The woman may have been trying to convince the man to do something he did not wish to do. But their words were not discernible, even though they continued in this way for several minutes.

Then, there was a knock on her door. Flo fumbled into her bathrobe and turned on a light. She looked at the clock. 8:12 a.m. At home in Indiana, it would be just after six. She opened the door. There stood a man in a uniform and a woman in a nurse's dress. The man introduced himself as a Communications Officer. The Nurse was from the medical offices. They entered the tiny cabin and stood, with Flo, in the narrow space around the bed. Later, Flo was glad she paid the outrageous single supplement for a private room, so she did not have to to deal with a room-mate.

The Communications Officer was clearly uncomfortable. He looked down at the floor and spoke formally, as if he had rehearsed.

"Ma'am, I'm afraid I have several pieces of bad news to convey." He paused, glancing up at her, then lowered his eyes again. "First, I regret to tell you that your mother is deceased as of last night at or around nine-thirty p.m."

"Oh!" Flo said. This was not entirely unexpected. Her mother was over ninety and had Alzheimer's Disorder. She had not spoken or seemed to recognize either of her children for at least three years.

"I'm afraid she didn't die of natural causes. She was.... She had head trauma. She was shot in the head with a firearm." He cleared his throat.

This was followed by silence. A strained chug was audible from the somewhere in the bowels of the ship.

The Communications Officer's lip quivered. The Nurse took over. Despite the confined space, she took a half-step forward.

"It is so very hard to tell you this. Your mother was murdered by your brother. And there is more. When you are ready, I'll continue."

Flo, sank down onto the bed. She clutched at the bedspread.

"After shooting your mother, your brother—Sid—Sid went to the nursing home where he was employed as a Maintenance Man. He shot ten residents there. We have no information about whether any survived."

Flo whispered. "Sid shot ten people?"

"There is just one more thing to tell you. Let me know when you are ready. It will be hard to hear."

"Okay…"

"Your brother is dead. Apparently, he was shot by the police. I'm afraid that's all the information I have."

"Yes," the Communications Officer added, lamely.

"Do you want me to go over what we know again?" The Nurse asked.

"No."

The Officer and the Nurse stood there stiffly, staring at her, waiting. Flo visualized her mother seeing a man she did not recognize as her son, lifting a gun to shoot her.

"Would you like some Valium?" A voice floated out to her, piercing her fog. It was the Nurse. Flo gestured vaguely, and it was left on her dresser, "In case you need it."

Now Flo became more agitated. "Sid killed Mom? Then ten people in the nursing home where he worked? And the police killed him?"

She repeated her questions out loud several times, shaking her head in disbelief, dry-eyed, running her hand obsessively through her hair. The day before, she treated herself to a spa package. Her gray hair was dyed red. The salon recommended make-up to cover up age spots and brighten her complexion. Seldom before had she bothered about her looks. She intended to show off her new look to her brother when she returned home.

This was the cruise's day at sea. There was no way for Flo to disembark until they reached a port the next morning. Then, she was given to understand, she would be flown to a bigger island that had an international airport. An FBI agent would be waiting to interview her.

In the meantime, she was invited to spend the day with the Nurse in the medical department so she would not be alone. She was encouraged to contact relatives and friends who might give her support in the tough days ahead.

Who could she contact? Her mother had been the youngest in her family. Her father had died years before. The aunts and uncles on both her mother's and her father's side were already gone. There were cousins, none close. As for friends, they seemed to drop off after she retired. Most had been work friends. In the two years since she had left her job, they had disappeared after a few scattered lunch dates.

Both she and Sid took turns caring for their mother, who lived in their old family home with Sid. Flo lived nearby. She came to the house during the day while Sid was at work and left when he returned. Neither married, and by the time they reached their mid-sixties, their relationships dwindled to just each other. Even then, they bickered constantly about their mother. Flo was of the opinion that her mother belonged in a nursing home. Sid, who worked in a fancy dementia care facility out of their combined price range, insisted on keeping their mother with him.

After the Communications Officer left, Flo dressed and followed the Nurse through the ship's labyrinth until they reached the medical department. Flo was directed to one of the exam rooms. She sat uncomfortably on a round stool. The only other place was the exam table. The Nurse hustled back and forth outside the open door with other staff and a white coated physician, conducting the ship's routine medical business.

In a daze, Flo decided to go back to her cabin. After getting lost a couple of times, she finally found it, and collapsed on the bed, face-up. The lighting in the room was dim. She had chosen an inside room in one of the less expensive bottom decks. There was no window or balcony. Despite modern stabilizers, she sensed the ship rocking. In a glass on her nightstand, the water sloshed gently from side to side. Until that moment, she had not been sea sick. Suddenly, she had to vomit and barely made it to the bathroom.

A few minutes later, there was a knock. On the floor outside her door was a tray of cheese and crackers, along with two bottles of red wine, gratis, with a condolence note from the cruise company. She left the tray and brought the bottles in. After dumping the water in the bathroom sink, she filled the glass with wine and remembered the Valium. There were two pills. She took both, before starting in on the wine. Ordinarily, she did not drink. But there no longer was an "ordinarily." In a short while, she finished the first bottle.

She must have slept for an hour or so. When she awakened, the cabin seemed smaller. The walls seemed closer together. Unable to breathe in a room that felt like a trap, she left and started wandering aimlessly. It hit her. Her mother was dead. Her brother was dead. Her brother was a murderer. She began weeping and ranting. Ahead of her were a handsome older couple. Both were wearing white resort wear.

As she approached them, she burbled hysterically, "My brother…dead…murdered eleven..my mother, my mother…gone…"

The appalled couple retreated, backing into their cabin and shutting their door with a loud click. Flo stood outside, sobbing. After a few minutes, she walked in the other direction, still crying. Passengers gave her a wide berth. When she entered an elevator, the others who were inside quickly stepped out.

On an upper deck, Flo found herself in the casino. There was a lot of activity, and no one took notice of her, now that she had quieted. She found her Ship-N-Sail card in her purse and used it to get a whiskey sour at the bar. This was a drink she never had before. The first swallow went painfully down her throat, but she could bear it as long as she took small sips.

Flo had only been to a casino once before, a land-based one in Indiana. She had gone with a girl friend from work, whose name she could not recall at the moment. She won enough to pay for dinner that time. It was beginner's luck, her friend told her.

Now the colorful blinking lights, the clanging and chiming sounds, the machine exhaust smell, and the smoke made it hard to believe she was still on a ship or in any familiar place on earth. She seemed to be standing behind her own back, watching herself, directing her movements. She instructed herself to finish her drink and place the glass on the bar. Then she instructed herself to stand up and walk further inside the casino. The self in front of her kept stopping, as if she were going to faint, or simply lie down on the floor, unwilling to go a step further. Flo was forced to order herself to sit as soon as she was able, perhaps at the slot machine a few feet away.

Once seated, she focused her gaze on the machine. The display window had five rows of images, the same that were found on a deck of playing cards. There was a slot for Ship-N-Sail cards and unintelligible buttons, with dollars or cents amounts, numbers of lines, and embossed with other meaningless icons. She inserted the card, after telling herself to do so, then pressed the "Max" and the "Auto Play" buttons.

The machine came to life, clamoring and spinning, blinking its strobe lights. She watched the red digital numbers tally the amount to be debited from her credit card. A server came by and asked for her order. Soon, another whiskey sour was in her hand. Someone must have given her a cigarette, although she had not smoked in thirty years. Nothing was required of her. All she had to do was keep sitting there with her head facing the machine. At some point, she noticed the red digital numbers were approaching two thousand. But she did not have to understand. She looked without seeing. Her inhalations and the pounding in her chest drowned out the clangs. She instructed herself to stay as she was, seated at the slot machine, until the casino closed at three a.m.

Flo was aware she was outside on a deck. She did not recall how she came to be there or which deck it was. The sky was overcast, and it was very dark. Somewhere below was the vast ocean, undulating unseen like an enormous snake, slapping itself against the hull as it passed.

How tempting it would be to pick an unoccupied corner, hoist herself over the rail, and drop into the mouth of the beast. She could do that. Or she could stay on board. When daylight came, the plan was to be escorted to a two-engine plane, which would bounce her from the small island owned by the cruise company to a larger, inhabited island. From there, she would be flown back to Miami where an FBI agent would be waiting to grill her about her brother's motive and the possibility of coconspirators. When she could not answer, who knows what the agent would be capable of— surveillance? prison? contempt charges? Media people could telephone at all hours, chase her down in the street, photograph her through a crack in her curtains. Neighbors could shun her. The relatives of the victims could blame her, send her hate mail, make death threats, sue her.

There was an announcement being made over the public address system. She thought it was about her. Was the Nurse and the Communications Officer looking for her?

Or, she thought, as she stumbled toward the rail, maybe it was someone else's voice, calling to her from the sea, urging her into the blackness, where—if she looked hard enough—she dimly made out the shape of her brother Sid.

"Why did you do it, Sid? Tell me why," she called out to him.

Sid began swimming toward the ship, using a powerful breaststroke. Once alongside, he bobbed in the water, smiling up at her and waving.

Come on in, Sis. The water's fine.

12. THE FAMILY

Ruby heaved with sobs while still on the phone. She listened to the other party without replying. With her free hand, she gripped the back of the kitchen chair. Her husband, Don, stared at her with a piece of half-eaten buttered toast in his hand.

"What? What is it?"

When she finally put the phone down, she collapsed toward him with tears streaming down her face. He managed to lay the toast on the granite counter.

"It's Mom. My mother."

"Oh, Sweetheart. I'm so sorry. Has she passed?"

Ruby pushed away, waving her fingers in front of her face like stirred-up hornets.

"No, no. I mean yes. But...."

He did not expect her to be so distraught. Edith, his mother-in-law, had been comatose in the hospice section of a nursing home. She might die at any time. Ruby had been sad, but seemed to accept the inevitable. She even said it would be a relief when it was finally over. But now?

She allowed him to guide her to a chair in the family room. She was so dear to him when she was helpless, when she relied on his strength, although he knew better than to say so. She was not the type to show vulnerability very often.

After taking several deep breaths, she was able to tell him. "It was someone from Hospice. Mom has been shot. Murdered."

"Shot?" He stood back, incredulous.

"Oh, my God! My God!" She began panting again.

"Tell me!"

"Okay, okay," She smoothed the air with her hands, as if ironing. After another deep breathe, she looked at him. "Someone shot ten Level Four residents. They think it was the Maintenance Man. He was killed by the police. The police are on their way over here to tell us, but this person from Hospice wanted to tell us first."

The doorbell rang. It was two officers, male and female. They asked if they could come in.

"We already know." Don led the officers into the family room. The children were still asleep upstairs. They did not need to hear this before their parents processed it.

"I'm Officer Brady, and this is Officer Evans," the female officer said. "Is Edith Fineberg your mother, Ma'am?"

"Yes," Ruby said.

"Is this your husband, Ma'am?" She indicated Don.

"Yes."

The male policeman, Officer Evans, was filling out a report. He took their names.

"Even if you already know, I'm afraid I must tell you that your mother died at or around ten p.m. this evening from a gunshot wound."

She paused, allowing time for the news to be absorbed. Ruby nodded. Don put an arm around his wife. She did not brush it away. Officer Brady told them that after shooting her mother and nine other residents in Hospice, the killer pointed his gun at a deputy, who was forced to shoot him in self-defense. Ruby listened intently. Don was stunned by the news and by the presence of police in his home.

Officer Brady gave them the information in stages, not wanting to overwhelm them any more than necessary. They were told to expect to be questioned by homicide detectives and the FBI the next day and to expect attention from the media. This was a big story of national interest. The first mass murder in a nursing home.

After a pause, the Officer said it would be necessary for the victim, Professor Fineberg, to be formally identified at the town morgue where the body had been taken. They should presume that the body was in damaged condition, especially in the facial area.

Ruby shuddered.

"You should go now, before the media arrives," Officer Brady said. "Arrangements have been made for the morgue to remain open all night so you and other relatives of the deceased can make identifications in privacy."

Ruby eased out from under Don's arm. She regained composure. They decided to leave a note for their adolescent children saying they were going to the supermarket. When they returned, they would tell them about their grandmother's murder.

Don had married into an educated German Jewish family of powerful articulate women and successful silent men. He converted to Judaism after the wedding to please Ruby. Although he was not a religious man, he accompanied his wife and children—Adam, Rachel, and Ben—to services. Before her illness, Edith attended with them.

All the adults in the family had academic positions at the nearby university. Ruby's grandfather, once an eminent mathematician, now deceased, was the first Jewish faculty member hired for a minuscule salary during the Depression. His daughter, Edith, started out in the History Department in the flusher 1960s, and later inaugurated one of the nation's early Women's Studies programs. Ruby was a new hire in the Jewish Studies Department when Don, an Assistant Professor in Philosophy, met her. The children were being prepared for admission to prestigious colleges.

In the morgue waiting room, some of the other families, familiar to each other from visits to Hospice before the murders, had already arrived. Nobody spoke as they waited for the grim task ahead. Each family was led into the next room one at a time.

Edith Fineberg at age sixty was the second youngest of the deceased. She had been riding her bicycle to her office two years earlier when a speeding car hit her and threw her twenty feet. Even though she was wearing a helmet, she had severe head trauma. Other than that, she did not have a single bruise, or a single broken bone. But she never regained her cognitive abilities. After futile weeks in a rehabilitation facility, she was discharged to the nursing home. Within a year, after a series of infections common to people in her condition, her body began to fail. Ruby believed she was willing herself to die.

When it was their turn to enter the morgue room, Don took Ruby's hand. She did not resist. The room look like a mausoleum, with rows of stacked cubicles. The Coroner motioned them to a table pulled out from one of the cubicles. A sheet covered the corpse. The room was very cold. Ruby shivered.

The identification was quick and gruesome. The Coroner lifted the sheet just enough for a glimpse of Edith's devastated face. Without saying anything, the Coroner looked inquisitively at Edith. She nodded. The face was covered again. Edith sniffled but remained silent.

Back home, they assembled the children and told them. The boys were stunned. Rachel wailed. Their grandmother delighted in all three of them, but especially in her granddaughter, who was named after Edith's mother. Ruby held her. Don put his arms around his sons. Ben, the youngest, broke into tears. Adam, the oldest, was indignant.

"You mean the murderer is dead? He won't even be punished for killing Granny?"

As Jews, they did not believe in heaven or hell. Anyone not punished for their transgressions while alive would not be punished after death. According to the Torah, it was four generations of descendants who were supposed to pay for major transgressions. If the murderer had children or grandchildren, they might be punished—which might be psychologically true even if not legally true. That is how modern Reform Jews interpreted it.

Yet, Don had been raised by Christian parents. He still clung to a belief in an afterlife. The murderer faced judgment there. He kept the thought to himself.

What lay before the family now was a series of rituals meant to comfort. As soon as Edith's body was released from the morgue, it was ceremonially washed—an especially complicated task when any part of the body was mutilated. The funeral would be the day after.

During the next two days, there was a whirlwind of ritual activities, interspersed with the expected interviews with a homicide detective and an FBI agent, condolence contacts from the nursing home Administrator, phone calls from family and friends, and—as foreseen—hounding by reporters. The funeral itself had the largest attendance of any in the history of the synagogue. Almost the whole congregation, many in the university community, the Hospice staff, and many from the town who had been touched by Edith's generosity, crammed into the inadequate space at the synagogue.

By the third day after Edith's death, there was quiet. The children returned to school—Adam and Rachel to the high school and Ben to middle school. Don taught his classes. Ruby, however, was not ready to go back to the university. A candlelight vigil for Edith had been organized by Gender Studies, as Women's Studies was now called. This vigil was to be joined by another arranged by Jewish Studies. Ruby was expected to speak. She was expected to have something to say.

What was there to say? Her mother had been murdered. She had been robbed of the dignity of a natural death. Her face had been blasted away by the shot to the back of her head. This was an image of her mother she would never forget. It overtook all other images of her, as if the mother she loved for close to forty years had been eradicated by the bullet that killed her. That horrible image, seen for a mere second or two, haunted her. In her dreams, her mother engaged in her normal activities—reading, cooking, public speaking, walking through airports, dining in restaurants—but with her face devastated by her wound.

As stricken as she was, Ruby wound up leaving the care of her bewildered children to Don.

"Why did this happen?" Rachel kept asking him, hugging the old teddy bear that still lay among the pillows on her bed. "I don't understand."

Don referred her to Kushner's classic book, "When Bad Things Happen to Good People." God was either all good or all powerful. If God was all-powerful, God would not let anything bad happen. If bad things happened, God was good but not all powerful.

Rachel snorted. "I'm talking about Granny, not God! Don't turn all academic on me. I'm not a student in one of your classes." She sulked off to her room.

Even though no one had an appetite, Ruby insisted that the family eat dinner together. On the third night, they all quietly helped prepare a meal they barely touched. At the table, despite everyone's exhaustion with the topic, Don took the risk of speaking about the murderer.

"There was an article in the newspaper about the killer. Seems he never married. He was taking care of his mother, who had Alzheimer's. He killed her first, and then the others to put them out of their misery. That's what he thought, apparently, according to one theory."

"Are you making excuses for this man, Don?" Ruby snapped. "You know, I don't care why he did it. It makes no difference to me if he had a reason for doing what he did. He shot my mother!"

"Dad," Adam said. "Granny was already out of her misery. She was in a coma. The others were probably also out of their misery if they were in Hospice. If the killer had a reason, it wasn't what you're saying."

Don leaned back in his chair while raising his hands palms outwards. He meant no harm.

Ben was tearful. "I'm not hungry."

Rachel was the only one eating. She was on her third helping.

"This is your fault, Mom," Adam said. "You're the one who stuck Granny in the nursing home."

"Adam!" Don said. "Apologize!"

Ruby put her hand on Don's arm as if to hold him back.

"As I recall, you didn't want to give up your room and bunk with Ben so we would have enough room for live-in help, correct?" Ruby said.

"If Granny had been here, the killer could have come here and killed her and us, too," Ben said.

"You are such an idiot," Rachel said to Ben.

"Shut up!" Ben yelled back.

"Okay, kids. That's enough," Don said.

"No, Don. The kids have to express themselves about this. We all do. No one shuts anyone up.".

"Fine." Don balled up his napkin. One day, he would express himself to Ruby about the way she contradicted him in front of the children.

If Edith were alive, she would have cooked a bounty of Jewish food—chopped liver, matzo ball soup, brisket. She would have used food to keep order and harmony, passing a dish to whoever raised their voice saying "Here. Just eat a little of this. A taste, Sweetheart." Acceptable dinner topics revolved around the latest opera production at the university, recent books read, restaurants tried, gentle gossip about relatives and friends, and the children's school work. After dinner conversation might be loud, raucous, and even wounding, but Edith, the queen of the dinner table, kept control during the meal.

After Edith's accident, the job fell to Ruby. But Ruby's academic pursuits never gave her time to shoehorn cooking into her schedule the way her mother had. She did not have her mother's way of charming others into submission. And Don never quite understood the basic rule for the men of the tribe: eat, study, and leave the rest to the women. That ancient rule still hid beneath modern feminist rhetoric about equality in relationships.

The difference between Don and his deceased father-in-law was that he cared about his second place status at the table. His own father, gruff and fueled by alcohol, never tolerated "back talk" from his wife or children. Don wanted to be more like his father-in-law than his father. He adopted the middle ground by giving in to Ruby but then resenting her for it.

Later, she said, "I just don't know how I'm going to go to this vigil tonight. The students mean well, but I'm exhausted."

This was a familiar trap. He fell into it anyway. "Don't go. Just don't show up. Stay here and rest."

"I can't rest. Open your eyes. Can't you see how agitated I am? How am I supposed to rest? My mother has been shot! What do you expect?"

His father-in-law would have shrugged off her outburst, viewed it as perfectly normal, and returned to his book. Don was hurt, frustrated. Couldn't she accept his offer of help for what it was? Does everything he says have to be answered with an attack?

In the end, Ruby did not attend the vigil. Her exhaustion continued for days. She could not concentrate. She reluctantly decided to take a leave of absence from the university for the rest of the semester. There would still be genders, even if she did not teach Gender Studies. For the next few weeks, she paced around the house irritably, drank wine, snapped at Don and the children, and spent long hours in bed. For several days in a row, she forgot about dinner, which she always organized even if she did not do the actual cooking herself. Everyone was left to fend for themselves, eating bowls of cereal or peanut butter sandwiches, unless someone from the congregation left a casserole. Finally, Don took over the task of preparing simple meals without Ruby's supervision. Hot dogs and mashed potatoes. Hamburgers. Roasted chicken from the supermarket. The family dined together. The children ate in silence. Ruby came to the table in a wine-splattered bathrobe, taking a few bites before retiring to the bedroom again.

After washing up, Don tried talking to Ruby. "Hon, you can't go on like this. You're depressed. You should talk to someone."

She turned on him. "Talk to someone? Will that bring Mom back? Depressed? Yeah, I'm depressed. What do you expect, Don? My mother was murdered!"

Ruby was no longer in the mood to allow any intimacy with Don, any warmth, any conversation, any interest in his existence. His electrifying and sensual wife, who had fascinated him as much as annoyed him, made only one response to him now, if she responded at all.

"My mother was murdered. What do you expect?"

Eventually, Don retreated to the university, no longer cooking, spending more hours in his office. One of his PhD students, a blond young woman, began bringing him small gifts of consolation—a chocolate bar, a plaque inscribed with part of the Twenty-third Psalm: *Though I walk through the valley of the shadow of death, I will fear no evil.*

This brought Don to tears. The student put her hand on his fist. His fist relaxed.

Meanwhile, Rachel had a dream. In it, her grandmother was in the kitchen. When she saw Rachel, she smiled.

"This is how you make chopped liver. Take an onion, two hard-boiled eggs and two pounds of chicken liver and…"

As soon as Rachel woke up, she went to Adam's room and woke him.

"Hey," she said, "I have to go to the supermarket after school. You have to drive me."

"Go away." He pulled the quilt over his head, but she pummeled him until he agreed.

Later, Rachel secretly borrowed her mother's credit card and bought the chopped liver ingredients. As she was unloading the bags in the kitchen, Ruby came in and asked what she was doing.

"Making chopped liver."

Ruby did not say anything. She poured herself a glass of wine.

"Go away, Mom." Rachel lifted the ancient meat grinder down from the high shelf reserved for Edith's vintage kitchen equipment—a Kenmore twelve-speed mixer, an original Tappan microwave, a Revere Ware copper percolator.

Several nights later, Edith taught her how to make matzo ball soup, and several nights after that, brisket.

The instructions in the dream extended beyond recipes. Rachel demanded the family have dinner together again, even if no one spoke. She brought in the familiar food. Her mother rarely finished everything on her plate. Her brothers ate with gusto. Her father complimented her.

"Very tasty, Rachel." He seemed relieved that order was being restored.

Over the course of time, the boys, particularly Adam, started to talk. He addressed his remarks to his dinner plate. Ruby and Don rarely responded, not looking at the others. It was Rachel who kept the conversation, as well as the food, moving along.

"I don't think there is a God," Adam said.

"Okay, Jerk, why not?" Rachel said.

"Because, like, there is no evidence that God exists. It's all superstition, because, like, in ancient times, before science, no one could explain anything. Like why day and night happen, for instance."

"That's stupid," Rachael said. "What about the things we can't explain now, like how to cure cancer or why that guy killed Granny. We don't go around inventing religions just because we don't have the answer to everything."

"I think God could save us from climate change and tornados and stuff, if God wanted to," Ben said.

"You're such a retard, Ben," Rachel said.

Don did not stop them, and Ruby did not take charge. They were both checked out.

The next time Rachel dreamed, Edith said, "You don't have a mother and a father anymore. You mustn't rely on them."

Rachel saw this was true. Her mother was a shadow of the woman she was before the murder, the woman who taught at the university, and who took care of her children. Now she paced through the house in her pajamas, drinking and muttering to herself like one of the crazy people in the streets. And her father was disappearing. Although he still showed up for meals, he left immediately after to work in his office or went into his den to make long phone calls. He no longer attended Ben's soccer practices or Adam's basketball games. She did not expect either parent to show up for her school play, although she only had one line.

"You're on your own, now. Don't think anyone will help you," Edith told her. "You must take care of your brothers."

As time went on, her parents stopped coming to the table for dinner. Her mother carried a tray to her room with a bottle of wine. Her father took a tray to his den, when he came home at all. But Adam and Ben continued to come, as usual, to eat the brisket or roast chicken or schnitzel or kugel Rachel made. She also took on the laundry and the vacuuming, making sure that Adam had clean underwear and that Ben took his asthma medicine.

In her dreams, Rachel complained to her grandmother.

"It's too much. I have school work, too. It isn't fair. I'm only fifteen."

"I was murdered and your parents identified my remains," Edith said. "I had no face left. What do you expect?"

Somehow, Rachel still managed to get all As in her classes. In order to find the time to do her homework on top of her other responsibilities, she had to go to bed later. She wanted to follow in the footsteps of her mother and grandmother by having a career. Academia appealed to her. She wanted a future of immersion in research, writing, and teaching. But first, she had to go to college. If her mother did not get better, she would have to commute to the local university until Ben graduated from high school. Or college would have to be delayed until he graduated. Somebody had to take care of him.

Every so often, she would harass her parents, hoping they would be parents again. Charging into the bedroom, now occupied solely by her mother, she would say.

"Come on, Mom. Get up. Take a shower. Get dressed. You've been lying around for weeks. What are you going to do, turn into a drunk?"

"I will. I will. Give me five minutes." Ruby spoke drowsily, as if drugged. "I think your father left me. I think he is seeing somebody."

This was a jolt for Rachel. She thought her father was working.

"Well, can you blame him?" She did not care if she was mean.

She also pitched into her father when she saw him.

"Dad, you're never home. Do you have a girlfriend? Are you divorcing Mom?"

"No, no. I'm just getting my book ready for publication. The editor wants the index yesterday. I have to push through."

"Liar."

She hated them both. She hoped they would die, then feared they would.

During her brief sleep at night, Edith said, "You're alone now. Do what you have to do."

Rachel woke up and got a knife from the kitchen. Back in her bedroom, she took her old teddy bear and stabbed it many times, grunting with the effort. When she was finished, Adam stood in her doorway.

"Have you killed that bear enough yet?"

She threw the knife in his direction.

At the dinner table, Adam, Rachel, and Ben returned to the same spiritual theme again and again. Adam usually started.

"I used to be an Agnostic, but now I'm an Atheist. Like, I don't believe in God anymore. I'm not going to the synagogue anymore."

"If there is a God, It sure isn't interested in us," Rachel said.

"I think God must be angry at us. We must've done something wrong," Ben said.

"Like what?" Rachel said. "Are we the ones who murdered Granny? Are we the ones who decided to stay in our bedroom and never come out? Are we the ones who never come home?"

"We're not being punished, Ben. Everything is just...like, random. Granny happened to be murdered. It could have been someone else. Or at another nursing home," Adam said.

"Yeah," Rachel said, acidly, "And we could have been born into a different family that knows how to stick together."

"I think God just doesn't like us," Ben said.

"I think I just don't like God," Rachel said.

Lately, Adam stopped going to school. He did not like it when other kids asked him questions about Granny. He did not like it when they did not ask him questions. He did not like it when they said stupid things like, "Hey, Man, that sucks" and "I don't know how you stand it. I'd want to die if someone was murdered in my family." The counselors and teachers were no better when they said, "Anytime you want to talk about it, my door is open," sometimes with a hand on his shoulder.

He did not see the point of studying calculus or Spanish or anything. He once cared about college. Not anymore. He stayed home, mostly in his room, playing video games.

Rachel went to school, but sometimes had to skip. There was too much work to do at home and not enough time for everything. Her friends got tired of asking her to hang out or texting her without receiving an answer. She no longer had friends, she realized.

She forced Ben to go to school. He was only thirteen, and she was scared of trouble if he did not show up. She was pretty sure he stopped doing homework, even math, which he used to love. Eventually, both he and Adam quit sports. Rachel was too busy to stay in the drama club.

"You're alone. You'll always be alone. Take care of the boys," Edith told her at night. In dreams about Edith, her face was slowly blurring, deteriorating. There seemed to be a large hole approximately between her eyes, extending down the bridge of her nose. Something wet tricked down to her chin. It was both comforting and disturbing when Edith appeared to her. It was her Granny who she loved. But it was her Granny who was shot dead and had no face. Moreover, Granny said things that were true but hard to hear.

Her aunts and uncles, all living out of state, left voice messages and emails for Ruby. She did not answer. The Rabbi, as well as friends from the university and the synagogue, sometimes knocked on the door. Rachel was not going to open it if Ruby was too lazy to move herself from the bedroom to the door. And her useless father, of course, was never around to respond. Eventually, people stopped dropping by.

"It's better that way," Edith told Rachel. "Being alone is better. You don't get shot if you're alone."

Ben had some kind of attack before going to school each day. It wasn't asthma. Rachel looked up the symptoms. Not seizures. Rapid breathing, sweating, shaking, pounding heart. They were panic attacks. He feared he would be killed if he went to school. There had been a number of school shootings in other states.

In a dream, Edith said to Rachel, "You must home school Ben. You all have to home school. That way you'll be safe."

With Adam's help, they looked up the home school requirements in the state of Indiana. There was no registration needed to be a home school or attend a home school. There were no course requirements. The only requirement was that attendance be taken by a parent. That was easy enough to fake. None of them planned to go to school anymore.

Ben's panic attacks stopped.

Edith told Rachel, "Your father is not one of us. He is not really Jewish. If he were, he wouldn't betray your mother. He doesn't belong with you anymore. Don't let him in the house."

Rachel was fully in charge of her brothers by now. When she told them what to do, they did not object. She told Adam to take the credit card to the hardware store and buy two lock sets, one for the front door and one for the back. They changed the locks themselves. Their father could not get in. After unplugging the automatic garage opener, they controlled who entered the house.

The next time Don tried, first through the garage, then through the front door, he realized his key did not work. He guessed that Ruby had kicked him out. He resigned himself to having to ask a third party to get his belongings, the most important of which he already secretly moved, and to make arrangements to see the children. He went away. Peeking at his departing car through the window, Rachel and her brothers felt bitter satisfaction.

"He doesn't belong here anymore," Rachel said.

At night, Edith said "Your mother will leave soon. Then you'll be truly alone."

The loss of her father was one thing, but her mother? Rachel was not ready. She took a black marker and made a black circle between her eyes, just above the bridge of her nose.

That night, at dinner, the phones of Adam, Rachel, and Ben kept lighting up with their father's number. He also sent texts. "I want to see you. I'll come and get you whenever you say. I love you." Rachel told the boys to block his number.

They talked to each other about God while they ate.

"In the Torah, God tells Abraham to kill Isaac. And he nearly does," Adam said. "What kind of a God wants a father to kill a son, anyway? Is that a God you want to believe in?"

Ben said, "But God doesn't let Abraham kill Isaac."

Rachel said, "He would have killed Isaac if God didn't stop him. Abraham does whatever God wants."

Adam said, "Abraham also tries to murder his other son, Ishmael, by sending him to the desert without water. God is the one who saves Isaac and Ishmael."

Ben said, "No. God tells Abraham to murder his sons."

Rachel said, "Sarah is the one who tells Abraham to kill Ishmael. And she doesn't try to stop Abraham from murdering Isaac."

Adam said, "It's lucky there were no guns back then. Or they'd both be dead."

Ben said, "What about daughters. Didn't Abraham have any daughters?"

Rachel said, "I bet he'd try to kill them, too, if he did have them. I bet God wouldn't save the daughters."

Adam said, "God, Sarah, and Abraham. They all wanted to kill the children. Their own children. God lets them try even though God knows Isaac and Ishmael will live."

Ben said, "I think Isaac and Ishmael must have been really really scared. And they probably didn't think Abraham loved them. I bet they wondered why they were born."

The next day, Rachel was shocked to find her mother in the kitchen, dressed in her wool blazer and skirt, hair combed, with make-up applied. The night before, her mother had been a drunken zombie. Now, suddenly, she was upright and normal.

When she spoke, it was in the voice she used to have, not the hoarse slurred whisper of a few hours ago.

"You kids are going back to school tomorrow. I'm better now. I'm going to my office," she said, "I'll be home later to make dinner. And who unplugged the garage door?"

Rachel just stared.

"What's that black mark on your face? Go and wash it off. And wake up your brothers."

Ruby left the kitchen. There was the sound of the garage door opening and the car backing out.

As soon as she heard the garage door close, Rachel unplugged it again. Then she woke her brothers and told them what happened.

The three of them gathered together at the table. They waited. Their mother would be back. When she tried and failed to get in, she would call the police.

That is what they expected. Rachel put her head down on her arms and tried to doze off. If she could do that, Edith would tell her what to do next.

13. THE SURVIVING SON

Abagail was able to tell from the type of knock that the police were at her door. It was a distinct sound, almost a banging. The time was well after midnight, and she feared they would disturb the neighbors if she did not get to the door before they rapped a second time. She was so accustomed to having them show up, she momentarily forgot Ned was in a nursing home now. There was no longer any reason for a police presence.

Puzzled, she managed to open the door before they knocked again. Almost always, there were two. This time there was a young male— probably a Rookie—and an older female. Neither had been to her house before. They both looked somber, unlike the cynical pursed-lip expressions of the police who had regularly arrived to break up fights between Ned and their son, Kevin.

Instead of barging in, they politely asked if they could enter. She opened the door wider. Their crisp blue uniforms, the light glinting off their badges, and the prominent holstered weapon on their belts reminded Abagail of times she was glad of their presence, when she was unable to restore peace in the house by herself. She asked if they wanted to sit. They preferred to stand.

The Rookie was the one who spoke. His tone was matter-of-fact.

"Ma'am, it is our sad duty to tell you that your husband, Ned Sparks, is dead."

He paused to give that information time to sink in.

"Ned is dead? That can't be. The doctor said he had another month." Abagail looked at the female officer, as if another woman knew the male officer was mistaken.

The Rookie continued. "Ma'am, I regret to inform you that between nine-thirty and ten p.m. this evening, your husband Ned Sparks was murdered along with nine other nursing home residents. All were shot. The alleged shooter has been identified as the Maintenance Man, a member of the nursing home staff."

"They let someone on staff shoot the residents? He shot Ned dead? Why would anyone shoot Ned?" What the young man was saying did not seem to be plausible. Perhaps this was a training exercise for him.

"The alleged shooter was killed when he aimed his weapon at the police. Later, it was discovered that his weapon was unloaded." The Rookie removed his hat.

Abagail looked from one officer to the other, trying to absorb what the Rookie had said. Now the female officer spoke up. Her approach was warmer.

"This must be so hard for you to believe. Do you want to sit down? You might be lightheaded. We don't want you to fall." She held out her hand, but did not touch Abagail. Her hand was there if Abagail needed it to steady herself. Abigail did not seem to notice. She remained standing. Two deep creases appeared on her forehead, between her eyes.

"Where is Ned? Is he still in his room? I should see him."

"Your husband has been moved to the city morgue. Whenever there is an unnatural death, the Coroner is required to do an autopsy. When she is finished, the body will be released to a funeral home of your choice. It may take a few days because of the number of victims," the female officer said softly.

Ned in a morgue. He would not like that. It had been hard enough when he was admitted to the nursing home. But, she realized, he was dead, according to these officers. He would not know one way or the other.

"Do you have someone you can call to be with you tonight?" The female officer asked.

"I'm not alone. My son is upstairs."

"Right," the Rookie said. "Then unless there is some way we can assist you, we have to go. Other relatives of other deceased victims need to be informed."

If there were a checklist somewhere, Abagail's name would now be crossed off. She opened the door so the officers could leave. On their way out, the female officer paused to give Abagail a sorrowful smile.

When she was alone, she went into the family room and sat in her LaZyBoy, pushing the lever that raised the bottom so her aching legs could be elevated. She would be spending the rest of the night in the chair, thinking. There were two other LaZyBoys in the room, one for Ned and the other for Kevin. All three were upholstered in the same plaid material, and they all faced the wall with the flat-screen TV. After Ned had gone to live in the nursing home, Abagail seldom turned it on. Kevin did not understand the programs anyway, although sometimes he watched cartoons.

She struggled to take in what she had been told. Ned was dead, but not in the regular way men in their eighties with brain tumors die. He had been murdered. What was the point? He was close to dying anyway, with only weeks to go. It was not as if he was suffering and needed to be put out of his misery like a horse with a broken leg. Mostly, he just slept. She anticipated a peaceful end.

She saw her reflection in the shiny black screen of the TV. Frail and short haired, she looked like a child in the over-sized recliner. All three recliners had been purchased at the same time in a model suitable for the two larger men. Ned had been big enough before the tumor caused the weight loss. But Kevin was a giant, over six feet tall and close to three hundred pounds.

It was best to wait until morning to tell Kevin about his father, after breakfast. It was always a bad idea to do anything that disrupted Kevin's routine. This was something Ned never understood. He might insist Kevin take his cereal bowl to the sink before rather than after Kevin finished drinking his mug of milk. It was this kind of thing that led to the awful fights, often violent fights in which they got into a clutch, then punched each other until she called 911.

Kevin had several developmental disabilities—low vision, autism, cognitive impairments—that Abagail considered her fault. When she was pregnant, all of her friends took pride in having "natural childbirth," which was unmedicated and vaginal, using the breathing techniques taught in Lamaze classes. Mandalas were hung in the delivery rooms to provide laboring mothers with a meditative focus. Fathers gave back massages and breathing instructions. Obstetricians were mere "baby catchers."

When Abagail had been in labor for eight hours, her physician determined that she was not dilating properly and suggested a medication.

She refused to break her no-drugs vow. In that case, she was told, a caesarian might be necessary. She refused again.

In the end, the baby was born vaginally with the cord wrapped around his neck. He had to be resuscitated after birth. The newborn was a limp baby, with little muscle tone—a bad sign. As he grew older, the developmental delays mounted. Abagail and Ned acknowledged their son would never become an independent adult, able to live on his own. Once he matured, either he would be placed in a group home or he would continue to live with his parents, who would be his guardians.

But Ned always believed that Kevin could do more than Abagail knew he could manage.

"He can learn to mow the lawn," Ned insisted, "Any idiot can mow a lawn."

"He might pick up twigs. But mow the lawn? No. He'd wind up destroying the flower beds. And don't call him an 'idiot.' He's our son!"

"Have it your way. I'm wrong again, according to you."

Slowly, the marriage disintegrated around this difference of opinion. At the same time, the couple was tightly bound to each other by their obligation to their son. By the time Ned was diagnosed with a glioblastoma, they had been caring for Kevin for over fifty years. They had no plan for what would happen to him once they were both dead.

Abagail had to admit that Kevin was easier to handle with Ned out of the house. She understood her son's anxieties and his guttural speech. When it was just the two of them, she anticipated the triggers that might set him off and attempted to remove them. That did not mean she was glad when her husband moved to the nursing home. His murder was a horrifying conclusion to a life nearly destroyed by their son's disabilities. This, too, was her fault for being the cause of the congenital defects.

The next morning, Kevin awoke at the usual time, ate his breakfast, brushed his teeth, and dressed in the clothes she laid out for him in the exact order he preferred. Once this was accomplished, Abagail thought it was a good time to tell Kevin about his father.

"Kevin, dear, we need to talk."

Although he was still seated at the kitchen table, he began rocking back and forth, no doubt stressed by not knowing what she would say.

"You know your father doesn't live here anymore. He lives in the nursing home."

She paused to give him time to recall this, although Ned had not lived at home for months. It was hard to figure out what Kevin knew or did not care to know.

"Last night, a man who works at the nursing home where your father lives killed your father. Your father is dead, Kevin."

Abagail spoke to Kevin without looking at him. Eye contact was unbearable to him. He did not say anything. She stole a glance. He still rocked. Then he asked a question. What time had his father died?

"Between nine-thirty and ten is what I was told. I'm sorry I don't know the exact time."

Kevin rocked harder. He wanted her to tell him the precise time. That would help to calm him. She decided to lie.

"Nine-forty-five. He was killed at nine-forty-five p.m."

"Nine-forty-five p.m.," he repeated. The rocking slowed.

"Would you rather watch cartoons now or go to your room?"

"Room."

Kevin normally spent the unstructured parts of the day in his room with the door closed. He rose and lumbered out of the kitchen. Abagail took a breath. That had gone better than she thought.

The phone rang. It was the minister from her church who was calling to express condolences. He suggested they talk in person when she was ready to discuss funeral arrangements.

Shortly after the call, a loud noise came from Kevin's room. He seemed to be wailing. Crash sounds, as if items were being hurled against the walls, followed. She rushed to his room and cracked the door. Kevin was destroying the room. There was nothing to do but stand there and wait for him to wind down. If she entered before then, he might hurt her unintentionally, with his wildly swinging arms.

When his emotional upheaval was finally spent, Kevin sank onto the pile of broken and shattered items on the floor, sobbing loudly. Cautiously, Abagail entered the room and stood off to the side. Standing directly in front of him might have agitated him again. He was saying something while weeping.

"I kill Ned Sparks. I kill Ned Sparks."

"No, no, sweetheart," she said in as soothing a tone as she could manage. "You did not kill your father. A man in the nursing home did. The Maintenance Man who fixes things. He killed your father."

"I kill Ned Sparks." Kevin blubbered, smashing his fist on the rubble.

The phone rang again. It was Kevin's case manager. Abagail took the call to give Kevin some more time to cool down. She stepped out into the hallway. This case manager was one of a succession, most only lasting a year or two, who had been assigned to her son since infancy. Like the minister, the case manager first expressed her shock and condolences, then asked how Kevin was doing. Abagail told her.

Over time, she had been given advice about how to handle Kevin's mood swings. Every two or three years, the advice changed. Hand slaps to stop unacceptable behavior, tokens to redeem for treats for good behavior, beating a mattress with a foam bat to vent frustrations, M&Ms of different colors for different sorts of acceptable behaviors, distraction, reasoning, gold stars, proving delusions wrong, accepting delusions even if wrong— none of these had been particularly effective. The case manager suggested the latest technique:

"Respond to the emotions, not the thoughts. Tell Kevin he must be very sad to think he killed his father."

This was so patently ridiculous that Abagail did not even bother to pretend to go along, as she usually did to keep the peace with the agency in charge of Kevin's welfare. She simply hung up, but not before the case manager added the suggestion of doubling Kevin's Haldol. This Abagail agreed do as soon as it was possible.

No further sound came from Kevin's room. She might have time for a quick nap. The lack of sleep and the stress took a toll. She was, after all, almost eighty. She only had a few good years left, if that, to be able to take care of Kevin, not to mention herself. She knew she was slowing down, tiring more quickly, gradually losing strength. As careful as she was, it was possible that Kevin would inadvertently cause her to fall. Anything could make her slip—a patch of ice, a wet leaf, spilled oil on the kitchen linoleum. A broken bone meant spending the rest of her days in a wheel chair, probably in an assisted living facility. Kevin would be forced into a group home or some type of institution.

It did not help to dwell on these gloomy prospects.

She seated herself in the recliner, raised the bottom, and almost immediately dozed off. She dreamed that Ned was calling her name. His voice was urgent, loud, and higher-pitched than usual. But it was not Ned she was hearing. It was Kevin, she realized, waking into alertness. He was the one making what sounded like something between a squeal and a shriek. Abagail lowered the recliner bottom and stood up.

"Kevin?"

Now he was moaning. He was not in his room when Abagail looked. He had to be in the kitchen. She rushed in. There she saw him with the kitchen knives laid out on the table. He was sitting on one of the chairs. The little paring knife was stuck in his upper left arm. Blood was running down his arm and pooling onto the table top. The next sized knife was thrust into his neck. It must have missed an artery because while blood was copiously flowing, it was not spurting. There was a cleaver in his fist.

Abagail gasped. She dared not move. What words would mean anything to her stricken son? What would make him put down the cleaver?

"I kill Ned Sparks," he groaned, without looking at her. His face was a mask of tragedy.

Where was her phone? She must have left it on the LaZyBoy. Turning back toward the family room, she felt her arms and legs go numb. She saw the recliner and the phone lying on its seat. She commanded herself to hurry toward it. *Faster.* But every step she took seemed to make it recede, as if she were moving backward instead of forward.

While Kevin howled in the kitchen, Abagail desperately inched toward the device that enabled her to call 911. But she could never get more than half-way there. Once at the half-way point, the remaining space could also be divided in two. When she reached the next divide, yet another space opened that was divisible. An infinite series of half-way points had to be traversed. The phone remained in sight, but—although she tried for the rest of her days—it would always be just a half-distance beyond the reach of her tautly outstretched hand.

14. THE ADMINISTRATOR'S DAUGHTER

Glee made an entry in "The Book of Me," which she fashioned from a spiral-bound lined note book. She used colored tabs to divide the book into sections. "Future," tabbed yellow, the color of optimism, for ideas for achieving her main goal in life—becoming rich. It was in this section that she wrote her Mission Statement concerning college. She was enrolled as a commuting freshman.

"Do minimum one semester to get the hang of it. I can always say I did more. Even graduated. Who's going to check?"

She cross-reference to the "Past Not To Be Repeated" section, tabbed black.

No way am I going to wind up like my mother and grandmother, being a single parent with three jobs and not a minute to myself. Or wind up married to an ass like my step-grandfather, Jack. I'll stay single until I meet a rich guy. Maybe one of those very wealthy Middle Easterners who like American girls.

As for her major, *I'm majoring in "me."*

Even though the campus swarmed with people her age, she spent most of her free time off-campus, at home with her mother thumbing through People Magazine and studying online fashion blogs. They contained great lessons on how the wealthy conduct themselves. Her entire focus was on the major of "me." What worried her was that she would be derailed like a lot of girls by falling in love. There was a whole section called "Love" in the Book of Me tabbed in pink and written in red ink. Falling in love with a boy her age meant grinding poverty, or at least many years of it, while she and the boy scrabbled together an income while waiting for one or both of them to become an officer or a doctor or successful in business. Years at a military base or in student housing or worse. Then paying off student loans until the end of time.

Not for me. I'll stay home and not take any chances.

She was writing her latest entries on an ordinary morning when her mother, Jill, came home after spending all night at work. Glee did not think much about it. Her mother was the Administrator of a nursing home and was often called back to work after hours to deal with emergencies. Glee was going to head to the campus when she saw her mother taking off her shoes and rubbing her feet, looking exhausted.

"No sleep again?"

"Haven't you heard the news? There was a shooting early last night while I was out of the building. Ten of our residents were killed. I never got home until now."

"I don't watch the news."

"Corporate is on my tail. They blame me for hiring the Maintenance Man—he's the one who was the shooter. I've got to go right back as soon as I change clothes."

"Old people are murdered and they blame you? Well, I wouldn't take your kind of shit job for shit pay where murders happen, and then you get blamed. *Geez.*"

"Then I guess you better get good grades and graduate."

"And those brainless old people who were killed should've been sent out to sea on icebergs to die, anyway."

"Nice, Glee. Very nice. Those are human beings you're talking about."

"Well, that's what my American History Professor said Native Americans used to do."

"And did your Professor tell you that nomadic people maybe didn't have nursing homes back then? Or that mass shootings are somehow okay?"

After her mother left, Glee lost interest in the murders. They had nothing to do with her future as a rich person. She went to her English class, weaving her way through student anti-gun demonstrators. There was a lecture on "Pride and Prejudice." She had not bought the book, but instead downloaded a movie version. If only she had a mother like the mother in the movie, one who shrewdly helped her daughter find a moneyed husband. Not like her own mother. Her do-gooder feminist mother.

When Jill returned from work the next evening, she was in a somber mood. Before she even took off her coat, she told Glee they had to have a serious talk right away. They sat at the kitchen table, where the unpaid bills piled up.

"Look, Glee. My job is on the line. Corporate thinks I mismanaged, and that's why the murders happened. They even say it's my fault our resident census is down and we've lost staff since the shootings yesterday."

"Okay." Glee played with a fork.

"I'm broke. I don't know how I'm going to make the mortgage this month. And that's if I get to keep my job. I may be fired."

Jill looked so pale and worn that Glee almost felt sorry for her.

"I do have a solution, the only one I can think of. You know the monthly bill for Jack to live in the nursing home is paid for by his long-term insurance."

Jack lived in the nursing home Jill managed.

"Yeah," Glee said, "You mean from the money that Grandma paid for him to have that insurance. That money belongs to us."

"That money belongs to Jack. He was legally married to her."

Jill continued. "I found out that the insurance will pay us if we let him live here and if we take care of him ourselves. Thank goodness he wasn't one of those who was shot."

There was a moment of silence, then the refrigerator gurgled, a sound like chuckling.

"No fucking way, Mom. No fucking way!" Glee shouted, standing up.

"It's the only way. We have to have that income. Otherwise, the bank gets the house, and we're out on the street. I won't be able to support you anymore. Even if I keep my job." She sounded weary.

"Fuck!"

"Jack's fee is paid up for this month, and I have to give thirty days notice before he leaves. So the rest of this month and next month are covered. We'll have to move him here by December first. You'll almost be finished with your fall semester then. I'll use personal days to be here while you take your finals. But after that, you'll have to be here for the day shift. Whether I have this job or work at Walmart."

"Fuck! Fuck! Fuck!" Glee shouted, stamping around the kitchen.

"I've thought this out. Jack can't talk. He can hardly move. Someone does have to be with him at all times, but there's not much more to do than feed him, give him his medicines, and change his Depends."

"His Depends? Are you shitting me?"

"Medicare pays for an aide to come once a week and bathe him, so we wouldn't have to do that. We can clear out the living room and put a hospital bed in it. That way you can keep your room."

"What about college? Next semester?" Glee whined, forgetting she had thought one semester would be enough.

"You can do online courses. But you'll have to be here while I'm at work. It'd be illegal to leave Jack alone. That would be dependent adult neglect. A felony."

"Fuck!"

Glee went slamming into her room. She opened the Book of Me, resisting the temptation to rip it up. In the section called Future, she wrote "None."

She was nineteen years old. That ass Jack would probably live another ten years, with her luck. Once she was twenty-nine, the window of time when young women appealed to rich old guys would have closed. She was screwed!

Throwing herself on her bed, Glee sobbed into her pillow. The Book of Me slid onto the floor.

Two months later, Jill still managed the nursing home. Classes had ended, and Glee had become Jack's caretaker. She discovered that the worst thing about him was that he grunted about once a second.

"Uh…..Uh…..Uh….."

It drove her crazier than changing his diapers, although that made her gag. He resisted everything she did to see to his needs. He pushed and stiffened when she changed him or dressed him. He spat out food he did not like, often in her direction. When he was sitting in a chair instead of lying in bed, he tried to trip her with his big feet. If she wore ear buds to drown out his grunting, he grunted louder. This was not going to be as easy or as simple as Jill promised. The old fucker was going to make this as hard as possible.

"I can't do this," Glee wept to Jill. "I won't do this. He's horrible!"

"Here's your choice," Jill repeated. "You can leave home and fend for yourself. That would mean I'd have to leave Jack alone all day. If something happens to him while I am gone, I'm in jail for neglect. Is that what you want?"

"No," Glee conceded, even though she hated her mother for doing this to her. Besides, if she left home, it would mean taking some shit job that could be as bad as taking care of Jack. And rent would leave no money to pay for college, even with loans. Goodbye to all that.

After all she had deprived herself of, she thought bitterly, in order to get rich. Friends. Hanging out. Sex. Weed. Love. Parties. Movies. And now, even if she had a chance to have those things, she was too depleted by caring for Jack to go out at night. Where would she go, anyway?

And even though she hated her mother, she knew her mother could not come home from work and tend to Jack all by herself. Not to mention leaving him alone to get food and supplies. Glee was forced to help out even when her "shift" was over. All she could do was give her mother evil looks to let her know how much she loathed her. She did not know who she hated more—Jack or Jill.

When Glee was alone with Jack, she had to make him cooperate. At first she tried Jill's advice: Validate the emotions that cause Jack's bad behaviors. "I know you're angry/scared/ashamed that I have to help you when you can't help yourself." Be respectful and apologetic. "I'm so sorry I have to move you in this way." Be positive and optimistic. "We'll get through this together." Reassure. "Don't worry. I won't leave you." Reward. "If you let me do this, I'll give you some M&Ms."

These were close to the polite, positive ways of speaking she had listed under "Language" in the Book of Me. But they did not work with Jack. He remained mean and resistant no matter what she said nicely. It was better, or at least it felt better, to bully Jack. After all, he was bullying her, wasn't he?

"Open your god-damned mouth so I can brush your god-damned teeth," she wound up saying.

"Uh…..Uh…..Uh….." Jack closed his mouth tightly.

"Fine. See if I care if your teeth rot in your mouth, you old bastard. Don't blame me if you get toothaches."

The most effective way to get Jack to cooperate was through pain. She knew she could not hit him and leave a bruise, as much as she wanted to. Jill would find out. Pulling his hair, yanking his ears, or pinching his testicles did the trick.

"Okay. Open your mouth, Jack."

Pull. Yank.

"Uh…..Uh…..Uh…." He opened his mouth.

"Are you going to let me clean the shit off of you or not?"

Pinch.

"Uh…..Uh…..Uh……"

"Okay. Good. Finished."

The aide who came once a week to bathe Jack was named Jose. Glee was amazed to see that Jack did whatever Jose instructed. He let Jose undress him, put him in the shower, soap and rinse him without any struggling. Jose spoke softly in Spanish and sang while he worked. It was almost as if Jack enjoyed it.

"Hey," Glee said, after he had come several times. "Are you legal?"

"Hey, are you bitchy?" He pronounced it *beechee.*

He was a short, muscular man, heavily tattooed, with shiny black hair combed into a pony tail.

"I bet you belong to one of those gangs for illegals."

"I bet you belong to one of those *beech* gangs." He grinned at her.

"How about if I *geeve* you a bath now. Let's take off your clothes," he said.

"No fucking way." She smiled without letting him see.

Soon she found herself waiting for the day of the week when Jose was scheduled. She told herself it was only because it was a break in the super boring routine of her days with Jack, of her life, in fact.

Opening the Book of Me, she started a new red section called "Don't." It was to consist of a list of forbidden things. She jotted down the first entry.

"Jose."

Under the sub-heading Technique, she wrote: *"Remind myself that he is an ugly little illegal, not an older rich man."*

One day, when Jose had finished dressing Jack, he spied the Book of Me. Glee had carelessly left it near Jack's bed.

"What is *thees*?" He opened it.

"It's mine. Give it to me." Glee reached for it.

He scanned it, turning pages as he twisted away from her each time she lunged for it.

"Well, look," he said, in a mock-amazed tone. "Here *ees* my name, Jose, under the part called "Don't'."

"That's not you. That's another Jose."

They entangled themselves, Glee trying to get the book, and Jose struggling to read it. Now she was hitting him. Then, somehow, they were kissing and falling onto Jack's hospital bed. Jack was sitting nearby in his chair, in clean clothes, hair shampooed and neatly combed.

"Uh…..Uh…..Uh….."

This became a weekly ritual. Glee waited for Jose. The days without him slowed to a crawl. Although she tried not to care about him, telling herself she was only letting herself be entertained, she could not stop thinking about his touch. It was just sex, she insisted.

"*I am not, not, not falling in love with Jose,*" she wrote in the "Don't" section.

But she spent hours craving him, more than she craved the major of "me." She read her English class copy of "Pride and Prejudice" despite herself, and daydreamed about the ways Elizabeth refused to fall in love with Mr. Darcy, comparing it to herself and Jose. As if Jose would ever be wealthy, like Mr. Darcy.

Jose never seemed to want more of Glee than their weekly sexual encounters. He never asked to see her in-between. He never seemed in a hurry to be with her. When he came in the door, he nodded to her then immediately began attending to Jack, while softly singing a Latino song. He barely glanced at her until he finished bathing Jack. Then he tumbled her onto the hospital bed.

There was very little talking at first. But Glee was becoming curious, knowing she should not be.

"So, where are you from?" She tried to be nonchalant.

"*Mejico* City."

She pursed her lips, considering this.

"Did you—like—have a girlfriend there?"

He laughed. "No. My *mujer*, my wife *ees* there. And my *ninos*. One day I *breeng* them to here."

Wife? Ninos? Oh, my God!

Pushing him away, she rushed into her room, shutting the door.

Fool, fool, she muttered to herself. Opening the Book of Me, she wrote: *"He's married, you idiot. Don't ever think about him again."*

When she heard the door close and knew Jose was gone, she paced around the living room, talking to Jack.

"Okay. Laugh at me. I've fucked a married man, an illegal, a loser. Go ahead, laugh. I hate him. I hate you. I hate me."

Her teeth ground with rage. She hit the mattress they had lain on together with both fists, sobbing and cursing.

Then it came to her. Jose probably was undocumented. Still furious, she looked up the contact number for ICE on the computer. There was a tip line. Immediately, she called it. It was automated. She was given the option to leave an anonymous tip.

No! She wanted Jose to know exactly who denounced him. She wanted him to know that she was getting even for *his* betrayal. She left her identifying information, what she knew of Jose, and when he could be expected at her house again.

Then she waited. When the day came, Jose arrived as usual and nodded at her before attending to Jack. Glee did not say a thing. She stayed near the door.

Still, she was surprised to see the ICE van pull up. She had not believed anyone really paid attention to her tip. And if they did, she had not thought they would come so soon. She felt goose bumps on her arms.

Two ICE agents knocked on the door and politely asked to see Jose. She called him. It would be the last time she called his name. He knew exactly what was happening and did not resist. After quietly answering a few of the agent's questions, he was handcuffed.

Turning to look at her before being taken to the van, he said. "Dry Jack."

She never saw him again. That evening, after Jill returned, Glee went to CVS and bought a pregnancy test kit. She was not surprised when she tested positive. She had Jose's child within her. She wanted to hate it, but could not. It was all she had of Jose. For some reason, she could not get rid of it the way she got rid of Jose, in a fit of rage.

What she would get rid of was the goal of the Book of Me. Instead, she would be like her mother and grandmother. A single parent at twenty.

She did make one decision. She stopped being cruel to Jack. Instead, she gained his cooperation by giving him a hand job whenever she changed his Depends. That worked. Now Jack did whatever she wanted. This is what Jose had taught her. People can be controlled with pleasure. Like Jose had controlled her. You don't have to hurt them.

She wrote it in The Book of Me under the new part, tabbed green, called "Power."

15. THE CERTIFIED NURSING ASSISTANT

When the Maintenance Man at the nursing home went postal and began murdering residents, Marie ran out the front door as soon as she heard shots coming from the back area.

Hell, she was not about to get killed for ten dollars an hour, even though she passed the Certified Nursing Assistant test. If her husband, Tom, said anything about it, let him get a fucking job changing shit-filled diapers of dead brains dumped there by their families. That should shut his mouth.

She and Tom fought all the time. They had been fighting ever since they started dating in their sophomore year in high school, not stopping when Marie got pregnant in her junior year, and they both dropped out. When they were not fighting, they asked each other why they fought. It was the littlest thing that got them going. Two minutes into the fight, neither could remember what it was about.

Their children, Clair and Junior, also fought. Even while their parents squabbled, screams of "You're not fair!" and "You did so. I saw you!" out-shouted the raised voices of the adults. Tom's parents, fueled by their after-lunch drinks, also spoke their minds. Doors slammed, fists banged the table, toys were hurled across the room. It was constant bloody hell.

They all lived together in the creaky farm house owned by Tom's parents. If Marie lost any income because of the shooting, there was no way they could afford the cigarettes and beer keeping them from killing each other. Tom was looking for work, supposedly. His parents only had their monthly Social Security. They all listened to Marie's account of her narrow escape and agreed she should not return to the nursing home for a while. It was too spooky to work in a place where murders happened. It might even be haunted.

But the thought of doing without made them irritable, and soon the squabbling started again. Marie was at the point she always reached with Tom.

"That's right! Whenever I want to talk about our issues, you zip up your damn lips."

To which Tom, as usual, replied in the usual way.

"What's the point of going over the same fucking thing again. How many times do we have to do this?"

Tom's mother had to have her say. "Here, Tom, a drink. You have to watch your blood pressure. Your face is red as a beet."

Tom's father interceded. "Hey, hey! I'm trying to watch the game. Everyone shut the fuck up."

In the midst of this commotion, the doorbell rang. Nobody moved.

"Somebody get the fucking door!" Tom's father thundered.

Naturally, it was Marie who rose from the sofa, smirking at Tom to indicate it would be her and not him, proving her point in the unfinished argument.

Standing on the front steps were two men in navy blue wool coats.

"Are you Marie Green?"

Marie was alarmed. These people knew her name and where she lived. They were unlikely to be Mormons or salesmen.

"Who are you?" She did not hide her suspicion.

"F.B.I., Ma'am. National Security Branch. I'm Agent Price. This is Agent Jefferson." Both men showed her their badges. Agent Jefferson carried a briefcase.

The National Security Branch? Was she in trouble?

"Ma'am, we'd like to speak with you. If this is an inconvenient time, we can make an appointment for you to come to the FBI office in Indianapolis."

The long trip to Indianapolis cost gas money. But she was unprepared for their visit. The F.B.I. That was worse than the police. This had to be bad.

"If you could wait here a minute…," she said.

"Yes, Ma'am. We will."

Closing the door, she said in a stage-whisper, "It's the F.B.I!"

The room instantly quieted. Everyone stared at her.

"The F.B.I? What the fuck do they want?" Tom whispered.

"They want to talk to me. What should I do?"

They looked at one another. The children ran to her side.

Finally, Tom's father said, "We've got nothing to hide. Let them in."

Marie opened the door and stood back. The agents entered the room, introduced themselves, and showed their badges again. They said they wished to speak to Marie in private. Tom said that as he was her husband, by rights he should be with her. The agents did not respond, which Tom took to be affirmative. The only place was the upstairs bedroom. The children could stay downstairs with their grandparents.

The two agents, Tom, and Marie climbed the squeaky staircase and crammed into the small room.

"How did you know where to find us?" Tom asked.

"Background check by Mrs. Green's employer when she was hired," Agent Jefferson said.

"What is this about?" Marie asked.

"We'd like to ask you some questions about the man known to you as Sidney Stone, Ma'am," Agent Price said.

Marie and Tom looked at each other. The Maintenance Man? The one who shot all those people?

"I thought he was killed or something." Marie had heard on TV that Sidney Stone was shot to death in the back garden of the nursing home, where Marie sometimes took residents for a bit of sun.

"Yes, Ma'am." That was all Agent Price offered. "Do you mind if we record this interview?"

"And may I have permission to take your photographs with my phone for our records?" Agent Jefferson said.

Marie and Tom gave each other another a consulting look.

"Whatever," Tom said.

"Mrs. Green, please tell us all you know about the man known to you as Sidney Stone," Agent Price said.

"All us girls met him the same way. Our supervisor, Mrs. Watson, introduced us when we were hired. She introduced us to everyone on the staff, not just him."

"You said 'all us girls'," Agent Price said.

"I meant all us CNAs."

"What was your relationship with Sidney Stone in the nursing home?"

"What do you mean "relationship," Tom said, testily.

"Did you and Sidney Stone ever work together as part of your job, Mrs. Green?"

"No, not really. I mean, if I noticed a faucet was leaking or something, I'd, like, tell Mrs. Watson, and she'd tell him to fix it."

"Did you and Sidney Stone ever have a conversation?"

Marie gave Tom a confused glance.

"About what?"

"Anything at all."

She paused, thinking. "No. Not that I remember. I was too busy for conversations."

"Can you tell us anything at all about Sidney Stone?"

"No. Nothing. I didn't think about him, much."

Agent Price looked at Tom.

"And you, Sir? Do you have any knowledge about Sidney Stone?"

"No. Nothing."

Agent Jefferson opened his briefcase.

"Ma'am, I'm going to show you and your husband some photographs of some men. I will also say their names. Some are Hungarian names. Please tell us if you have seen or heard Sidney Stone talk about any of these men, or if you saw any of them at the nursing home."

Agent Jefferson placed about a dozen photographs of mostly beefy-looking older men around Sid Stone's age on the bed. He pointed to each one and said the name. Marie and Tom shook their heads as each was said. They never saw or heard of them, including the non-American ones.

Agent Jefferson returned the photos to his briefcase. "Thank you both. That is all we need to know, for now. Here is my card. If you recall any of those men later, please contact me."

Once the two agents were out of the house, Marie nervously chattered about how scared she had been, how she was afraid she and Tom would be arrested, about the photographs, about how polite the agents were but who knew what they were up to.

Tom did not say much at first. He took a deep swig from the whiskey bottle his father handed him. Junior sat on his lap. Tom let him have a small sip. Marie hoisted Claire onto her hip. The child sucked her thumb and leaned into Marie. Tom's mother lit a cigarette, and said she did not appreciate those agents scaring the family.

Then Tom said, "You know what I think. I think Sidney Stone was a fucking spy. That's what I think. The photos? I bet they were all spies. Or terrorists. They were Hungarians, right? Sidney Stone must have been a Hungarian terrorist, if he killed a bunch of people and all. Maybe he's a foreigner. You can't always tell from how a person looks."

For once, Marie did not contradict Tom. She said he was probably right. That made Tom like Marie a lot better than he had for a while. Even his father nodded approvingly, observing that the agents did say they were from the National Security Branch. That was more than regular F.B.I. It sure sounded to him like the kind of outfit that goes after spies and terrorists.

Later, Marie and Tom shared the same bed. Neither went to the couch or to one of the children's beds in a huff. Instead, Marie lay her head on Tom's chest. They talked into the night about the interview. Tom told Marie that she hadn't said anything wrong. They wondered about Sid Stone being a terrorist. Wasn't it the quiet kind who you'd never suspect who always turned out to be a terrorist? What if he had been one of those suicide bombers? Marie could have got herself killed.

But, Tom wondered, what if the F.B.I. interviewed them to trick them into confessing that Sid Stone recruited them? Not that he had, but what if the FBI thought he planned to? Maybe they were terrorism suspects! Both were scared and thrilled by these ideas.

Before she fell asleep, Marie told Tom she loved him. Tom said he loved Marie, too. It had been a long time since they said that to each other.

For the rest of the week, everyone talked of nothing but the interview. Even the children had opinions. Junior thought Sid Stone hid a bomb somewhere in his house. Claire said he probably bit people, like in the movies about vampires. Junior called his sister an idiot, but not in a yelling voice. He was just saying it. Tom did not even have to threaten to whip his ass if he was mean to his sister.

Tom's father said, "No fucking foreigners better not show up in my house. I'll show them who the terrorist is with my shot gun. It's loaded and ready. I'll shoot their asses off if they don't leave on the spot. And no fucking F.B.I. agents better come around either, or I don't care if I shoot them, too. But right now, someone better get me a beer to steady my nerves."

Tom's mother got him the beer even before he had to curse her to get her to do it.

Everyone was getting along.

Marie, Tom, and Tom's parents had long discussions about the terrorist plot. They speculated that the only two targets in southern Indiana worth a dime were the college and the naval base where weapons were developed. Marie thought that since maintenance men were good with their hands, Sid Stone was probably going to blow up the naval base next. Who in their right mind would want to blow up a damn college? Everyone thought she had a point.

Finally, Marie and Tom wore out the topic. There was nothing more to say. The F.B.I. agents did not come back. Neither the college nor the naval base were blown up. Sid Stone was dead. Soon, Marie and Tom were fighting again and sleeping in separate beds.

This went on for the next few weeks. No one mentioned the mass shooting or the F.B.I. anymore. Everyone in the family was back to endless squabbling about nothing anyone remembered the next day. Marie returned to her job at the nursing home, which at least limited the time they had to squabble.

One day, when her shift finished, Marie was walking through the employee parking lot towards her car, when a man spoke to her.

"Excuse me," he said.

He looked familiar. Where had Marie seen him before? She stopped and starred.

"I'm Max Stone. Sidney Stone was my cousin. May I talk to you for a minute?"

He did look like Sidney Stone. And maybe a little like one of the Hungarians in the photos the agents had shown her, although she did not remember them saying any of the men in the photos were named Max Stone.

"I don't care." She held her purse tightly across her chest, as if Max Stone might steal it.

"Do you work in the nursing home?"

"Yeah. I'm a CNA."

"And that is…?"

"Certified Nursing Assistant."

"I see. The thing is…you see…my cousin killed ten people here before he was killed. And he also shot my Aunt Mary, his mother. My cousin Flo, Sid's sister, well…it seems she committed suicide. So, you see…I've lost half of my family."

Tears were welling in Max Stone's eyes. He took a handkerchief from his pocket, blotted his eyes, and blew his nose.

Marie was silent. She had never seen Tom or any man cry before.

"I have a daughter. Francine. We call her Francie. She's fourteen, in high school. The thing is, the other kids know. They say awful things to her. My wife might have to quit her job and home-school her. Even though we won't have enough money if she does. I don't know what we're going to do." He closed his eyes and slowly shook his sad head.

"Geez, Mister. I'm so sorry."

He opened his eyes and looked at her. "I'm not from here. But I drove over here to see if I could get some answers. Why would my cousin do something that would ruin so many lives? Even Francie's? She loved him and Flo and Aunt Mary. Now they call Sid a mass murderer and Francie a mass murderer's cousin. Why would Sid do that to her?"

Marie felt her own eyes tear up. "I don't know, Mister. I didn't really know your cousin."

Max Stone stared at her for another moment. "Well, okay. That's alright. I thank you for your time, Miss." He walked away.

Later, Marie discussed the conversation with Tom. Neither could think of any way Marie herself could have helped Max Stone or his daughter. Their cousin killed ten people, eleven—counting his mother. It was what it was.

"What the girl should do is give a hard kick right where it hurts to any son of a bitch who says anything about it. That would fucking stop them. If she did that, her mom could keep her job," Tom said.

For the next day or two, Marie and Tom enjoyed an improved relationship. There was little squabbling. They slept in the same bed every night. The children played well together and shared toys. Tom's parents remained in a state of alcoholic tranquility. The house was peaceful.

"Maybe it's time for another baby," Marie whispered to Tom.

Tom smiled. "Maybe another boy," he said.

V. A FEW DAYS LATER

16. THE FRIEND

Larry heard the news of the mass killing on TV before the two policemen knocked on the door to deliver the terrible information that his mother had been among the victims. He slumped to the floor at the sight of the red blinking lights of emergency vehicles on the screen, while the anchor stated the grim facts. The murders occurred in the nursing home where his mother resided. The killer was identified as the Maintenance Man on the staff of the facility. He died by police gun fire. He was thought to be the lone killer.

"If only's" circled in Larry's mind. If only he had been visiting when the killer entered. If only he visited more frequently. If only he kept his mother at home instead of placing her in a nursing home. If only he picked a different nursing home. If only the killer lived to face punishment on earth before going to everlasting Hell, where he belonged.

Vengeful thoughts rocketed through him. His hands tightened into fists. His nails dug into his palms.

"I wanted to see the killer roast in the electric chair. I'd take a front row seat. I'd pull the switch myself. It would've given me pleasure to watch the man writhe in pain as the electricity cooked him. I wanted to see smoke rising from his head and to smell his burning hair before he was pronounced dead. Then the killer's body could've been thrown into the county dump for the rats and maggots to eat, for all I care."

His mother had been the best woman, the best mother in the world. He never remarried after his divorce. When his father died, he moved back home to keep his mother company. It had been just the two of them for years. But he realized he could not take care of her himself after her dementia diagnosis. It was too undignified and even repugnant for him, a man, to see to his mother's hygiene needs. Reluctantly, he moved her to the nursing home. He visited nearly every day after work, but as time passed, she did not seem to notice.

Then his mother had a stroke and was not expected to survive. She was moved to a Hospice room, where she was only conscious at brief intervals. It was only a matter of time, he was told. He took vacation days in order to spend time with her, holding her hand. It was important to him to be with her for her last breathe. When he went home to sleep, he gave the staff instructions to phone him if death was imminent.

The killer deprived him of a last opportunity to tell his mother he loved her. He wanted her to leave this world knowing she was loved. Of course he told her he loved her constantly, but he thought it was vital for her to hear it in her last moments. And it was possible she had some last loving words for him. It would have meant the world to Larry to hear his mother tell him she loved him just before she departed.

That is what the killer stole from him. He had been robbed!

The funeral was sparsely attended. Larry did not like it when the minister gave a standard account of his mother—that she was a good Christian woman. The minister recited the standard Twenty-Third Psalm. Clearly, although his mother had been a regular church-goer, the minister did not know her well enough to personalize the service. The minister did not appreciate or perhaps understand her uniqueness, her extraordinary kindness and exemplary character. True, she had been a quiet woman. But with a little effort, the minister could have discovered for himself that a humble member of his flock was nothing less than a saint.

His mother had been on to the minister, though. On more than one occasion she remarked that it would not surprise her if the minister ran off with church funds or with a twelve-year-old girl or both. When she said this, her mouth twisted into a sarcastic-looking smile at odds with her sweet nature.

At home after the funeral, Larry paced from room to room, wringing his hands. If he sat down, he jumped up again in a few seconds and continued his pacing. He could not rest. His mind raced. Where could he find justice? How could he obtain vengeance when the killer had died? Suicide-by-cop, it was called. It was explained to him that some individuals kill to force the police to kill them in a "hail of bullets."

He spoke out loud, although there was no one to listen.

"Who am I supposed to hate? The dead killer? The staff at the nursing home who did not protect my mother? God?"

He did not return to work. HR faxed him family leave forms. He was too on edge and distracted to work. During the rare times he slept, he ground his teeth so hard his jaw ached for hours the next day. He forgot to eat, lost weight. For days, he did little more than pace and stew about what had happened.

At times, he wept, pulling his hair, remembering those youthful occasions when his mother chastised him for his insolent attitude. Or, when he was an adult and caused her to rebuke him for flippant remarks. Fortunately, those occasions were rare breaches in a loving relationship. Larry vigorously apologized to her whenever she brought them up.

How he missed their quiet evenings together, studying the Bible after dinner and praying. They watched older shows on TV, decent family comedies made before the modern era of unrelenting sex and violence. The only one his mother objected to was "I Love Lucy" because she did not find a mixed-race couple amusing.

Ten days after the murders, Larry received a notice from the Homicide Division of the Police Department. The families and close friends of the victims were invited to attend an update. Grief counselors would be available if requested. Following the update in a private room at police headquarters, there would be a press conference on the front steps.

Without hesitation, he sent back the RSVP form. Yes, he would attend. What he wanted was answers.

He was one of the first to arrive at the meeting. He took a seat in the back. Others came mostly in groups of three or four. Often an older person accompanied by others a generation younger. Spouses of victims, he supposed, and their adult children. He was one of the solitary attendees. There was only one other. A man in his sixties, around his own age, who also sat grimly in the back.

A detective entered and spoke. He introduced himself and launched into the update. The Maintenance Man, named Sid Stone, acted alone. He took care of his mother, who had Alzheimer's, with the help of his sister in his home. He killed her before killing the nursing home residents. He left no note, and his motive was unknown. Both the staff at the nursing home and Mr. Stone's neighbors claimed he showed no sign of distress. They described him as a man who minded his own business. No one knew him well. The Department was satisfied there was little more to learn and would soon be closing the case. Did anyone have any questions?

Someone asked about the type of handgun. Someone else asked if the gun was loaded when the killer refused the demand to drop his weapon. Someone asked if this was the first "suicide-by-cop" in the county. After each of the detective's answers, the other solitary man gave a little snort. Larry wondered if anyone else heard him.

After the update, as people were filing out, the man approached him and extended his hand. His grip was strong.

"Ralph," he said.

"Larry."

"Care to have a bite to eat and a drink with me, Friend?" Ralph asked.

It can't hurt, Larry thought. He had to force himself to eat anyway, even if he had no appetite. And perhaps the tension from the update would lessen if he had someone to talk to who had been through what he had been through. He soon found himself in a sports bar with Ralph. When the waiter asked for their beverage order, Ralph asked for two shots. He gave one to Larry.

"It's on me, Friend."

Larry was not one to drink, and especially at lunchtime, especially whiskey. In the heat of the summer, he and his mother had an occasional cider. On holidays, they might indulge in a little sherry. But his mother disapproved of hard liquor and of people who drank to excess.

"No character. That's their problem," she said with a sniff.

During the slow wait for their food order, Larry was aware that he should pay for a round, too. He promised himself he would sip it slowly, unlike Ralph, who tossed his down immediately.

"Who did you lose, Friend?"

"My mother."

Ralph grimaced. "Tough one. Mothers. That's rough."

Maybe Ralph understood.

"And you?" Larry asked.

"My dad. We weren't close. And he didn't say a word for the past three years. Not that he was ever much of a talker. He likely didn't know anymore that he had a nose on his face when that freak killed him. He sure as hell didn't know me anymore."

Larry was not sure what to say. "That's rough, too," he managed.

Ralph reached into his back pocket and produced a folded piece of paper. He spread it on the table and slid it over to Larry. It was a printout of a list of names of the corporate owners of the nursing home.

"What's this?" Larry asked.

Ralph pointed to the paper. "Read the names."

There were seven names.

"I don't understand."

"Look again. It'll come to you."

Larry stared, uncomprehending. Then Ralph pointed at four of the names, one by one.

"See?"

Larry was silent.

"Those four are Jew names," Ralph said.

Larry saw that they could have been.

"And this one? Brown? Typical nigra name," Ralph said.

Larry was shocked to hear anyone in anyone say "nigra."

"I'm not very PC, am I." Ralph smiled. Larry guessed that Ralph meant not being PC was a good thing.

"What about the other two names?" Larry asked.

Ralph gave the paper a quarter turn and stared at it.

"Ah. This one, Pavel, is a common name from India. Another nigra. And that one, might be anything. Hard to say. But that's six out of seven for sure."

"Six out of seven?" Larry repeated.

Ralph leaned forward and said, softly, "Four Jews and two nigras. And everyone knows that Jews control nigras."

He paused to let that sink in.

"I don't think I get your point."

"The point, Friend, is that the nursing home is owned and controlled by Jews. Now, take a look at the killer's name, Sid *Stone*. Stone...*Stein*. Stein. Jewish. Get it? They change their Jew names to normal names. The Jews do. Like Stein to Stone."

"I still don't see the..."

"Friend, it's clear. The Jew owners arranged for Sid Stone or Stein to do the killing. Then they arranged for the police to kill Sid Stein. Like Oswald and Jack Ruby when Kennedy was killed. See? The assassin is assassinated. So no one will know what really happened."

"Why would the owners want residents killed?"

Ralph looked around, as if he did not want anyone to hear what he was going to say.

"The ten who were killed? All Level Fours. You must have received the letter."

"What letter?"

"The one about raising the fees for Level Fours. Not for the ones who were already paying, like your mother and my father. For the next lot. They wanted the ten Hospice beds emptied pronto. Then they could get the next in who they could charge more. The Jews, you know. They'll do anything for money."

Larry felt lightheaded from the two shots.

"Are you saying my mother was killed so the nursing home could charge the next resident more?"

Ralph sat back in his chair. "What do you think, Friend?"

Larry was aware that Ralph's logic was faulty, somehow. Or was it?

Ralph called the waiter over.

"Let's have one for the road," he said, winking.

"I don't think I..."

"It's on me, Friend. This is a special occasion. It's not every day two victims of injustice meet and get to the truth so quick."

By the time Larry rose to leave, he was staggering.

"Whoa!" Ralph said. "I better drive you home. I can pick you up tomorrow and bring you back here. So we can finish our conversation."

Larry wondered what there was to finish. But he was in no state to argue.

Once home, Larry fell into a long restless nap. When he awoke, it was dark. He had a headache. A hangover, he supposed. He was nauseous, too. He recalled the odd conversation he had with Ralph. About Jews arranging the murders of the Hospice patients. To get more money from the raised fees for the next residents.

He wondered if Ralph was crazy. Or exaggerating. But then he remembered that long ago, his mother had called Jews "Christ-killers." He thought about that. If Jews killed Jesus, the very son of God, it was surely no stretch to think they could kill a human, or even ten humans, was it?

He went to the kitchen and found the aspirin. He took three. Even if they made his stomach worse, they would stop his headache. He wanted to be able to think straight. He remained awake all night pondering Ralph's words. More than half the owners of the nursing home business had Jewish names. Jews often change their names, so the killer might be a Jew. Stone, Stein. Close enough to pass for a non-Jew but still let other Jews know who he was. Like a secret signal. Like Oswald and Ruby. Ruby—another Jew. Another assassin.

By morning, Larry was leaning toward thinking Ralph was on to something. No one wanted to kill Hospice patients who were days from death anyway. What was the sense to it? Unless there was another reason. Follow the money, it was said.

Just before noon, there was a knock on the door. Ralph was there to drive Larry back to his car.

"Doing okay, Friend?"

"I'm afraid I'm not used to drinking so much. I'm still a bit queasy."

Ralph took a flask out of the pocket of his jacket. "Here's what you need. Hair of the dog."

Larry put the flask to his lips and swallowed. Within a few minutes, he was feeling like himself again. Ralph drove him to his car, then parked next to it instead of just dropping Larry off.

"Friend, here's what I'm thinking. We should sue the nursing home. Both the corporation and the corporate owners. And we should do it before any of the others decide to do it. Let them dick around. If we do it ASAP, we'll drain the corporate funds dry before the others figure out they want a share."

Ralph paused to give Larry a moment to reflect.

"Sue." He said.

"Correct. Sue the Jew bastards. The only way to get any justice is to hit them in the pocketbook. Make them sorry they were raising fees and couldn't even wait a month or two to get a few dollars more. That's all they had to do—wait for the residents to die. Not murder them. The sons of bitches!"

Ralph slammed his fist on the top of the dashboard. Larry startled.

Ralph took two deep breaths. "Sorry, Friend. Gotta keep control of myself better than that." Taking out the flask again, he took a swig and offered it to Larry.

"Here's the thing. I've consulted a lawyer experienced in doing malpractice suits. He says suing a corporation is expensive for individuals because corporations have more legal resources. But he's willing to take our case. He thinks the award could be in the millions."

Larry was astounded. The millions!

"Usually the lawyer gets half of the settlement. But he's willing to take a third. That's a third for him, a third for you, and a third for me. But he wants ten thousand up front as a retainer. To show we're serious."

Ralph took the flask Larry passed back to him.

"Thing is, Friend, I'm divorced times four and my exes have been cleaning me out for years for child support. Of course, that's all over now that all the kids are grown. But now it's the kids asking for help with this payment or that payment. I'm flat broke, Pal."

He gave Larry a long look.

"Think you could come up with the ten K? I'd pay you back out of my third. With interest, if you'd like. Say three, four percent?"

"I don't know. It's a lot."

"Think it over, Friend." Ralph took the folded paper with the seven names out of his pocket. "That's my phone number I wrote on the bottom. Think it over and phone me if you want in."

Larry took the paper. He got out of the car.

Back home, Larry paced again. How he wished he could talk Ralph's ideas over with his mother. He imagined her agreeing that she may have been shot in the head by a Christ-killer. She might also agree that the corporation was run by Christ-killers who convinced a Christ-killer-patsy to do the mass killings. He would have been a patsy if the plan was to have him killed, too. That would mean the Christ-killers also controlled the police.

For hours, Larry went back and forth between belief and doubt. Often he talked out loud to himself.

"Four Jew owners...*but three non-Jew names*...two nigra names...*controlled by Jews*...Sid Stone...*Sid Stein*...The owners would be able to control him...*they could have ordered him to kill*...Everyone knows all Jews stick together...*Christ-killers stick together no matter what*...but they had to kill the killer in case he weakened..."

In the end, Larry could not imagine his mother agreeing to a lawsuit.

"We don't wash our dirty linen in public." That is what she would say.

Besides, he could not take money for his mother's death. No, that would be taking advantage. Money would not bring him justice. And it would bring one more undignified element to his mother's death.

He could not, would not profit from her death!

Having made that decision, he felt better. He took Ralph's folded paper, tore it up, and threw it in the garbage can.

The feeling of relief lasted about an hour. Then the pounding in Larry's head started again. This time, it was not a hangover. He paced again, railing out loud.

"Christ-killers! Christ-killers killed my mother! They think they can get away with it because they're big shots. I don't want their filthy money. Insurance would just give it back to them anyway. Filthy pigs! They should die. Why should they live if they killed my mother, took her from me?"

Just before dawn, He went into his garage and looked on the shelf where he kept used paint. He took what he wanted. Then he drove to the nearest synagogue. He did not park in the parking lot, but a little further up the street instead. Walking to the synagogue, he saw that no one was around.

Starting at one end of the building, He used one of the black spray paint cans he had brought with him from the garage to cover the walls with swastikas and the words "Kill all Jews". He continued around the building until the paint ran out in all three cans. Then he left.

The next day, the local news broadcast the story of the anonymous hate crime. It was satisfying to see his work in daylight on TV. It had come out better than he thought, considering he was hardly able to see what he was doing the night before.

There was a big gathering of outraged citizens, many of them Christ-killers and many of their sympathizers, "nigra" and white Ministers, and city officials who all helped scrub away the offensive images.

A rumor started that perhaps Sid Stone had not been a lone nursing home mass murderer. Perhaps he had an accomplice who was responsible for the antisemitic vandalism. After all, four of the ten victims had been Jewish. Maybe the motive was antisemitism. The six other victims might have been killed as distractions from the four real targets. Some thought they had seen Sid Stone at an alt-right gathering.

This was reported in the media as an unverified story.

Larry's sense of satisfaction lasted about as long as the media attention did. Then his anger began to build again. He did not achieve justice with a can of spray paint. "An eye for an eye, a tooth for a tooth." This was a quote from the Old Testament. His mother proclaimed it several times over the years. Larry now thought she had been instructing him. As if she knew it was a lesson he had to learn as he had learned other teachings from the Bible.

Using the Internet, Larry discovered that the corporate headquarters of the nursing home was in the Jew city, Cleveland. This was where the Christ-killers worked. He would drive there. It would take about eight hours. One long day. Briefly, he thought of asking Ralph to go with him. But he no longer had Ralph's phone number. Besides, this was something he had to do himself. It was for his mother, and no one should think it was for any other victim.

As he drove the speed limit on Interstate 70, he planned. He would get a hotel room in the outskirts of Cleveland. He would pray. He did not know what should happen after that. He would play it by ear.

17. THE SOCIOLOGIST

How lucky the Sociologist was! A mass killing in the very town in which his university was located. This was his special area: a study of how mass killings affect communities. And what good fortune that the local killing—in a nursing home, a first of its kind—occurred in a small, self-contained southern Indiana town adjacent to the campus.

Just as he was in the midst of a dry spell, tearing his thinning hair out trying to come up with a new hypothesis, a research subject fell right into his lap. Immediately, he instructed his graduate students to construct an instrument for surveying different demographics in the town, grouped cross-sectionally by race, gender, religion, age, and social class. He anticipated the mathematical model he would present at the annual meeting of the American Sociological Society in Washington, D.C. He envisioned a peer review journal, such as the New Sociologist Quarterly, publishing his conclusions.

At last, he would be promoted to Full Professor, as he should have been and deserved to be years ago, if it were not for the interference of Harvey R., the Chairman of the Tenure and Promotions Committee. The Sociologist seethed at the thought of Harvey R. The elderly man, well past the normal age for retirement but not yet at the mandatory age, clung to both his committee assignments and to his desirable corner office, with windows overlooking the university arboretum. By rights, the Sociologist, who still carried a full teaching load, should have had that office instead of the much smaller one in the back of the building. It galled him that Harvey R. no longer taught classes. Instead, he supervised a handful of PhD candidates, meeting them for a few hours a week, and spending the rest of his time on campus lounging in the Faculty Club.

In the back of the Sociologist's mind was time Harvey R. and a group of his associates tried to get the already-tenured Sociologist fired on ethical grounds. The bogus claim was that his published article, "Decontextualized Measurement of the White Male Voter," was strikingly similar to Harvey R's "Implicit Bias in the Party Identification of Upper Class Men." The word "plagiarism" was bandied about among the faculty, and the Sociologist received disdainful looks from some. All because of a few sentences that were somewhat alike and the appearance of methodological similarity. No action was taken, but it left a bad taste. It had jeopardized the Sociologist's earlier advancement from Assistant to Associate Professor.

Two or three years later, there was the scurrilous charge by certain female students, no doubt under the thrall of Harvey R., as so many naively were at the time, that the Sociologist made them "uncomfortable" by "invading their personal space." Such nonsense! While it was true that, when in passionate discourse about his subject, the Sociologist might pace and gesticulate, possibly moving too close to students for brief moments, or perhaps some lingering moments, this was entirely unconscious and without any inappropriate intent. This was a conclusion the Ethics Team, a university-level investigative unit, eventually made, after months of harrowing interviews.

Naturally Harvey R. used this as an excuse to further hold up the Sociologist's overdue promotion. But the murder of ten residents in a nursing home by the staff Maintenance Man was a game changer. When his article was accepted for publication, no one on the Promotions Committee would have the temerity to deny him his due. In fact, such an important contribution to scholarship in his area might propel him to Harvard, Yale, or Stanford, where the best Sociology Departments were located. It would be where he belonged, finally rid of his position at the tin-pot Indiana college, fine for the likes of Harvey R., whose statistics were—after all— not first class, in the Sociologist's considered opinion.

The only challenge would be if the old man tried to beat him to it, assembling his own team of graduate students to survey the community. Harvey R. was the one faculty member whose specialty overlapped with the Sociologist's. The others were either deadwood who never published, languishing in the lower ranks, or who did fieldwork in Africa, the American west, or the Caribbean.

The Sociologist had to work fast and hard to publish before Harvey R. This meant a period of forgoing vacations and invitations, although he was seldom asked to faculty gatherings. He had to double up on Synthroid to combat the inertia caused by hypothyroidism, which was also the reason for the roll of fat spreading across his midsection. He needed a more powerful sleeping pill to combat chronic insomnia, followed by strong coffee through the day to maintain alertness. He approached his research as if going into combat, preparing for a long ordeal, eating less of the unhealthy fast food he craved and doing a few hateful push-ups every morning upon arising.

He wondered if this was enough to motivate him to design, conduct, and synthesize his research before Harvey R. completed his, considering how much time the Sociologist wasted preparing for classes, teaching, grading, and attending tedious meetings of the many undergraduate committees so unfairly forced upon him. It was appalling to think that Harvey R. might beat him simply because he had fewer obligations than the Sociologist did. Something should happen to equalize their chances. But what?

If only Harvey R got hit by a bus. Weeks in a hospital would set him back decisively. There was, however, scant likelihood of that happening. Yet, it might be possible for the elderly man to fall or have some sort of accident.

The Sociologist could not believe that he, a highly educated faculty member, had such an unacceptable thought. He did not wish harm on anyone, even his worst enemy.

Unless it was in self-defense.

He considered. Wouldn't harming Harvey R., who spent years doing harm to the Sociologist's career, be a kind of self-defense? Hadn't the time come for the Sociologist to stand up for himself and stop allowing this man from taking what was his?

Back and forth his thinking went, from the kind of consideration a learned man was supposed to have to the kind of considerations a man cruelly victimized for so many years could be expected to have. The words of the great German sociologist, Ulrich Beck, came to him:

Conditions of inequality and historical injustice have given rise to a feeling of hate in the world—a deeply felt hate that cannot easily be overcome with a few good words.

If the Sociologist hated Harvey R., it was certainly with cause. And it could not be overcome with the usual high-minded words—"turn the other cheek," and the like. No. He must be a man and act, but only to protect himself.

He imagined accidents that might befall Harvey R. He could be hit by a vehicle. Perhaps not a bus, but a car, like the Sociologist's own Honda Accord. The main problem was the timing. How to get Harvey R. onto the road at the precise moment he was barreling toward the spot. What about witnesses? Someone might see and write down the number of the Sociologist's license plate. An intelligent man, like he undoubtedly was, should be able to come up with a much better plan, one that would do the job, one in which he would not be implicated.

He used the internet to research ways to cause accidents without detection. Many were fanciful, such as leaving a poisonous snake under the covers of a bed, or too risky, like arson. In the end, the Sociologist became convinced that the accident must happen on campus, ideally in Harvey R.'s own office—so that everything leading up to the accident seemed normal and routine. The accident should appear to be a random piece of bad luck. And he himself should not be suspected of having anything to do with it. That went without saying.

Fortunately, he was in the habit of working in his office late at night. It would not seem odd if he were in the building if the accident were to happen at that time. Also, he knew the rather annoying schedule of the janitorial staff. Twice a week, he had to stand outside for a few minutes while his office floor was mopped and his wastebasket emptied. However, the janitors might provide an alibi.

His three PhD students requested a meeting with him to discuss the survey questions. How eager they were. They would be doing original research on a horrific local crime. This was their opportunity to make a difference—and at the onset of their careers. If they could analyze the social factors giving rise to such a terrible incident by studying community attitudes toward gun ownership, dementia, and low-wage employment, they might be contributing to the improvement of society.

While the Sociologist was listening to them, he drifted back to his thoughts about an accident befalling Harvey R. The older man would have to be lured to his corner office at night, when the janitors were not around. As the students discussed their methodology, he developed his. As soon as the meeting ended, he wrote an email.

To: <u>harveyr@indiana.edu</u>
Subject: Document of interest to you
Dear Harvey,
My former student, now on the faculty at the University of Pittsburgh, sent me a hard copy of an untitled document that might bear a relationship to your last book, "The Intergenerational Transmission of Information: A Multilevel Study." I think you'd find it quite fascinating. I've no use for it myself, but I'd be happy to let you look it over and keep it if it is of interest. Shall we meet in your office on Thursday at 9 p.m.? Sorry for the late hour. I'm hopelessly behind with grading.

Having set the bait, the Sociologist hoped he had forced himself to follow through. He feared he might back down if he did not set things up in a way that left no exit. As soon as Harvey R. accepted the appointment, not more than a few minutes after receiving the enticing invitation, there was only one possible outcome. Otherwise, the Sociologist would have to admit he lied about the document. The email was evidence that could be used against him. Harvey R. might tell others the Sociologist was either amoral or mad. There would be another investigation.

That was not going to happen!

When Thursday came, the Sociologist went to his office at six-thirty, as usual, after dining in the campus cafeteria. This was a night the janitors were scheduled. After stalling for a few minutes, he left his office. The janitors would say they never saw him there. Taking the back stairway, he was careful not to be seen on his way to Harvey R.'s office, which was never locked. Without turning on a light, he entered, opened a window, took a book from a shelf, and sat on the sofa. If anyone came in, he would say he had fallen asleep while waiting.

Harvey R. was not expected for another two hours. The Sociologist found it hard to sit still. He was very anxious. Perspiration dripped from his head. His hands shook. His tongue felt swollen in his mouth. Dearly, he wanted to run. He had to resist the temptation. The idea of physical brutality sickened him. He had never been in so much as a fist fight as a boy. He had always been a bookish introvert, then an academic—not some sort of thug.

But, he reminded himself, this was self-defense. Pure and simple.

The wait was excruciating. Finally, the university carillon rang the hourly tone. It was nine. A few minutes later, the unmistakable sound of footsteps approached the office door. It opened, and the silhouette of the older man fumbled for the light switch. The Sociologist was nearly in a state of panic. He stood, frozen to the spot. Harvey R. managed to turn on the lights. Then he saw the Sociologist. He gave no indication of surprise at finding the Sociologist waiting in the dark.

"Why, there you are. Give me a minute to put these papers away, then let's see what you have."

Harvey R. crossed in front of the Sociologist to his desk, which was close to the open window. He noticed it immediately.

"Who opened this window? I can't tolerate drafts on my neck. It makes the arthritis much worse. Help me close it, please."

"Leave it." His voice was thickened, as if his mouth was filled with cotton.

"I've been asking for modern windows for years. These old-fashioned things are too heavy for me to manage."

"I can't let this continue."

"What? The window?"

"No. Your...your...you...."

The pain and outrage stored in his mind for years welled up in him. He chocked. Then he began sobbing out loud. Heavily, he sank down onto the sofa again. He balled his fists into his eyes like a boy.

"What's this, now?" Harvey said with gentleness. He went to the Sociologist and placed a hand on his shoulder, as if comforting weeping men were part of an ordinary days' work. "Perhaps if I brought you a glass of water?"

The Sociologist shook his head. His sobs turned to heaves.

"Ah, me," Harvey said. "Academic pursuit can be a rough sport. You start out thinking you might change the world. You wind up fighting trivial battles with your colleagues. Your values are lost along the way."

The Sociologist still heaved. His face was red and wet. He glanced at Harvey R., amazed not to see a trace of contempt.

"Let's go see if we can get that window closed and then have a talk. Can you stand?"

The Sociologist rose. Harvey R. moved to the window and tugged. The Sociologist, weak from his crying spell, stumbled after him.

That is when it happened.

A year later, the Sociologist's article titled "A Cross-Sectional Analysis of Community Attitudes in the Aftermath of a Mass Shooting" was published in a peer review journal. Shortly after, he was promoted to Full Professor by the new Chairperson of the Tenure and Promotions Committee.

18. THE HOUSEKEEPER

The names of the victims scrolled across the bottom of the TV screen. There had been a mass shooting in a nursing home. Ten residents and the shooter had died. The former Housekeeper was startled to see that Dr. Silvers was among them.

Dr. Silvers? My Dr. Silvers?

She stifled a sob, clamping her hand onto her mouth. Crying would have made her boyfriend Roger ask questions. It was seldom a good idea to let a boyfriend know your true feelings. Some things were better kept to yourself.

They both had worked at the same nursing home. She had been fired. Roger, on the other hand, returned to his old job as a Groundskeeper after quitting to go to Wichita. That did not work out, so he came back to Indiana. Well before the shooting happened and Roger became her boyfriend, the Housekeeper ran into him on the bus. It was the day she was hired. A familiar face sat down next to her. She tried to recall who he was. *Roger. It was Roger. Right?*

"Hey," she said.

He turned his blank eyes toward her, then smiled. "I know you. You used to hang out with my friends. Aren't you the one who worked at the Apple Store?"

"Used to. Until I got busted. I'm just out of jail. My first time. I'm on parole, now."

"That's the shits," he said.

"Yeah. College degree. Job with Apple that had a future. Poof! All gone. Have to start over now."

They both looked out the windows, he across the aisle to the left and she to the right. Snowflakes were dissolving on the smudged glass, creating grimy runnels. The bus stopped at the hospital in the medically zoned part of town.

"What've you been up to?" She asked.

"I was staying with my cousin in Kansas until things cooled off here for me after some trouble. Now, a few of us from the old gang are working at the dementia nursing home. Like Pete—remember him? The short guy? He's a Kitchen Prep. Steph is in Housekeeping on the demented side.

"Well, dang. That's where I've got a job, but in the Assisted Living unit. Today is my first day. Looks like I'll be working with the old fam."

Roger leaned closer. "If I had twenty dollars, I'd pay you to fuck. Unless you want to fuck for the fun of it. I'm broke."

"Nope. I'm not into that anymore."

"Too bad," Roger said, standing as the bus pulled into the behavioral health clinic. "This here is my stop. Gotta get off. I don't go to work today 'til after supper."

"Okay. See ya."

At the time, she never thought he would wind up being her boyfriend.

She continued on for a couple of stops until the bus reached the nursing home. She reported to the supervisor of Housekeeping. After filling out paperwork, she was given a set of keys, a locker, and two smocks to wear over street clothes. She was shown the supply closet and how to load a supply cart. She was taught how to clean one of the unoccupied rooms. Then she was given a list of rooms to clean that day, half the number she was expected to clean once her training ended.

Compared to the filth of the jail, the nursing home was a step up. The diaper brigade, as the CNAs were called by the rest of the staff, cleaned up most of the resident messes. Quickly, she became accustomed to the routine and within a week, tolerated the urine-soaked bedding and grossness in bathrooms that were the hazards of a nursing home job.

Occasionally, she saw Pete in the supply room getting dishwasher detergent or oven cleaner. A few times she met Steph in the staff break room, but their breaks came at different hours, and Steph took hers outside so she could smoke. They did not see each other often.

The best part of the job were the residents. They were all old and disabled to a degree, but they still talked like human beings, unlike those in the dementia unit, who were totally checked out. The Housekeeper enjoyed old people. She had been raised by her grandparents, now both deceased. Her mother, who she barely remembered, OD'd when she was three or four. She did not know who her father was.

Her Granny and Pappy were good to her. They saved to send her to college. How she missed them, yet she was glad they did not live to see her become an addict like her mother—a felon, arrested for dealing. For their sake, she wanted to do better. When they looked down from heaven, she wanted them to be proud of her.

Over time, she became friendly with the residents of her assigned rooms. She got along with them, even the grumpy ones. There was one she particularly liked. Doctor Silvers. He had been some sort of scientist. In his room, there were bookcases filled with scientific journals, although she never saw him read any. He used a walker but otherwise needed little help from the CNAs.

While she cleaned his room, she and Doctor Silvers had conversations. Most of the residents talked about themselves, but he seemed interested in her. He asked her questions about her life. She did not mention her legal problems. What she told him about was the kind of life she should have led.

"What were your parents like?"

"My parents died tragically in a traffic accident when I was very young, Doctor Silvers. I was raised by my grandparents, who were as sweet as can be. They're gone, too."

"So you are alone in the world."

"I guess that's true."

"That's very sad, my dear. I hope you at least have a boyfriend."

"Oh, no, Doctor Silvers. I'm not pretty enough for a boyfriend."

"I think you are very pretty, my dear."

Slowly, it came to her that Doctor Silvers may have been flirting. Although he was very old, he was still an appealing man. He was slender with affectionate brown eyes and a ring of fluffy white hair around his head, like a halo. Like most people his age, he was bent and stiff, but not badly.

At first the Housekeeper was amused. She could have an old man boyfriend, if she wanted. Gradually, it occurred to her that having a boyfriend like him, financially well-off enough to pay the exorbitant monthly fee charged by the nursing home, might be an answer to some of her problems. If he wanted to help her out, she might get back on her feet. She decided to encourage the flirting and see where it went. Besides, she was fond of Doctor Silvers.

The next time she entered his room to clean it, he was there as usual, waiting for her.

"I like the way you look with your hair up. You have a lovely long neck. I've always been attracted to women with long necks. They're like swans."

"Thank you."

"Will you be my little swan? Will you let me kiss your neck?"

She closed the door and went to him, curling downward in front of him. Tenderly, he kissed the back of her neck.

"Thank you, my dear."

The kiss was sensual. Her old man boyfriend was more erotic than the young guys who just wanted to fuck. She looked forward to the next time. But when it was his room's turn to be cleaned the next day, he was not there. The Housekeeper wondered if he might be in the cafeteria? Or the emergency room? Any time a resident fell, they were taken to the emergency room. Did he fall?

When she was near the nurses' station, she asked where Doctor Silvers was.

"He's around somewhere. I saw him a little while ago. Did you look in the craft room?"

So he had not waited for her after all. Possibly, one neck kiss was all he had wanted. She may have been just a staff person to him. Nothing special. It was foolish to expect much more.

But there he was the following day, sitting in his room when she reached it. She closed the door.

"What can I do for you, Doctor Silvers?"

This was taking a risk. If he did not like her, she could pretend the meaning of her question was about extra chores in his room. Instead, he surprised her.

"I'm a widower, my dear. It's been years since I've seen pussy. Will you show me your pussy?"

"I don't know if I should do that, Doctor Silvers."

"It would greatly please me, my dear."

She relented and showed him what he wanted to see.

"Oh, how beautiful. How extraordinarily beautiful."

The Housekeeper liked his appreciation. It was so different from the urgency of younger men. This was a new experience. She felt more like an art object than a sex object. For the following week, whenever Doctor Silvers and the Housekeeper were in his room together, she showed him her pussy. She began entering his room during breaks and after her shift, hoping her supervisor would not notice. Most of her visits were no longer than a few minutes. She feared getting caught.

She was starting to need Doctor Silvers' attention. He reminded her of her Pappy. As a child, she spent hours with him, sitting on his lap. Then, her grandmother would suddenly grab her arm and rush her into the kitchen. If Pappy tried to follow, Granny slammed the door hard.

The Housekeeper wondered if she was falling in love with Doctor Silvers. Or, if not exactly falling in love, caring for him like she would a younger man. He seemed interested in her as a person. While she cleaned his room, he still asked her about herself, her goals, and her dreams. He listened closely to whatever she said. He sometimes reminded her of what she had said at previous meetings. To her, this was proof of his caring. Who else ever asked about her deepest desires and remembered them? Only Pappy and Doctor Silvers.

Over the course of the next weeks, the Housekeeper grew more dependent on Doctor Silvers. She reminded herself that his interest might be in her youth. There was an almost sixty year difference in their ages. He might have enjoyed any young woman's willingness to do as he asked. Maybe it had nothing to do with liking her in particular and more to do with liking young women in general.

This possibility made her sad.

Then, one day, Doctor Silvers surprised her again.

"I'd like to take care of you, my dear, if you will allow me to. I'm quite wealthy, you see. I wonder if you would do me the honor of marrying me? I'm afraid I'm unable to get down on my knee."

She was so shaken, she sat right down, still holding the mop handle.

"People will say I'm too old for you, and they would be right if we were to have a conventional marriage. But I'll continue to live here. You'd visit me instead of cleaning my room. I'd give you money for an apartment. You wouldn't have to work. All I'd want is for you to come every day to talk for a while, as we have been doing. And I'd want to look at your pussy and kiss your neck, but nothing more than that. That would be enough."

"I don't know what to say."

"Don't say anything now. Go home and think it over. I can wait." Then he added, "But not too long, my dear. Who knows? I could die at any time."

For the next several days, Doctor Silvers repeated his proposal and went over the benefits for the Housekeeper if she accepted. The inheritance of his sizable estate. The immediate promise of a nice apartment. The ability to quit her job. The meagerness of his demands. His desire to take care of her. Strangely, he did not talk about feelings—his for her or hers for him. There was something both courtly and businesslike about his proposal.

When she was by herself, the Housekeeper took a piece of paper, folded it in half, and wrote "Pros" on one side and "Cons" on the other. Under "Pros," she wrote "Money" and "Caring for each other."

She paused to consider, then put a question mark after the second item. Did they really care for each other? Or did they each have a need the other could fulfill? Under "Con," she wrote "Age Difference." Why did it matter? Was marrying someone close to your age just a convention or was there good reason to limit the number of years between two people who wanted to marry? She did not know.

The next day, while she was busy cleaning her quota of rooms, one of the CNAs said she was wanted in the Administrator's office immediately. The Housekeeper wondered why. Leaving her supply cart in the hall, she followed the CNA.

In the office were the Administrator of the facility, the Housekeeping supervisor, and another woman in her fifties.

"This is Doctor Silvers' daughter, Mrs. Lux," the Administrator said. Mrs. Lux nodded grimly. "She has something to say to you."

Doctor Silvers had a daughter? The Housekeeper was light-headed. For some reason, she was reminded of her Granny rushing her into the kitchen, away from her Pappy.

"I don't know what you think you're doing, young lady." Mrs. Lux reprimanded her. "I understand my father has proposed to you, correct?"

"Yes, Ma'am."

"That isn't going to happen! I'm prepared to go to court to get guardianship of my father if you don't agree to stay away from him, right now."

"Yes, Ma'am."

Her Granny scolded her in the kitchen. She did not remember why.

"I have my suspicions about the reason you would marry someone so many years your senior. At any rate, I'm prepared to give you this check, to pay you to stay away from my father."

Mrs. Lux handed a check to the Administrator, who handed it to her. The Housekeeper looked at the amount with astonished eyes.

Mrs. Lux took a step toward the Housekeeper. "Do you agree?"

"Yes, Ma'am."

At that, Mrs. Lux gathered her coat and purse and left. Now it was her supervisor's turn.

"I don't know what you've been doing, but whatever it is, it's totally unacceptable. I'm afraid we'll have to let you go immediately. Please turn in your keys and smocks."

"Yes, Ma'am."

She left the office and went into the break room. There was Steph, eating a meal cooked by the kitchen staff. The Housekeeper sat down at her table.

"Hey," Steph said. "What's happening."

"Nothing. I just got fired."

Steph held her fork in mid-air. "Really? You were fired? What'd you do?"

"Showed Doctor Silvers my pussy." She did not mention his proposal.

"How did administration find out?"

"I guess he told his daughter and his daughter told them. She was there when they fired me."

"He told his daughter he looked at your pussy? Oh, my God. That's like incest or something."

"You don't know the half of it."

That was a month before the mass shooting. The victims had been in Hospice. Dr. Silvers must have become gravely ill shortly after the Housekeeper was fired. Was it her fault he had become so sick? As a child, she thought it was her fault Pappy died. Granny looked at her in such an angry way at the funeral.

Now she had a new loser boyfriend—Roger. They had been meeting on the bus on the way to work whenever their shifts coincided. After she was fired, he showed up at the place she rented with Mrs. Lux's money. Because she was lonely, she let him fuck her, then move in.

She was twenty-four, and already several paths to a good future had been gated shut—her position at the Apple store, her housekeeping job, marriage to Dr. Silver. And now she had a criminal record with a parole violation, too. She knew she and Roger would burn their way through the rest of Mrs. Lux's money, probably on drugs. And then what? Without anyone to take care of her, it was hard to imagine making it to her twenty-fifth birthday.

Dr. Silvers. My old man boyfriend. Murdered. My fault. I deserve nothing.

19. THE ARTISTS

The morning after his mother was murdered, a CBS affiliate correspondent interviewed Martin. He wore a lapel microphone. The interview took place in his parent's log cabin. In the background, portraits of his mother nearly covered the walls.

"Your father was the late Kent Barry, the well-known painter famous for his portraits of your mother. What went through your mind when your mother was killed in the nursing home?"

"Actually, I was glad my father didn't live to see this day. He would have regretted not being with my mother during her last moments." Martin swiped his tearing eyes with his palm.

Before his own death, Kent painted Nan for seventy years. In all that time, he never had another subject. Martin had never seen him show real interest in any other human being, including his children. His father claimed that something about his mother always eluded him. Whatever it was, he was still pursuing it in his eight-eighth year.

"The purpose of my art is to capture the mystery of your mother on canvas."

He said this to Martin whenever he finished a new painting, shaking his head at what he regarded as his latest failure. They both stood in front of the work, arms crossed over their chests, as if whatever it was Kent was looking for would become apparent if they stared long enough.

Before his powers declined, Kent had an urgent need to find, at last, the pigment, shape, or angle that would open his wife to him just as her mouth opened to his insistent tongue. Then, he might truly know her as a husband ought to know his wife. She had always been a quiet woman. That was part of her allure. Kent painted hundreds of portraits of her since he met her when she was fifteen years old, and he persuaded her to undress for him.

Over the years, he had been fascinated by the way her heavy breasts changed shape as she changed position or raised her arms.

"But it's not your mother's physicality that really interests me," he explained, while dabbing at a canvas with a paintbrush. "I want to paint her soul, her essence, the part of herself she keeps hidden from me."

Nan would be posing while he said this. It was unclear if she paid attention.

"If I ever know all there is to know about your mother, she might no longer be fascinating to me. I might lose interest in her and painting both. It's the hunting that drives me. Not necessarily the gathering."

"It sounds like being careful what you wish for," Martin said.

Kent retired from the university located in the same Indiana town as the nursing home. He had been a member of the Fine Arts faculty for his whole career. His paintings of Nan had been exhibited frequently in the gallery in the Fine Arts Building and in the more established galleries in town. The university museum purchased two of his larger works, and art museums in Indianapolis, Evansville, and Louisville also made purchases. The Art Institute of Chicago had one under consideration.

Critics placed his style in the Thomas Hart Benton School without the working-class social consciousness of that genre. The interest in Kent's work was in seeing how his skill at portraiture developed over time. As reviewers commented, to view Kent's work was to view the history of an obsession.

When he was not painting and Nan was quietly going about her chores, Kent could not leave her alone. He insisted they be in the same room, as near to each other as possible. If she was washing dishes, he stood next to the sink. He did not need to touch her. He needed to see her close up.

She, on the other hand, seemed to exist without reference to him or their children. She rarely looked back at him. Instead, she focused on the work at hand—cooking, sewing, laundry.

"Nan!"

He called her name sharply when he had been patient long enough. She blinked three or four times, as if awakening, and then looked in his direction.

When in bed with Nan at night, Kent could not tolerate a complete darkness. There had to be some light. He had to be able to watch her sleep.

He kept a small lamp turned on beside the bed, awaking frequently to gaze at her. Often, he put his face a half-inch from hers, even though his vision blurred at close range.

There had been occasions over the years when Kent would go into a rage when he thought Nan was deliberately evading him. He lashed out. There were times that he struck her to get her attention. Each time, she fell over soundlessly.

"You made me do that to you!" He thrust a furious finger in her face.

When he calmed down, he disrobed her and posed her so he could paint the bruises. These were the works in the most demand. He titled them "Nan Beaten 1", "Nan Beaten 2," and so on. Kent had been careful to never let his son or daughter, Jean, see the "Nan Beaten" series. These were only shown to dealers during private appointments.

Martin, who lived on his parents' property, was a photographer. His main subject matter was nature, especially the surrounding woods. But the only way to have a relationship with his father was by developing an interest in his mother as an art object. Like Kent, Martin exhibited portraits of her. Now that she had Alzheimers, he photographed her more frequently.

He always showed his work to his father.

"I have some new photos of Mom here."

"Oh?" Kent looked at them.

"I used the Opteka 85mm f/1.8 Manual Focus lens on these."

"Uh-huh."

"These here have more contrast than those."

"Uh-huh."

"What do you think of these two?"

"Mmmm."

Then they had the same argument they had been having since Martin was a boy with his first camera. Over time, it became a way for Martin to have an opinion of his own while fighting for his father's meager attention and grudging approval.

"Photography has as much in common with portraiture as a mirror does. Whatever it is, it isn't art," Kent said.

"A mirror doesn't have a human being directing and manipulating the reflection. That's why a mirror image isn't art. A photograph is art."

"Those photos of your mother capture her appearance, not her soul. Her eyes look outward, not inward."

"If Mom is looking outward, it's because she had more interest in the world than you ever gave her credit for. That's what my work says about her. This is a woman curious about her surroundings."

"That's what is wrong with your work. Your mother was one of the most internally focused people I ever met. A photograph can't convey that."

"And you think your paintings do? Reveal her inner life?"

"More so than any photograph could."

Despite their controversy, Kent and Martin planned to have a joint exhibit of their portraits of Nan since her diagnosis. The title of the exhibit was "Nan with Alzheimer's." It was going to be sponsored by the American Alzheimer Association and to travel to six cities across the country.

But then Jean stepped in when, during one of her visits, she saw Martin with his camera.

"What are you doing?" She asked.

"Photographing Mom,"

"Stop! Don't do that!"

"Why not?"

"It's disrespectful."

The argument continued when Kent took down all the paintings of the healthier Nan from the walls of the cabin and replaced them with the "Nan with Alzheimer's" series. The wall space also contained those few of Martin's photographs that were included in the exhibit. He and Martin discussed several placements to see which order of hangings was the most effective.

Jean was appalled.

"These are grotesque. You can't allow the public to see them. It's unethical."

"Unethical?" Kent's eyebrows raised.

"Unethical, yes. Because Mom doesn't consent to this." Jean waved her hand at the walls.

"A tree doesn't consent when I photograph it," Martin said.

"A tree isn't a human being. I doubt Mom ever really consented to what either of you forced her to do, but this…this…is a kind of blasphemy. A kind of elder abuse."

"My paintings always honored your mother. And this series is about the humanity, the soul of someone with dementia."

"What soul? Mom is a shell of a human. Her soul is gone. That's what you're painting. I suppose you'd say you're honoring a corpse if you paint it."

"Exactly," Martin said. "Art dignifies whatever is its subject. Even a corpse."

Kent looked with interest at the way the afternoon light deepened his daughter's furrowing brow. He would have to sketch it when she was gone. After Nan died, perhaps he could paint a series called "Jean's Rage." He would have to include an ambiguity, perhaps in the way he painted her mouth, to reproduce the intriguing element in the Nan portraits.

"I hate these," Jean said.

"Good. An intense response to art is what the artist wants. Even a hateful response."

"He's right," Martin said. "A negative response from a viewer is better than no response."

Jean stormed out. Later Kent sketched the interesting rigidity of her back as it spurned him.

Nan began to wander into the heavily wooded area outside their door. Kent tried watching her more carefully. It was easy for healthy people to lose their bearings when hiking there. For someone in Nan's condition, walking away from home was treacherous. Even though Kent locked the doors at night, somehow Nan was getting out while he slept. It was clear there was no recourse other than having her cared for in a locked door dementia facility.

What Kent missed the most after moving Nan out of their house was posing her. She never objected to sitting in the same position for hours with only one or two breaks. At such times, her expression was dreamy or trance-like. She could be right in front of him, yet at a great distance, too. He was transfixed by the contrast.

By the time Nan was moved from their rural home to the nursing home, the mystery had deepened. Now his ambition was to capture on canvas the gap between the past Nan and the even blanker present Nan. Kent and Martin both recorded the gradual masking of her spirit and the deterioration of her appearance—the thinning of her hair, the fading of her features, the hunching of her back.

Kent visited his wife frequently. He sat with her for hours, just staring at her, memorizing her, locating the little glint in her cornea that was a dab of titanium zinc white with a touch of cerulean blue and dioxazine purple. If he placed her near the window in her room, he watched the interplay of the changing light on her skin as the time passed. When he thought he had seen what he needed, he hurried to his old Subaru Outback and drove the two lane route before the light failed, and it was useless to go to his studio.

But after a few months, Kent had second thoughts about the nursing home.

"You know, your mother doesn't walk much anymore. Mostly, she stays in bed or sits in a chair. Now that she doesn't wander, I'm going to bring her back home. The light is so much better in the cabin. At home I can pose her again."

"How are you going to take care of her at your age?" Martin asked.

"I'll hire a caretaker. She'll probably wind up having to take care of both of us." Kent chuckled.

At the end of the month, over the objections of Jean, Kent and Martin arranged for Nan to leave the nursing home and return to their rural home. The social worker who discharged Nan contacted an agency that sent someone three times a week to bathe Nan. Between Kent and Martin, her other needs could be managed.

Kent was delighted. If he worked quickly enough, there might be good additions for the exhibit.

Once she was home and back in bed again at night, Kent was too excited to sleep. He stayed up looking at the angle at which her head rested on the pillow, the motion of her eyes under her closed lids, the way her breathing moved her chest. He made sketches while propping himself up in the bed. He envisioned another series called "Nan Asleep."

One morning around five a.m., he got up to urinate, although he had been up twice before in the night for the same reason. This was not unusual. He took a step onto the small braided rug Nan made for one of his birthdays. Suddenly, he was losing his balance, falling backwards with his arms flailing. His head hit the night table. Then he slid to the floor. He did not exactly lose consciousness. He was aware of something being terribly wrong. He tried to cry out to Nan. Although it seemed like he was yelling loudly, he did not hear the sound of his voice.

Neither could he stand. Something was the matter with his legs. After a brief struggle, he gave up, exhausted. His head lay uncomfortably on the edge of the rug, which bunched up when he fell. He could not move. Martin checked in before leaving for work around seven-thirty. Kent was relieved his mind still worked well enough to remember that. Nan was likely to continue sleeping. He would have to lay on the floor until his son arrived.

When Martin came in and found his father unable to move, the first thing he did was grab his camera and take a few shots. Then he called 911. It would take the ambulance a half-hour to find the isolated cabin, which Kent had originally purchased precisely because it was so far from a paved road and so private.

Martin knew that if his father had a stroke, he needed medical treatment within three hours to have a chance of recovering. He had no idea if the ambulance would arrive within that window of time, since he did not know when his father had fallen. He had no idea whether his father would live or die.

Taking out the array of lenses he always carried along with his camera in his backpack, he began taking photographs of his father: extreme close-ups, close ups, and middle distance shots. Then the same from other angles. Changing the lens, he stood back and photographed his mother still asleep in the bed in the same frame as his father on the floor.

He saw Kent following his actions with his eyes. Was his father approving or objecting? Kent had to think he was approving. He had to think he was giving his father the highest respect possible by turning what might be the old man's last moments into art.

It was not without a thrill that Martin imagined having his own exhibit, no longer under the shadow of his father's paintings. He would title it "Nan's Alzheimer's and Kent's stroke."

Then he took his phone out of his pocket and sent Jean a text.

"Dad fell. Looks bad."

20. THE DEPUTY

They said all the right things to the Deputy.

"How were you to know?"

"It was his choice; not your fault."

It did not help.

He was on administrative leave pending an investigation by Internal Affairs. That was just a necessary formality. It was paid leave—at least there was that. Janet and the kids would not have to pinch pennies. But if he stayed home, what was he supposed to do with himself all day while his wife was at work and the kids were in school?

He washed the breakfast dishes, fed the dog, mowed the lawn, and chopped wood until his shoulder felt ready to fall off. Then, there was nothing to do but hang his head in his hands and think about what happened.

I wish the alleged perp had a loaded weapon. I wish he had dropped his weapon. I wish I had not been the first one to confront the perp. A million "I wish's" did not alter the bare fact that he shot and killed a harmless man who was no longer a threat.

After his suicide-by-cop, the perp was ID'd as Sid Stone. No record. Not even a traffic violation. He purchased his firearm—a Glock 4th generation—legally. Not much was known about him other than he was employed as the Maintenance Man in the very nursing home where he shot ten Hospice patients before aiming his weapon at the first officer to respond to the 911 call.

It was later learned that Sid Stone never married, living quietly in his home with his aged mother. The Deputy tried to figure the perp out.

Maybe he hated her. How else to explain his murdering her right before doing the same to ten other old people like her? Or maybe he just lost it.

If the Deputy had taken a bullet in his big gut, a beer belly that had crept up on him now that he passed his fortieth birthday, it would have been preferable. As it was, he never felt such bone-agonizing guilt before, not even the time he cheated on Janet, and she found out.

The marriage had been through a rough patch. They separated, almost divorced, but in the end she forgave him. Now she was sticking by him again. He did not deserve her.

It was a week after the incident. The Deputy was too agitated to sit at home any longer. Although it was before noon, he decided to go to Thursday's, one of the local dives not frequented by police officers. It was unlikely he would run into anyone who recognized him. It was a dreary place matching his mood—dark, narrow, dusty. The reflective surface of the mirror behind the bar was peeling in spots. A sour-looking Irish guy owned it and tended the bar. He was so short he used a step-stool to reach the bottles on higher shelves.

"What'll you have?" He asked.

"Whiskey. Neat."

"What kind?"

"Cheapest."

After the bartender served him a shot, the Deputy looked around. Customers who drank their lunch were sitting at the bar and in the booths. The TV was turned to CNN, with the sound muted and the closed captions on. There had been another mass shooting, this time in a school in Florida. The video showed a helicopter shot of kids running out the door. There was a cut to anxious parents, waiting somewhere at a safe distance. The shooting in the nursing home was old news, now.

He heard a voice saying "Are you present or absent with the Lord?"

It was the middle-aged man in a light gray suit sitting next to him, possibly a businessman, thumbing through a pocket bible, while his drink waited on the counter.

Turning to the Deputy, he recited, "When you pass over, you will appear before the judgment seat of Christ. You shall receive according to the things you have done, whether good or whether bad."

"Are you talking to me?" The Deputy swallowed his whiskey.

"It's something for you to think about today."

The Deputy wore civilian clothes, a T-shirt, jeans, and jeans jacket. His badge had been confiscated. There was no way the businessman could have known he was the one who shot the perp, in self-defense, although this had yet to be officially ascertained. He remembered racing down a long hallway with his weapon drawn. Someone shouted, "He's out back." When he reached the rear door, the Deputy threw it open. The perp was there, sitting on a bench, his handgun raised and aimed squarely at the doorway. There was not a second to think. His trigger finger acted, and his mind trailed behind.

"I want to tell you this: Today is a good day to get right with the Lord."

The Deputy got up and moved to an empty seat at the other end of the bar. He ordered another whiskey. The businessman watched him with somber eyes.

His mind wandered to the time in Eye-raq, his third deployment. The mission was to search houses for young men who were suspected of being ISIS. On the way to the village, he traded seats with his buddy, PeeJay. They took turns sheltering themselves from the ruthless afternoon sun that roasted those on the left side of the convoy. Immediately after the switch, an IED exploded up front. He felt it before he saw the flash. A piece of shrapnel flew back and lodged in PeeJay's neck, severing the carotid artery. His buddy bled to death in his useless arms.

When they reached the village, he shoved in the door of the first house. A boy of about fifteen confronted him with his arm raised. The boy was preparing to hurl at a stone in his direction. Behind him in the dark interior were a dozen silent women and children. Even the babies were quiet. Without thought, he shot. Even after all the occupants were dead, he kept shooting, round after round. The ear-splitting sound drowned his sobs until he was pulled away. When the mission was over, no one said anything about it.

The Deputy was not sure what he remembered in Eye-raq or in the back of the nursing home really happened. Both times, he had been present and absent. On the one hand, he could see the boy and the perp in front of him, at point blank range. On the other, it was as if he were a hundred feet away, up in a helicopter, looking down.

Throwing back his head, the Deputy downed his second whiskey and ordered a third. At his weight, he could carry liquor without getting much of a buzz. Pushing two twenty-five, he was more than fifty pounds overweight. He might not pass his next physical. That, too, would put him on administrative leave until he got himself in shape.

As the noon hour passed, the bar began emptying. The businessman finished his drink, put his bible in his briefcase, and rose to leave, without looking at him. Soon, there were only a few customers. The Deputy moved to a booth, ordering again. As he often did when changing positions, he unobtrusively checked his personal handgun, concealed in an OWB holster. All the officers had licenses to carry concealed while off-duty.

Like the others, he knew his first priority was his family. He would protect them with his life, he had sworn to Janet the time she caught him cheating. There had been days of interrogation.

"Why did you cheat? Do you love her? Did you go down on her? How many times?" The same questions, over and over.

He did not know what to say. Finally, he lost it. He did not remember—exactly. The next day, she showed him her bruises and said she was getting a divorce.

"If you leave me, I'll shoot myself. I mean it." He wept on his knees, wrapping himself around her legs with both arms. She relented. He humiliated himself to keep his family together. He would do it again. But something in him broke. Janet stayed, but never looked at him again with the same trusting eyes.

Nevertheless, when he told her about the Internal Affairs investigation, she was outraged. "You should get a medal for taking out a killer of helpless old people—in self-defense, mind you. You saved the taxpayers the cost of a trial and three square meals in prison for life. And they take away your badge? Disgusting!" She smoldered, her chunky face reddening.

Since then, she had been friendlier. He wished it meant more. He did not want her to leave him, but he did not know if that meant he loved her. Loyalty, was what it probably was. Only that.

"Another whiskey, here, please," he called to the little bartender. How many had he had? Four? Five?

He needed to piss. Stumbling his way to the Men's, he turned on the light. There on the ancient yellowing tile wall above the urinal, someone had written in black marking pen:

"Get right with the Lord."

By the time he returned to his booth, he remembered the businessman, who had said those same words to him not an hour before. It was about him passing over, dying, and facing the Lord's judgment. There was an emptying in his head, as if his brain suddenly collapsed. A spell of sitting in a kind of stupor, not thinking, followed. Another whiskey was on the table. Perhaps he asked for it. He should order a coffee the next time. He needed to sober up, go home. He downed the whiskey.

There was only a smattering of customers in the bar, mostly men middle-aged and older. This was not the kind of place attractive to young men or women. As he looked the others over, not only did he fail to connect with any of them, he felt no love for his family or anyone in this world.

He thought of Sid Stone, sitting out back of the nursing home, by himself, knowing he was doomed, waiting to be killed by whoever stormed through the door. The Deputy wished they could have a conversation.

He imagined asking Sid, "Did you do it because you couldn't feel anything?"

"I was not present to the Lord."

"Is that what it means when you can't love?"

"I shall receive according to the things I have done."

They were both lost and unredeemable. Strangely, he could not be sad about it. The guilt was gone. All that was left was a crushing numbness, as if lying under a very heavy stone.

It was after five. Customers were trickling in for after-work drinking. The Deputy ordered a double this time. He should head home. Janet expected him to help prepare dinner. But he would be of no use to her or the kids. He only dragged them down. They were better off without him.

Suddenly, he was dead sure Internal Affairs would find him at fault for the death of Sid Stone. They would charge him with manslaughter, maybe even with murder one. Didn't he intend to kill Sid Stone, armed or unarmed? Wasn't he relieved to learn the perp did not stand a chance? There would be a trial, then he would stand before the judge for sentencing. Long, hard time.

He needed fresh air. He made his way to the back and out the rear entrance. It led to a brick-walled alley, littered with cigarette butts and syringes. A rusty metal chair was opposite the door. The Deputy sat down.

He dozed off, waking after dark. He checked this gun. It was still in its holster.

I don't care if I shoot the next person who comes out the door. It was a crazy thought. Surely, he did not mean it.

As if under independent control that had nothing to do with him, his hand reached under his jacket and removed the gun from the holster. The hand aimed the gun at the rear door.

He waited. He could hear his raspy breath. Sooner or later, someone would open the door. His hand would shoot first, ask questions later. His hand would appear before the judgment seat of Christ, not he.

Unless he were to get right with the Lord by stopping his hand. It was his only chance at redemption, the only way Janet and his buddies in the Department would not despise him. Internal Affairs would close the case. When he died, there would be a memorial service. A photograph of himself, in his uniform, taken in his younger, fitter days, would be on display. That is how he wished to be remembered.

But he could not get his hand to cooperate. He would have to ask for assistance.

"Sid," he called. "Sid Stone. I'm requesting your help."

Sid Stone, or maybe it was PeeJay—it was hard to tell in the dark—appeared, smiling.

"I'm here now. You can relax. Leave everything to me."

Gently, the hand holding the gun was raised to his right temple.

Sid or PeeJay, or perhaps it was the Redeemer Himself, put a finger on top of the Deputy's and tenderly helped him pull the trigger.

VI. A WEEK OR TWO LATER

21. THE FOLLOWER

Standing in her doorway, Ruth watched the red taillights of the police car recede. At a distance, they merged with the Christmas lights the Christian neighbors put up, twinkling and swaying in the biting wind. Her arms were crossed tightly over her chest. All she had on was a light sweater over flannel pajamas. She went back inside and shut the door. She was shivering.

Her children would have to be told before they saw the incident on TV, or read it on a banner appearing on their phones or laptops. Hell, even the grandchildren had smart phones. They could text their parents before Ruth reached them. At least Mahl had not lived to hear that his mother, Naomi, had been murdered. Even though it was before dawn, Ruth called her daughter.

"Are you still in bed? Have you heard the news?"

She told the shocked younger woman the grim details just as the police had told her minutes before. Her grandmother had been murdered, along with nine other elderly Hospice victims, by an employee of the nursing home. The employee had been killed by the police.

After speaking to her daughter, Ruth phoned her son. These were hard calls. Her children adored their grandmother, who lived with them while they were growing up. Naomi was fond of slipping them candy or allowing them to watch cartoons behind Ruth's back. No wonder they loved her. Ruth vowed never to undermine her children in that way when she had grandchildren. Her grandchildren seemed to like her, anyway. She was more likely to take them to the science museum or the library than to feed them candy.

The next day, both children, their spouses, the five grandchildren, and the Rabbi all showed up to be together and plan the funeral. During the intense discussion of Naomi's murder, the unanswered questions about the killer, the indignation, and the tears, Ruth came and went into the kitchen. She served coffee or wine to the adults and Cokes or milk to the children. She made cheese sandwiches. She took chocolate chip cookies out of the freezer and put them on the coffee table on a green Depression glass plate that had belonged to Naomi. She put three chickens in the oven for dinner. She restocked towels in the bathrooms. Discretely, she placed boxes of tissues around the family room.

After the funeral, everyone went home. Ruth was alone again, as she had been for the years after Mahl died suddenly of a heart attack when he was not yet sixty. That had been an awful shock. He had just had a physical three days before and was declared to be in excellent health. He jogged and cycled. Then, boom! She found him dead on the living room floor, holding the remote in his hand. Stephen Colbert was on TV pretending to be a right-winger.

Ruth knew that if Mahl lived, he would have blamed her for his mother's death. It was she who persuaded him to put Naomi in a nursing home. The two women always had a contentious relationship. It started when Ruth and Mahl began dating, before she converted to Judaism. Her future mother-in-law let it be known that, besides being a *shiksa,* Ruth was not good enough for her college-educated son. Ruth did not have a degree.

"Di shiksa iz nicht gut far ir"

Nothing she did for all the years after pleased her mother-in-law. Even before the older woman's dementia, she treated Ruth like a servant. It just grew worse after her illness began. The more her memory faded, the meaner she became. If Ruth helped her bathe, bought her Kosher food, did her laundry, and took her on outings to Macys, she took it as her due. She constantly criticized.

"Di vaser iz kalt. Di matzo balls zenen aoykl gross."

Finally, Ruth had enough. She talked to Mahl in the privacy of their bedroom, even though Naomi was not above bursting in on them even if the door was closed. Ruth was fed up and beyond caring.

"You can have me or your mother but not both. I'll leave. You can take care of your mother yourself." She spoke through gritted teeth, eyes blazing.

Mahl tried to get her to be reasonable.

"I'll hire someone. I'll talk to her. She's only difficult because she's ill."

When he understood Ruth was giving an ultimatum, not negotiating, he reluctantly made arrangements for his mother to be admitted. But he spent so much time with her that he might as well have moved into the nursing home himself.

After his fatal heart attack, Ruth did not tell Naomi her son was dead. There was no point. Naomi might not have remembered who Mahl was, or that she had a daughter-in-law.

Ruth supposed she did bear some responsibility for the manner of her mother-in-law's death. The older woman was days from passing away from natural causes. Thankfully, she slept most of the time and was probably not awake when the murderer shot her. If Ruth had known this would happen, she certainly would have allowed Naomi to die with dignity in her old bedroom.

Guilt was the reason why Ruth decided to attend the survivors' support group organized by the nursing home. It was for friends and relatives of the victims. The meetings were going to be held once a week in the activity room of the facility. There would be an opportunity to get updates from the police and for the participants to talk among themselves.

At the first meeting, ten people showed up, eight of them women. They sat on folding chairs in a circle. The nursing home social worker facilitated. The rules were that participants could either talk or pass, and that everything said at meetings was confidential. During the first round, everyone said their first name and who they had lost. Then the homicide detective in charge of the case was invited to give an update. All he said was that the killer had no known accomplices, and that his motive was unknown.

After the detective left, the social worker asked everyone to talk about their feelings about what the detective had said. Ruth passed, as did three other people. The six others spoke about their confusion, their wish for vengeance, and their theories about the killer. Some cried and some spoke angrily. Ruth did not find the meeting especially helpful.

As she walked to her car, one of the two male participants approached her. He reminded her that his name was Ralph. He was another who passed when it was his turn to speak. They stood in the parking lot and talked. Both agreed they would not be attending future meetings. Ruth learned that Ralph's father had been murdered. He mentioned that he was divorced. She mentioned that she was widowed. The next thing she knew, they were having coffee together in a nearby Starbucks.

Ralph planned to sue the killer's estate. Another victim's relative might put up the money to retain a lawyer. Was she interested in being named in the suit? Ruth was dubious, but she said she would think it over. Then they branched out to other topics. It almost seemed like a date. Ruth had not had a date since Mahl died. When they parted, Ralph took her phone number.

Several days later, Ralph phoned her and asked her out to dinner. While they were looking at the menu, Ruth revealed she did not eat pork because she was Jewish. To her surprise, Ralph said he was Jewish, too, but not practicing. At the end of the meal, he asked to see her again. By the third time they were together, they could be said to be "dating." Ralph was now her "boyfriend." How odd it was for a woman in her sixties to say she had a "boyfriend." She had not used that word since high school.

Ralph talked a lot about the mass killing and the lawsuit. He had a theory about the motive of the killer that he revealed during a meal they shared at an Italian restaurant.

"Four of the ten victims were Jewish. It is not often that forty percent of the residents in the Hospice rooms happen to be Jewish, especially when the Jewish population in the nursing home is only around five percent. Since the killer was an employee, he would notice the large Jewish percentage in Hospice. Maybe he waited for a large number."

"I'm not sure I understand." Ruth twirled spaghetti on her fork

"I'm just saying. His motive could have been antisemitic. I'm just saying, that's all." He chewed thoughtfully.

"The killer was an antisemite?"

"It's possible, isn't it?" Ralph swallowed, looking straight into her eyes.

When he looked at her in that deep way, she wondered if she was falling in love with him. Do people in their sixties "fall in love"? It seemed so teenage. Although they spoke about other things—music, Israeli politics, climate change—whenever they spoke about the murders, Ralph's voice softened. It was as if he was crooning, even though the subject was grisly. He seemed to be inviting her to something special the two of them could share, something no one else would understand.

"I can talk to you about this because you won't think I'm crazy. We are the only two relatives not drowning in emotion. We can think rationally, right Ruth?"

"I know you're not crazy, Ralph. But there may be other ways of looking at the same facts."

"Such as?"

"I don't know. Maybe it's a coincidence that the killer murdered so many Jews."

Ralph furrowed his brow. "It isn't a coincidence, Ruth. The corporation that owns the nursing home is a Jewish corporation. The majority of the owners are Jewish. The employees would know that."

His low tone, and the way he looked at her were more persuasive than his actual words. And he had his hand over hers as he spoke. His touch was warm.

But then he looked away, removed his hand, and sat back.

"Think it over, Ruth," he said, dismissively.

After the meal, Ruth did not hear from Ralph. Had she been wrong? Maybe he wasn't her boyfriend after all. She had been fooling herself. She was just someone for him to talk to. She sent him texts. He did not reply. She found herself pacing through the night. Had she let him down by not agreeing with his theory immediately? Was he angry at her? Was she like the other Jewish relatives of victims, too emotional to see the obvious?

Ten days later, he phoned and asked to see her. She invited him for dinner. He accepted. Naomi had taught her how to cook a good Jewish meal. She made chicken soup, brisket, and challah. She was being given a second chance.

When Ralph showed up, he was warm to Ruth again. He brought flowers and wine. He ate without bringing up the topic of the murders. It occurred to Ruth that it was up to her to reintroduce the topic. She did not want to disappoint him. When it was time for coffee, they went into the family room and sat on the sofa.

"I've been thinking about your theory of the killer's motivation," she said.

Now Ralph looked into her eyes and softly crooned, "Yes?"

"I suppose the killer could be an antisemite."

Ralph leaned over and kissed her. It was their first kiss. Ruth had not been kissed in years. She realized how deprived she had been. Then, Ralph leaned away from her.

"It's the only thing that makes sense, Ruth," he said. "But there's a problem. I don't know what to do." He turned and leaned his elbows on his knees with his hands loosely clasped in front of him. He hung his head.

"What is it?" She put a hand on his shoulder. "You can tell me."

Ralph signed. "It's about the lawsuit. Remember I told you that one of the victim's relatives was going to pay the lawyer's retainer? He pulled out. It's ridiculous. The lawyer says a settlement is sure to result in the killer's estate paying out millions. Turns out the killer was worth at least five million. And this guy won't pay ten thousand."

"Ten thousand? Dollars?"

"Yes. I'm broke. I need ten thousand to hire the lawyer, and I don't know where to get it."

Ruth knew there was something wrong, but she heard herself say, "Maybe I can find the money."

Ralph looked at her. "I wouldn't dream of taking money from a widow, Ruth. I would worry you'd think we are friends because of money. You have to know how I feel about you. I just want you to believe me and stand by me."

Now Ruth felt the need to persuade him, to prove her feeling for him.

"It's what I want to do, Ralph. My mother-in-law was killed by an antisemite, just like your father was. If his heirs are antisemites, I don't want them to inherit anything." She almost believed her words.

Ralph looked at her with shining eyes. That was the first time they were intimate.

The next day, after Ralph left, Ruth paced excitedly. She was not naive. She knew Ralph might be scamming her. Ten thousand dollars was a lot of money to pay for a boyfriend. No one better find out. How else was a woman in her sixties supposed to find a man as attractive as Ralph? She guessed he was a good ten years younger than her. She guessed he lied when he said he was Jewish, but she did not care.

She found herself channeling Naomi, who, whatever else she had been, was no fool. She would help Ruth not to be a fool, either.

"*Er iz a gonif. Ikh vet zogn ir vi.* I will tell you how."

Naomi recommended doling out the money a bit at a time. If she gave him the whole amount right away, he would probably disappear with it.

"You're right!" Ruth said.

The next time she and Ralph got together, Ruth gave him five hundred dollars. She said she was working on getting the rest. He shouldn't worry. She was good for it. Perhaps the lawyer would take the money as an installment. After the briefest of frowns, Ralph leaned into her. They had a perfect date.

It took a number of weeks for Ruth to come up with the rest of the money. Meanwhile, they celebrated the certainty that a settlement in the millions was only a few months off. They talked about how they would each spend the money. Ralph hinted that they might have a future together. Holding her close, he imagined out loud vacations they could take, condos they could buy, the kind of car they would both enjoy driving.

Ruth was not surprised when Ralph told her that the lawyer needed another ten thousand.

"*Ir visn vos tus ton.* You know what to do. String him along," she imagined the older woman saying.

She and her mother-in-law began to have the relationship—imaginary, of course—that they never achieved during Naomi's lifetime. They were becoming collaborators. Her mother-in-law looked out for her, schemed with her, helped her keep Ralph in line. For the first time, Ruth appreciated her mother-in-law. Maybe they had misjudged each other.

Over the course of the next few months, Ruth kept giving Ralph money, and the settlement kept vanishing into the distance. She controlled him by giving and withholding money. He controlled her by giving and withholding intimacy. They seemed to be at a stalemate.

She continued to imagine what her mother-in-law would advise. She was increasingly able to understand Yiddish.

"*Dos iz nicht gut genug.* The situation is not good enough. You need to get others involved. *Ir isn vi.* You know how."

Ruth went back to the support group, which still met weekly. Six of the original ten members were there, but two new ones had joined. This time, Ruth did not pass. She spoke with honesty about missing her mother-in-law, not revealing that it was her imaginary one.

After the meeting, she invited one of the other Jewish women out for coffee. In the same Starbucks where she and Ralph had their first coffee. She talked to her new friend about the possible antisemitic motivation of the killer, of the size of the killer's estate, of the lawsuit.

"There's a lawyer who will represent us. The problem is he wants ten thousand dollars. I don't have that kind of money, myself." She looked down at her coffee, biting her lip, then up into her new friend's eyes.

The other woman would think it over. She agreed to meet again.

Naomi was right behind Ruth, whispering in her ear.

"Gut. Das iz gut."

22. THE ADMINISTRATOR

In the student parking lot at the university, the Administrator's daughter, Glee, rushed into her car and immediately locked the doors. Rubbing her swelling hand, she sat there stunned and weeping. She was able to move all the joints. If her hand were broken, how would she type her papers? Would the stress cause her to miscarry? The Professor who hurt her knew how to inflict pain without leaving evidence. Broken bones would have been hard for him to explain. He had made his point.

This was the same Hungarian Professor she had known years before, while still in high school. He had been arrested for photographing teen girls in exchange for drugs. She did not expect to see him again. She thought he had been fired.

Glee still lived with her mother, Jill. She was back in college, now that her step-grandfather had died and had left her mother some money. Her plan was to finish the spring semester before the baby was born. After that, college might have to be put on hold.

Her Spanish class was in the Language Hall, on the same floor as the Uraltic Department, where Hungarian was taught. The bright murals on the walls of the Spanish Department side gave way to the steel gray of the much smaller Uraltic side. Glee avoided that side. It actually seemed chillier there. She did not like remembering how she had been manipulated by one of the professors when she was younger.

But one night, she slipped a late paper under her Spanish instructor's door. The hallway that teamed with students during the day was uncomfortably silent. Quickly, she went to the elevator. Just as she entered, a man appeared from nowhere and followed her inside. The doors closed.

"Professor!" She said. It was unmistakably the same portly older man with the ruddy cheeks. She took a step back to the rear wall. He stood between her and the control panel.

"Who you?"

"You wouldn't remember. I came to parties at your house a couple times years ago, but I didn't stay long."

He stared at her.

"Weren't you fired or something? Are you allowed to be here?"

The Professor turned and pressed a button. The elevator stopped descending. The doors remained closed.

"What are you doing?"

"Give me a hand," he said.

Before she could react, he grabbed her hand and squeezed it hard. Glee gasped. Then he let go.

"I no like hurt you. I just impress you not say you see me in coolege. I here is secret. You not say secret, and I not hurt you more. Yes?"

Glee rubbed her hand, wincing.

"Okay. I won't tell anyone I saw you. Just don't hurt me again."

"I only hurt if have to."

He pressed the button again, and the elevator restarted with a groan. The doors opened in the lobby. Glee got out first. She did not look back. She hurried to her car and fumbled for her key in her backpack. Finally, she was inside. Had that been him, right behind her? It was too dark to see. Every shadow looked like a figure. She backed out of the space, grateful the car had started.

She guessed the Professor had been trespassing, nosing around the Uraltic Department in the middle of the night for reasons she could not imagine. He did not expect to see anyone who recognized him. If he thought she might tell, he could really come after her. He must have guessed she had classes on that floor. All he had to do is wait for her and follow her.

She understood she was working herself into a frenzy. The Professor scared her. His way of scaring her worked. She would not tell. As time passed and nothing happened, he would know she had not told. He would lose interest in her.

She drove home with only one hand on the steering wheel. Once in her house, she iced her injured hand, then lay down for a few fitful hours. The next day, she had a ten a.m. Spanish class. She drove to the student parking lot, but could not make herself get out of the car. She just sat there, watching the time change on her phone. Finally, when she had missed more than half the class, she gave up and drove back home. The same thing happened the next three days.

There was no way she could return to the language building. When she tried, she shook like a leaf and could hardly breathe. Her thoughts scrambled. She would have to withdraw from her Spanish class. But this was the class needed to fulfill her language requirement. She was defeated. She might as well quit college. Probably, this was what the Professor wanted, anyway.

When her mother realized that Glee was spending her days at home in bed, she asked why she was not going to her classes.

"I thought you really wanted to return to college. What's going on?"

"Nothing. You wouldn't understand."

"Try me. Does it have to do with a boy? The one who got you pregnant?"

"No."

"I knew it. It's the baby's father, isn't it? Did he let you down again?"

"It's nothing like that. The father isn't here anymore. I just can't tell you. I can't tell anyone."

"Now you have me worried."

As Jill stared at her, Glee began to cry. Soon she was sobbing on her mother's shoulder. "Enough. We're going to sit here until you tell me. All night if we have to."

Glee knew she should keep her mouth shut. But she was so tired. She just wanted someone else to make everything okay. There was no one else as smart and as capable as her mother, who ran a whole nursing home by herself. Her mother was a single parent, like her grandmother, like she was going to be. Both had something Glee lacked—"street smarts," her mother called it. Her grandmother called it "grit." They were tall, thick-boned women. Here was delicate, little Glee, blowing her nose into an old tissue and scared to go into a building filled with hundreds of students.

Her mother looked at her over her glasses, waiting.

"It's, like, this Professor. Only maybe he isn't a Professor, anymore. I'm not sure."

"What's this Professor's name? Did he do something to you?"

"I don't think I should say his name. He could hurt me again if I told."

"Again?" Her mother leaned forward. "What did this Professor or not Professor do to you, Glee?"

"He hurt my hand."

"Your hand?"

"Yeah."

"He hurt your hand."

"I know it sounds stupid."

"Let me see your hand."

Glee held up her hand. The swelling had gone down. There was little to see.

"How did he hurt your hand?"

"In the elevator in the language building. He stopped the elevator, then squeezed my hand real tight. He said he'd hurt me again if I told anyone I saw him there."

"What's wrong with seeing him there?"

"He was fired after he was arrested. I don't think he was supposed to be there."

Jill insisted on hearing the whole story. Glee told her what she knew about the arrest and about the two times she had been to his house, leaving out the fact she had posed. Finally, she told her mother his name.

The first impulse Jill had was to go to the authorities, either the University police or the town police. But the police wouldn't do anything. Glee's hand had no visible injuries. There were no witnesses. And the Professor was sure to deny he had been on campus. It would be the word of a Professor, no matter how compromised, against the word of a student. Even if the #MeToo movement had gained young women some credibility in cases of sexual misconduct, it was still a man's world.

Jill knew this from her work as a nursing home Administrator. Corporate was mostly staffed by men. After a staff member she had hired went on a shooting spree and killed ten residents, she was criticized for her handling of the media, for staff turnover, and for the loss of census when a number of beds remained vacant. What she learned was never to show emotion. If she expressed a trace, the men at Corporate reacted as if she were hysterical. A polite assertive tone saved her job. She planned to use it to make sure her daughter was safe, even if she had to do it without help from the authorities.

The next evening, Jill knocked on the Professor's door. When he opened it, she said she was the mother of the student he hurt in the elevator, and she wished to speak to him.

"Coome in, please. I Professor Ladimer Bailik. You name?"

"You can call me Jill."

"Mrs. Jill. Please to sit. Vant drink? Vater? Vodka?"

"This isn't a social call, Professor, if you are still a Professor. You hurt my daughter. You hurt her hand. You forced her to remain with you inside an elevator. That is unacceptable."

"Regrettable. Sometimes, these things necessary."

"Necessary? How in the world do you justify hurting a young girl?"

"It necessary for me to be at Ooniversity undercoover. This is secret. Middle night. No one there but you daughter. I had to impress her to keep secret. Please to sit."

The Professor indicated a leather chair. She sat awkwardly. The chair was too deep even for a tall woman like her. He remained standing, requiring her to look up at him.

"What secret? In a language building. In the middle of the night. I don't believe you."

Reaching for a silver box on the mantle, he opened it and bent to offer her a cigarette. She refused. He took one and lit it with a silver lighter. He took a deep drag and exhaled toward the ceiling. He was making her wait. She kept her composure. At last he spoke.

"Mrs. Jill. You have daughter. You have grandchild one day. You care what happen to them, right?"

Jill stayed silent. This might be leading to a threat. She was not going to tell this man her daughter was pregnant. Did he somehow know, even though Glee was not showing yet? Why was he changing the direction of the conversation from his deplorable behavior toward her daughter? Instead, he was challenging her on whether she cared for her daughter and grandchild.

The Professor looked down at Jill pleasantly, with a slight tilt of his head, seeming to imply they were two reasonable adults. He could explain his thinking to her. She was an educated woman who would understand.

"In thirty years, 2050. Temperature of Earth up one-one-half or two degrees. Many places unlivable for humans. They die in summers. India, Pakistan, south Mexico. Agriculture change. Not enough food for all peoples. Of course, educated woman like yourself know this, Mrs. Jill."

He was playing her. Why was he talking about climate change? She had to be on guard. Even though she understood what he was doing, his confiding tone made her want to appear worldly, like him. Not like someone who was ignorant. After all, she did know that climate change was coming. She did not deny that, even if she did not know all the details. Absurdly, she wanted him to think they were both on the same side on this issue. Why did she care what he thought?

"Great migrations happen. Right now, one million peoples from Syria in Europe. That *oo*nly one country. From *oo*nly one civil war, not climate yet. In America, few thousands try come in Southern border. Not problem like in Europe. By 2050, problem even here. Coasts undervater. Most peoples go to interior of country. No resources for all," he said. "I hope not to upset you with facts."

She had to be careful not to convey any emotion, especially at this moment. He was one of those cold, logical types, like the men at Corporate. She shook her head, forcing herself to hide how confused she was becoming.

"Peoples who come not American peoples. Come from other parts world. Africa. Muslim. Mexico. Peoples like daughter—they minority then."

She stared straight at him, as her assertiveness training taught her to do. Losing eye contact would make her look weak.

"I think you are saying that white people would be the minority. That's racist talk, Professor."

"It no matter what color people. Black, white, rich, poor. They not American citizens. They make not-democracy if too many for resources. Food, water is enough for Americans, but not enough for all peoples."

These reasonable-sounding words were either racist or some sort of trick.

"Victor Orban, Prime Minister of Hungary, prepare for this future. Like American President. Even now, keep refugees out of Hungary. Protect borders. He has enemies in minority party. They not want Hungary be strong. Some these enemies in *oo*niversities with Uraltic Departments.

Teach Hungarian. Very few departments in America. Two. Three. I find out what enemies here do."

"So that's the secret? That's why you hurt my daughter?"

"In 2050, you daughter still alive. What world you *vant* for her when too many peoples here?"

"Are you saying that you hurt her in 2019 to save her in 2050?" Jill asked.

"Could say that. Intelligent way to put."

She caught herself being flattered. A Professor was saying she was smart. She could not let it go to her head. Instead, she confronted him on his lack of empathy.

"And you think it will take ruthless people like you, willing to allow millions to die—never mind nearly breaking my daughter's hand—to save humanity?"

"Could say that, too."

Jill took a deep breathe. "I'm not sure I want humanity saved under those circumstances."

"You talk about your daughter and grandchildren dying when say that."

She needed to restore the purpose of her visit and not let his toying speech continue.

"I only have one final thing to say to you, Professor. Do. Not. Touch. My. Daughter. Ever. Again. Understood?"

He took a step closer. "If you and she not say saw me."

Not promising anything, she left.

Driving home, Jill was in turmoil. He had threatened her. He tried to intimidate her. While she had held her own, she allowed him to control the conversation. She was unprepared for someone so masterful at manipulating others. She was accustomed to thinking of local solutions for the local problems of a nursing home, like finding the most effective brand of disinfectant at the least cost. The Professor had maneuvered her into considering the bigger picture. On a world-wide scale, not everyone would survive in the future. Her democratic values might doom Glee and the baby, in the bigger picture he painted.

Who would the Professor choose to save if his vision was accurate? That was an easy one. Other sociopaths like himself and enough slaves to serve them. She hated everything he was. She hated the way he justified scaring Glee.

And she hated how attracted she was to him.

At home, Glee asked what happened

"I made the Professor understand he cannot hurt you again. He knows I mean business. Tomorrow, you can return to classes. You will be safe."

Under her breath she added, "For now."

23. THE GIANT'S WIDOW

An eight pound bag of navel oranges was on sale for nearly five dollars. Frieda loved navel oranges, but it did not make sense for a widow to buy eight pounds of anything. After Fred was murdered along with nine others in the nursing home, she canceled her Sam's Club membership. It was not necessary to lug a thirty-six roll package of toilet paper into the house.

Fred had been a big man who did everything in a big way. He slathered toothpaste on his toothbrush and talked to her through billowing blue foam, then gargled loudly, spitting torrents of water into the basin. He ate three oranges at a time, leaving behind a mountain of rinds. They shopped at Sam's once a month. He ran through everything they purchased the month before by then.

Now that she was alone, Frieda was shocked by how little she consumed. A box of shredded wheat lasted for a month of breakfasts. A loaf of bread began to mold before she reached the bottom crust. She was a tiny woman, not even five feet tall. When Fred had been in his prime, with his booming voice and larger-than-life personality, she had been all but erased. This was never Fred's intention. It was just how it was.

Their residence had been built to contain a large man. Without him, the over-sized rooms, wide doorways, and two-story front room, seemed more like an airplane hanger than a house. In the enormous bedroom, the heft of Fred had shifted her to a small slice of the king-size bed, while his thundering snores had rattled her awake. All there were now were the quieter creaks of the house settling in the night.

She began spending most of her time in a small sewing room at the top of the house. Besides her old sewing machine, unused for years, it had a comfortable chair, a small bookshelf, and a side table. Frieda sat there and read or looked out the window at the doves bobbing on the gutter. Rather than cook in the huge downstairs kitchen, she brought up a hot plate to warm cans of tomato soup. Eventually, she took cushions from the living room sofa and made a bed for herself on the floor. This simple arrangement suited her.

She did go to the bedroom to change clothes. Two large walk-in closets were there—his and hers. She did not want to deal with Fred's or even see his row of custom-tailored suits and professionally laundered shirts. She shut the door of his closet. Her closet was equally dismaying. So many dresses for occasions and events, mostly accompanying Fred, and an equal number of luncheon outfits for gatherings with her friends. The events were sure to drop off in time, and she was in no mood to socialize. Choosing a couple of pairs of jeans, three sweaters, and underwear, she returned to the sewing room. She hung the garments on two over-the-door hooks.

Every morning, she went downstairs to shower, make coffee, and collect the mail that had fallen through the chute. Besides the usual flyers, there was a daily avalanche of condolence cards in square, hand-addressed envelopes, as well as invitations. Friends and acquaintances, shocked that Fred had been killed just days after his admission to the nursing home, requested her presence at dinner parties, theatrical outings, and company events. No one wanted to exclude her if she no longer stood in Fred's shadow with a glass of merlot in her hand. While she was flattered to be remembered, she wrote emails thanking the hosts and organizers, saying she was terribly sorry to miss the occasions due to scheduling conflicts.

Without Fred, she was becoming more clearly her true self: an introvert and a loner.

One day, the doorbell rang. Frieda rushed down stairs to answer it, thinking it was the person she hired to mow the lawn. When she opened the door, there was Essie, Fred's younger sister, carrying a Chihuahua in one arm. Frieda was surprised to see her sister-in-law, who had arrived unannounced.

"Hello. It's me," Essie said, looking down at Frieda. Although she was not as large as her brother, she was much taller than Frieda, especially in spiky high heels. "Let me in.'"

Frieda opened the door wide without saying anything. Fred had been a domineering personality. Yet he was solicitous of his wife. His sister was just plain bossy. When he was alive, he stood between the two women, protecting the gentler Frieda from Essie's pushiness.

"*Geez,*" she would start in. "That wallpaper is fucking boring. Look at it! White and yellow stripes! This place needs some God-damned color."

"Language, Essie. Watch it! Anyway, we like the wallpaper."

"Just saying, that's all."

Later, Fred would apologize for his sister's coarseness.

"I don't know where she gets it. Our parents were proper Germans. We never heard that kind of talk growing up."

Essie wobbled into the front room on her heels, flinging off her jacket and setting down the Chihuahua. Frieda noticed she was wearing a very short skirt and a peasant-style embroidered blouse with a low-cut neckline. With a toss of her head, her long bleached hair rippled across her back. But the effect was undermined by her leathery face, a casualty of age and too much time in a tanning salon.

After she plopped down into a wing chair, she took a cigarette and a lighter from her purse.

"Do you mind?"

Without waiting, she lit up.

"I...Fred would never..."

"Well, Fred isn't here, is he." She thrust her hand into her purse again and withdrew a folded tissue. She dabbed at her eyes. The Chihuahua raced around the room, sniffing at everything low enough for it to reach.

"No, he's..."

"He was my big brother. My only brother. I can't wrap my head around it. He was here one minute, then gone the next. Poof! Like that. Murdered. I still can't believe it. God damn! Sometimes, life is so, so, you know?"

"Yes."

"So how the fuck are you doing, sister?"

"Fine."

"It's gotta be hard. It just sucks. That's all I have to say." She paused to take a drag of her cigarette, then swept the smoke away with a flick of her hand. "Hey, you don't happen to have any whiskey, do you?"

Frieda fetched a glass and a bottle of Johnny Walker. Essie poured herself a double.

"I usually don't start drinking this early, but this house brings up memories. The three of us. You know. All the good times."

Frieda could not guess which good times Essie referred to. Fred called her a 'collection of bad habits—drink, drugs, gambling, men, you name it.' He warned Frieda against leaving her alone in the house. She stole things. Though he watched her carefully, she managed to take an antique silver bowl passed down from their grandparents and, even more galling, an expensive ivory chess set.

"We can't let her stay here. We'd have no peace," he said.

Frieda was thinking of Fred's words when Essie spoke again.

"Where's your remote? Let's hear the news."

The dog jumped onto Essie's lap and starred at Frieda with hostile eyes. She handed Essie the remote. On the TV, a newscaster summarized events in Washington.

"Fucking A! It's like a boxing match. You into boxing?"

Frieda shook her head.

"I watch women's boxing when I can. Boxing's not just a guy thing anymore.You should see how those bitches go for each other's asses. You can watch them on ESPN. What do you think, girl?"

"I don't pay attention to sports, much." She nervously watched the long chain of ash at the end of Essie's cigarette. There were no ashtrays in the house. "What your dog's name?"

"Edy. We are Essie and Edy. If you and my brother were fucking Fred and Frieda, we can be Edy and Essie." She planted kisses on the animal's head and snout. In return, Edy licked her mouth. "He's my baby, aren't you Edy?"

If Fred had been with them, he would have noticed the expression on his wife's face. He would have commented that she must be tired and asked why doesn't she go on up upstairs to rest. He would take care of his sister. Without him, Frieda did not know how to deal with Essie. It was exhausting to be around her.

"Would you like to stay for lunch?"

"Actually, I was going to ask you. I'm down on my luck right now. Broke. This guy I was with—it's a long story. He's after me. Look. I need a place to stay for a couple of days, okay?"

Frieda knew that if Fred were alive, he would tell Essie to leave. Frieda did not have his courage. All she wanted to do now was escape to the sewing room. Even though he took up all the space, she seldom needed to get away from her husband. Essie was a different matter.

Essie stood up, arched her back, stretched, and yawned. Just in time, Edy jumped down.

"God, I'm tired. I think I'll go to your guest room for a nap. I'll borrow a robe. Don't worry. I'll find one in your closet. I didn't have time to grab any clothes when I left that bastard." She started for the stairs, then turned. "Do me a favor. Take Edy for a walk. You don't want him wee-weeing on your nice carpet. His leash is in my purse."

It was a bad idea to leave Essie alone, but it was also a bad idea to avoid walking the dog. As her sister-in-law went up the stairs, Frieda and Edy eyed each other. She managed to hook his leash onto his collar even though he bared his teeth at her. Once outside, the Chihuahua ruled the walk, either by running ahead and yanking her along or by falling behind and pulling her backwards. What should have been a ten-minute stroll turned into a twenty-minute ordeal. Frieda planned to drop Edy off in the guest room after they got back and retreat to the sewing room.

When she returned, the front door was wide open. Inside, Essie screamed from the top of the stairs at a stranger staring up at her from the bottom.

"Fucking piece of shit!"

"Bitch! Get your ass down here, now."

"Try and make me."

"You don't want me get rough again."

"You and who else, dickhead!"

"Cunt!" He yelled, starting up the stairs.

Frieda held the leash while snapping up her car keys and wallet. She ran back out the door. Quickly, she climbed into Fred's car, which was in the carport. Edy jumped onto the passenger seat. She drove away, breathing heavily. She did not know where to go.

For the first time, it hit her. She really was a widow. Fred was not coming back. She was alone in the world. The whole earth lay before her, connected by a system of highways, flight routes, and shipping lanes. Her house, large as it was, was a mere speck on a Google map. She was free to go anywhere, live anywhere. The choices were abundant, and the abundance was daunting. The only thing she decided was not to return home. She did not want to be near Essie. Let her steal what she wished. Nothing in the house was that important, now that Fred was gone.

She pulled into the Sam's Club parking lot and chose a spot far from the entrance. She read that cars parked there overnight without being disturbed. She could get a motel room, if she found one accepting dogs. But the snugness of the car comforted her. The way she felt, even a motel room seemed too large.

She glanced toward Edy. He growled softly. They would have to get used to each other.

Her muscles loosened. Her breath slowed. The thought came to her that she did not have to leave the car. It was a larger model, bought to accommodate Fred. With the seat in a reclined position, there was room to stretch her legs out while sleeping.

She could join the drifting tide of vehicles that, by choice or necessity, washed up in the parking lots of Sam's, Walmart, malls, and supermarkets, and unlit residential streets. The next day, she would buy two dog bowls, one for water and one for kibble. Whatever else she needed, she would buy and store in the back seat or the trunk.

Fred had been such a large man. As she thought about him, he seemed to swell in her mind to an even larger size, gradually towering upward. Although she could not see him, she sensed his big-knuckled hands encasing the car in mammoth palms, closing huge fingers the size of tree trunks around the car body, cradling her, holding her, keeping her safe. As long as she stayed in the car, he would never be truly gone.

24. THE WIDOWER'S CHILD

Every weekday evening, the Widower snapped his MacBook Pro closed at precisely five-thirty and unlocked the wooden gate on his daughter's bedroom doorway. Because he worked from home, he could not allow interruptions other than for meals and potty breaks during business hours. Dinah's hair was kept very short to avoid time wasted brushing out snarls. Dark shirts and shorts meant less laundry. The child learned to play quietly with her stuffed animals or to turn the hard cardboard pages of colorful preschool books.

The Widower's wife had become too ill to be cared for at home. He placed her in a nursing home. Just after she had been moved to the Hospice section, she became the youngest victim of a staff person who shot her and ten others. As terrible as it was, the Widower knew better than to grieve in front of the child. He did not try to explain murder to a three-year-old.

"Mommy loves you, but she had to go away." That's all he said.

She was barely old enough to stop sucking her thumb. She stood there staring at him without blinking. He thought she took it well.

No one had to tell the Widower how to raise a child by himself. All it took was a strong dose of discipline backed by Scripture. For her next birthday, he gave her a Bible coloring book and a set of crayons. Before her bedtime, he spent a few minutes with the girl. He sat next to her at the kitchen table, telling her the story of each page of the coloring book, then allowing her to choose the crayons to color in the pictures by herself.

"Be sure you only color within the black lines." He slapped her hand lightly if she made a mistake.

Her favorite story was King Solomon. It became annoying when she asked for it every evening. He sighed with irritation and once again told her in language simplified for her age.

"King Solomon was very smart. There were two mommies who wanted the same baby. One was the true mommy, and one was a false mommy. The King said he would cut the baby in two and give each mommy half. The true mommy said she would go away and let the false mommy have the baby, if the King wouldn't cut it. The smart King knew that only a true mommy would leave to save her baby."

In the illustration of the story, King Solomon held the baby with one hand and raised a long knife with the other. The true mommy was on her knees, pleading. The false mommy just waited with closed eyes, not looking. Dinah tried to understand.

"Why did the false mommy want the baby?"

"Because she was a sinner. She was bad."

"Why did the true mommy want to leave the baby?"

"Because she was good."

Dinah was reminded of her own mommy, who often had her eyes closed like the false mommy, because of hurting in her head.

When her father gave permission, Dinah took out her drawing paper and crayons. She tried to copy the coloring book picture of King Solomon, starting with a circle for the baby's head, then attaching an oval for the body. The arms and legs were four lines sticking out of the oval at odd angles. She drew a line through both shapes with a red crayon. Red was for the blood that would come out of the baby if it were cut in half.

If the baby was sliced exactly in the middle, each half would have one of everything except a full mouth: eye, nostril, ear, hand, foot. If the slice was uneven, one half would have all the features and the other half would have none. Sometimes, she drew only a half baby with two dots for eyes on the side of its face. If it were up to her, she would want to be the half with two eyes. She wanted to be able to see when her mommy came back. She wanted to be able to see which mommy it was.

By the time she started school, Dinah gradually took over the housework and cooking, complicated by her father's very high standards. He supervised her work. If the dishes were not stacked correctly in the dishwasher, she had to remove them and re-stack them until he was satisfied. When she took piano lessons, she had to practice her *Etudes* until she did not miss a note.

"If I can be good enough, Mommy will come back. But what if the one who comes back is a false mommy?"

This thought came to her at night when she could not sleep. Very quietly so her father would not hear, she would get out of bed and take her drawing pad over to the nightlight. It helped to make pictures of the two mommies. If a mommy came back to tuck her in, even a false mommy, she would not have to draw her.

When he thought she was old enough, her father told her the truth—her mother had been murdered. She was fifteen by this time. Again, he thought she took it well when she did not cry. Now she knew nothing would bring her mother back. She googled newspaper accounts of the mass shooting. It interested her to read that the coroner performed autopsies on the victims.

She looked up "Autopsy Procedure" on the Internet.

An incision is made beginning at the shoulders that meets at the breast bone and continues vertically down to the pubic bone.

She no longer remembered her mother. The only way she knew what she looked like was from a framed wedding photo hanging in her father's bedroom. In it, her mother wore an elegant white dress. Dinah pictured her being sliced after her death. She tried to draw what she visualized. She drew her mother standing up, smiling on her wedding day, but with her dress ripped and her body cut open from neck to waist. .

Her artistic skills were improving. During her high school years, she kept illustrating the King Solomon story, trying to get it right, crumpling paper after paper of less than perfect drawings. In college, as a fine arts major, she refined her technique, spending months on each canvas. But sometimes, she sliced the canvases with a knife in frustration if they did not turn out the way she wanted. Sometimes, she had the urge to slice herself downward through her torso. She imagined King Solomon nodding his head with approval.

That's crazy thinking. I mustn't....

She knew she shouldn't dwell on such bizarre thoughts. It was better to turn them into art, and then rip them to shreds before anyone could see. She especially did not want her father to see.

After graduation, she obtained a certification in medical illustration, specializing in anatomy of babies who were born with rare congenital or inherited defects. She continued to live with her demanding father after getting a job in that field. Her salary was used to rent a studio. She was gaining a reputation for paintings of huge wailing baby heads above divided newborn bodies on eight-foot canvases. Her work was included in exhibits and had good reviews, but there were few purchases of the horrific, over-sized canvases. No one wanted this kind of art over their fireplace mantel.

Her father remarried. He sold the house and moved to a condo with his new wife. Dinah moved into her studio. He visited her from time to time to watch her paint. He commented on her work.

"A little more crimson for King Solomon's robe. And the eyes are not level."

The subject matter did not disturb him. However distantly, it was backed by Scripture. And it pleased him that his daughter developed a detailed, realistic style, rather than an abstract mess he was sure was a sin.

Her paintings were changing. The split infant was decreasing in size. The two mothers were enlarged. One resembled her mother in the wedding photograph, the other her new step-mother. In a series of paintings, they overlapped with each other, until they were united. In the final painting of the series, they were conjoined twins. Each had half a face—one with an eye on the baby, the other with her eye closed. She stacked these canvases facing backwards when her father visited, in case he disapproved of the way she depicted his two wives.

Her step-mother was polite but distant. Although she did not try to replace Dinah's real mother, her presence made Dinah wonder about women who wanted the children of other women. There was no longer any doubt about true mothers. In certain circumstances, they could love their children enough to give them up. In theory. She could not think of what those circumstances were, but surely they existed.

But false mothers—how could they, how could anyone—bear to see a human baby harmed? Sliced in two? What was wrong with them?

There were women who killed their own infants, and she supposed there were women who killed infants that were not their own. These women were not understandable. When they were sentenced, there was no mitigating circumstance that really explained them. Maybe they were mentally ill or abused as children, but so were many other mothers who did not harm their children. False mothers had it in them to kill a baby or to see one killed. Who knew why?

Then, Dinah discovered she was pregnant after a brief relationship. She did not tell her father while considering an abortion. With her lifestyle, there was no way to fit in a baby. She slept in a corner of her studio, cooking over an electric burner, and sharing a bathroom with other tenants. Poisonous chemicals used for her art were stored on open shelves. Fumes from the oil paints and turpentine were probably unhealthy. It was not a place for a child.

She decided to let her painting hand make the decision about whether to keep the baby. Preparing the canvas, she emptied her mind. She did not want to get into a struggle with her hand. It dipped the brush onto the ivory black paint it squeezed onto the palette. She watched it guide the brush. It was as if it had nothing to do with her. Something went through her directly to her hand, bypassing her will.

Her hand painted an outline of a portrait, coloring book style, in which there were two figures, both herself. She was Queen Solomon, wearing a crown and a judicial robe. On her lap was a newborn girl in a swaddling blanket decorated with tiny pink lambs. Eerily, the baby had her own adult face. The Queen Solomon figure cradled the infant in one arm while her other was raised holding the knife. The Queen's face was unevenly divided: half had two eyes and half had none. The title of the painting was "Queen Solomon Making a Judgment".

When color was added, the painting was her masterwork. It might be purchasable by a museum. Yet, she found herself reluctant to call her agent or her dealer. It revealed an image of herself she was not sure she wanted seen by the public. It was a part of herself that was not understandable.

The painting needed more work. The hand repainted the Queen's face as divided. This time, there was a true mother half and a false mother half. The true mother half had both eyes, while the false half had none. The hand smudged the true mother half. This made the blind false mother half the dominant one.

The drawing revealed the truth to Dinah. The false mother did not see her child. She would swat away the interrupting child and expect it to busy itself with chores. Only when the chores were finished to Dinah's satisfaction would her child be allowed get down her crayons and color.

25. THE RECEPTIONIST

The receptionist at the nursing home had earned the yearly "Most Valued Employee" award for her role in restoring calm after the ten residents had been murdered. The Mayor gave her the award himself. No one was surprised that such a warm and outgoing personality received an honor for her helpfulness during a time of tragedy.

She was very sociable. Besides her job, she belonged to the Sierra Club, the Audubon Society, two book clubs, a rotating gourmet group that cooked meals at each other's houses, and she was active in the Democratic Party. In addition, she was the president of the Single Women By Choice Society. After conditions returned to normal at work, she accepted an invitation for the Society to march in the July 4th parade.

At the next business meeting, the members decided to wear similar costumes during the march. A number of the Single Women by Choice were also celibate by choice. There had been a skirmish between those who wanted to wear all white to celebrate their celibacy and those who wanted to wear all red to celebrate their sexuality. In the end, they chose to wear both.

The Receptionist was one of the celibate by choice members. At forty-five, she was still attractive, with cropped blond hair and regular features. Although she could have had any number of relationships, she refused to date or have sex. It was not for her. Friendships were enough. When she traveled during her annual vacations, it was usually with a local group. She had reservations for a trip to Jerusalem with two friends who had time off when she did, later in the summer.

It was during her travels that she acquired exotic clothing. She kept them in a cedar chest. A dress from India decorated with tiny mirrors and beads. An embroidered peasant blouse from Poland. A hand-knit fisherman's sweater from Ireland. A red boa scarf from somewhere in the Caribbean. And—*aha!*—there was the white linen skirt from Belgium. Perfect for the parade.

She decided to wear all white to signal her celibacy, with just the red boa to comply with the Society's requirement. Her decision to remain celibate was not a recent one. As far back as she remembered, she hated being touched. She endured hand-shakes and hugs, but when someone laid a hand on her, she startled as if she had been burned. Being touched was painful. Often, she stifled a scream. Her mother called her unnatural. She especially did not want to be touched by her mother.

When she was in elementary school, her mother had her evaluated for autism. However, she readily made eye-contact and displayed normal empathy. Her sociability itself ruled out that diagnosis. The evaluator told her mother that her daughter's touch phobia was most likely an inherited personality trait.

"Not from my side," her mother said, stiffly.

Her father was unknown. Her mother had many boyfriends. The inherited trait must have come from her father.

After many years of secret shame, the Receptionist now wore her celibacy like a badge. She proudly spoke of her identity, even in lectures given to the Single Women By Choice Society and to other groups.

"Choosing to be celibate is a rational decision. It does not have to be due to a traumatic sexual history or even a dislike of sex. It can be philosophical or spiritual. It is as deliberate as the decision to become a vegetarian, a pet owner, or an avoider of social media. It is a personal choice and nothing to be embarrassed about."

July 4th was sweltering that year, but the Single Women By Choice Society members gamely marched, carrying their banner and wearing red and white. They were between the South High School Baton Twirlers, in colorful cheer-leader outfits, and a semi-cab pulling a cumbersome comic hero float. The pavement was so hot that the bottoms of the Receptionist's sandals stuck with every step. Perspiration streamed uncomfortably down her shirt. Many of the onlookers stood under umbrellas or grouped under shade trees.

They were nearing a local brewery when three young men banged out the door and began to catcall the twirlers. Clearly, they were drunk. As the twirlers moved ahead, the men noticed the women in the Society. For a moment, they quieted, as if puzzled by these older women with the unintelligible banner. Single By Choice? Were they a bunch of man-haters? Lesbos?

"Hey, Cunts. Wanna fuck?" one yelled out.

The three guffawed loudly and staggered.

As the Receptionist moved a few steps nearer to them, the one who had yelled reached out and grabbed the boa by each end, yanking her closer to him.

"I'm gonna fuck you, bitch," he slurred into her ear.

The women stopped marching. They shouted at him to release the Receptionist. As she struggled, he pulled the boa tighter. She began to choke. Then, in a fast swirl, both the club members and the two friends of the assailant rushed to rescue her. The driver of the semi was running in her direction. Further back, costumed comic heroes were climbing off the float. The onlookers were dragging their astonished children away from the scene. Finally, a motorcycled policeman arrived and ordered the assailant to let her go. The assailant did as he was told. The policeman told him to lay face down on the ground.

The Receptionist fell down next to him. She was having trouble breathing. Possibly, she passed out because the next thing she was aware of was an EMT taking her blood pressure in an ambulance. There was an oxygen tube in each nostril.

"Just try to relax. I'm making sure you are breathing properly. Don't try to talk."

During the next several hours under observation in the emergency room, a policeman came to take a report. She wrote answers to his questions, leaving her bruised larynx undisturbed. Her elderly mother showed up. Society members and coworkers came and went, observing the two visitor rule. Over time, her breathing and blood pressure stabilized. Someone brought a pair of yoga pants to replace the ruined linen skirt.

The emergency room was harder to endure than the memory of the attack during the parade, which seemed faded and unreal. The Receptionist could only recall sketchy moments. The heat. The tightness around her throat. The man's voice saying "I'm gonna fuck you, bitch." The inability to take a deep breath. The crumpled skirt. She did not remember fearing for her life or having any particular emotion.

In the hospital, she was examined by the medical professionals, who held her arm while taking blood, prodded her neck, placed the head of the stethoscope on her chest and back. Her friends patted her arm and kissed her. Only her mother spared her the agony of touch.

For the Receptionist, the assault continued for hours after the choking. She trembled whenever anyone approached her.

When she was discharged with instructions not to spend the night alone, she went to her mother's house and curled up in her old bed. She pulled on a quilt even though it was summer and later kicked it off. She was alternating between icy chills and feverish heat flashes. Far into the night, she stared at the ceiling while shivering, then sweating. Her throat hurt, reminding her of the sore throats and other illnesses of childhood, suffered in the same room. Her mother would try to put her hand on her forehead, but she would bat it away. Then her mother would turn and walk out. Now that the Receptionist was an adult, her mother left her alone.

When she finally fell asleep, she had a nightmare that startled her awake. She could not remember what it was. It was still very dark outside. She lay in bed, waiting with a sense of foreboding, not being able to make a sound—this seemed familiar, although she did not know why. The assailants's words replayed in her mind.

I'm gonna fuck you, bitch.

The next day, she returned to her apartment. She arranged to take several days off from work until her larynx healed. She spent the days as she had in her old bedroom, lying in bed, tossing the blankets on and off. The TV was on a news channel, with the volume turned low. She was unable to concentrate on anything but her own scattered thoughts. She wondered what happened to the boa. Was this what made her a target for the assailant? The bright red material on her white outfit? The assailant had been inebriated. That meant he was not in his right mind. Maybe the red color was enraging the way it was for a bull. What a bull who saw red tried to do was gore the one who enraged him. Sex is a kind of goring, isn't it?

The Receptionist shuddered. Her deepest objection to sex was the pain. She knew she could not tolerate it. Possibly, she could not survive such pain. When she pictured a man entering her, she imagined a bull's hot breath from its enormous flared nostrils, rough hooves scraping at her fragile skin, and an oversized, insistent penis pounding its way into an opening that was too small to accommodate it. She would be split, torn, and left bleeding, dying on the ground as she could have been when the ambulance arrived on the day of the parade. As this terrible vision subsided, she became aware of the twisted sheets beneath her. The pillows had been tossed onto the floor. The blankets lay in a crumbled wad beside her.

She dragged herself out of bed and to the shower. The bedding and her pajamas had to be laundered. She did not recall whether she drank any water that day. No doubt dehydration was partly responsible for her symptoms. And lack of food. She forgot to eat.

It was inexcusable to remain in this condition. She forced herself to put on a clean sweat shirt and sweat pants, make tea, strip the bed, and eat a banana. Her phone contained many texts, emails, and voice mails from friends. Outside her front door, she saw casseroles, flowers, and cards in a pile. She left them there.

The Receptionist would soon force herself to respond to her friends and then return to work. She would put on a mask of sociability. To those who knew her, she would remain the cheerful, outgoing persona who made a rational choice to abstain from relationships and sex. She always believed this was true. Now she understood she had been faking for most of her life. Beneath the cheerful exterior was stark terror. She was sociable to appear more normal than she felt. And her rational choice was based on irrational fear.

The image of the bull popped back again. She shuddered. Then, as if it had been there all along waiting for her to remember, Mr. Bull came into her mind. Mr. Bull. Her mother's boyfriend when she was a child. A big man, larger than most men. Sometimes he grabbed her, leaving bruises on her arm.

"He doesn't know his own strength," her mother would say.

Even more than the memory of the parade, the memory of Mr. Bull was shadowy and scattered. Mr. Bull gripping her arm with his enormous hand. Mr. Bull pushing her away from her mother with force. Mr. Bull red-faced with anger. Mr. Bull bellowing at her.

How terrified she had been of Mr. Bull.

Then he was gone. She never saw him again. She stopped thinking about him. Instead, she thought of other kids and clubs and activities and school work. She built a solid fence of friendships around herself. She did not allow anyone to touch her.

Her assailant at the parade was in jail awaiting sentencing. One day he would be back in the community when he was released. That did not bother her. Instead, she had another worry. Where was Mr. Bull? Was he still in the area? She dropped the mug of tea she had been holding when this occurred to her. Shards flew over the kitchen floor. She left them to look out the window. She needed to see if Mr. Bull was lurking outside of her apartment.

The Receptionist knew she was becoming crazy. It was highly unlikely that a man who must now be in his seventies would have any interest in her. She had simply been the young daughter of his old girlfriend, who sometimes got in the way. He could be a thousand miles away or dead. Surely she would have noticed such a strikingly tall man if he had been stalking her all these years.

Although she prided herself on her capacity for reason, she could not stop herself from looking for Mr. Bull wherever she went. Back at her job in the nursing home, she waited for him to come stomping to the reception desk. In public, she scanned the area to see if a towering figure was approaching. She startled at any loud angry voice, remembering his roar.

Slowly, the memory of the assailant who choked her was replaced by Mr. Bull. It was Mr. Bull who choked her. She was wearing her pretty white dress when he put one of his massive hands around her tiny neck and squeezed. Someone in the background screamed at him to let go.

The Receptionist's larynx healed and in a few days, her voice returned to normal. Anyone who did not know about the parade would have thought she recovered from laryngitis.

But although no medical reason could be found, her throat never stopped hurting.

26. THE RECORDS KEEPER

Every morning, the Records Keeper arose early to see the fox run across her rear lawn. Her yard backed onto a small grove of pines, where, she assumed, the fox found refuge. It returned there just after dawn each day. By then, she had made her coffee and started on the newspaper crossword puzzle while listening to NPR on the radio. She sat at the kitchen table and stared out the window, waiting for the fox.

It was a red fox, but its fur was closer to burnt orange. It was about the size of a small dog. When it turned its head in her direction, she could see its sharp snout and perky ears. On the whole, it looked well-nourished. The pickings of wildlife must have been good in her neighborhood. To have a red fox so close by seemed like an omen. For what she had no idea.

Then, the day came when the fox did not appear. Carrying her coffee mug, the Records Keeper went outside in her white terrycloth bathrobe and slippers, taken from her last hotel stay, and looked around. There on the west side of her house, near the garbage cans, she found the carcass. It was an awful sight. The disemboweled remains of bone and fur were a bloody mess. The eyes in the head stared at her.

One day you will know what it's like....

Horrified, the Record Keeper backed away, spilling the coffee on her robe. She ran back into the house. Quickly, she drank water to stop herself from vomiting. She did not know what to do. How would she ever be able to take the garbage cans to the curb the next day, as was required by the city? She did not think she could bear to see the fox carcass again.

She lived alone since the divorce. She won the house in the settlement. If she were still married, she could have asked Dale to take care of the fox remains. For two seconds, she considered phoning him.

With a brusque shake of her head, she decided against it. The next morning, she would simply use the garden shovel to move the remains into the garbage can. However disturbing, she would manage. Foolishly, she had allowed herself to become captivated by the fox. She forgot that nature has its ugly side. Eat or be eaten. Survival of the fittest. The fox ate mice and rabbits. And probably a coyote ate the fox. A mountain lion might eat the coyote. And a human might shoot the lion. That is what the natural world was like. A chain of ruthless horrors with a mask of beauty.

It reminded her of work. She was a manager of a medical records company that served several nursing homes. It was only efficient because she allowed herself to be overworked by those above her and disliked by those beneath her. The Records Keeper could be more popular if she did not demand eight hours work from those paid for eight hours. She expected the records to meet a certain standard demanded by her superiors. She was not one to tolerate laziness or sloppiness. Let the girls show each other photos of their babies and their puppies on their own time, not during company time.

The Records Keeper worked many hours overtime after there were several murders in one of the client nursing homes. The deaths of ten residents required a burdensome amount of specialized paperwork she would not trust to her staff. After work, she ate a simple supper of cheese, crackers, and wine. She was too tired to cook. Then she watched documentaries on PBS. No longer did she have to share the remote with Dale, who favored dumb crime shows.

"I'm just an ordinary guy. Not smart like you," he used to say. Excuses!

At ten, she went to bed. Now that Dale was gone, she could sleep in the center. She loved having the whole expanse of the bed for herself. For years, she crammed herself onto one side or made sure not to take more than her share of the blankets, but not since the divorce. She was soon asleep.

A noise awoke her. She looked at the clock. It was not even midnight. The noise sounded like weeping. It was high pitched, as if a child were crying. It seemed to be coming from just outside. She could almost believe it was coming from the back yard where she had seen the red fox so often. But more likely it was from a neighbor's house. Or it was an owl. She fell back to sleep. After what seemed like just a few minutes, the alarm was buzzing.

Putting on another robe—not the splattered white one—she went to the garage to get the shovel. Taking a couple of deep breaths to work up her nerve, she opened the side door bit by bit and sidled out. There were the two garbage cans. Now that Dale was gone, only one was half-filled. The other was empty, missing its top. Cautiously, she worked her way around the cans. There was nothing there. She stood the shovel up and leaned on it. Nothing. Not even a stain on the pavement. Had she dreamed up the carcass?

Was it possible that Dale knew it was there and came in the night to dispose of it for her? That was a crazy thought. The Oxy knocked him out for hours. He would have been too sedated to drive over. Unless he forgot to get his pills and careened into one of his agitated spells.

When she met Dale, he was thirty-five years old and already in bad shape. He worked as an aide at one of the nursing homes. Because of the Lexapro, he gained weight and lost his muscular good looks. His back was messed up from high school football and the army. Sciatica pain shot down his leg. His knees, ankles and wrists hurt. Only opioids gave him the relief he needed to be able to work. He had an Oxy prescription for a while, until the VA doctor refused to renew it, and then he bought it on the street.

After they married and began living together, the Records Keeper thought Dale exaggerated his suffering. He gained more weight. It seemed he just wanted to drink beer and play games on his phone. His medical condition was a way for him to wind up on Disability and lie around all day high from Oxy. By their first anniversary, she had lost all patience with him. He depended on her for everything. She did the finances, the cooking, the shopping, the housework.

"It's a good deal for you! I should get sick and let someone else do everything for me."

"I do what I can." This was always his reply.

When she told him she did not love him anymore and wanted a divorce, he wept. Then he took a double dose of whatever it was he had from the streets. Promptly, he fell asleep on the couch. She knew he would sleep on and off for the next twenty-four hours. She took the day off and used the time to rent a furnished apartment and move all of his belongings into it.

When he was awake but still groggy, she drove him there, handed him the key, and left in disgust.

"Whatever made me choose a man who was not only ill, but also almost ten years younger than me?"

She had fooled herself into thinking their age difference and state of health did not matter. Nearing her mid-forties, she had streaks of gray in her hair and crinkles around her eyes. A ring of fat had developed around her waist even though she kept strict control of her weight. Dale had been looking for a mother. She, who never wanted children, had resisted that role. He never gave up trying to get her to take it.

The Records Keeper had already been a caretaker. Her mother was diagnosed with cancer when she was fifteen. Ten years later, her mother died. Halfway through her illness, the new painkiller Oxycontin became available. It greatly reduced her mother's suffering. Toward the end, on a high dosage of the drug, her mother stared at her with dilated eyes.

One day you will know what it's like...

The Records Keeper shuddered. During the last weeks of her mother's life, the Records Keeper developed an itchy rash. Her skin was hardening. She had to get a special ointment from a dermatologist. From that point on, she wore long sleeves that covered the red, scaly eczema on her arms.

Dale was not bothered by it. But if he put his hand on her rash, she did not feel his touch.

After the mangling of the fox, the rash worsened. The Records Keeper had to use extra ointment. It required intense discipline not to scratch. To distract herself, she deep cleaned the house. After work and on weekends, she laundered curtains and tablecloths, dusted, vacuumed, scrubbed, and polished. When she finished the entire house, she began the process again. It was the way a house should be cleaned. Not just once in a while, but repeatedly.

Her sleep was still being interrupted by what sounded like weeping. It was no longer the noise a baby or child made. The sound deepened and became more adult-like. Still, she thought, it was probably an animal. A beagle or a coyote howling.

It made her wonder how Dale was doing. There had been occasions besides the divorce when he wept and mentioned suicide, especially when the VA refused to give him any more narcotics. At the time, she had been glad not to have to tell the doctor that he abused the narcotics, taking them more often than he should. Until he found another source for Oxy, Dale drank more. He was probably an alcoholic as well as an addict.

Looking around at her gleaming, uncluttered home, she imagined the state of the apartment she rented for Dale. He would not care what it was like when he was high.

The itching was worse. When it was unbearable, she scratched and bled. Finally, she had to admit feeling anxious about Dale. What if he had OD'd? How long would it be before his body was discovered? It was not her business. They were divorced. Dale had to take care of himself. If he died, so be it. The newspapers were full of reports on the opioid epidemic. Addicts took drugs laced with fentanyl. Many overdosed. Dale could become one of the statistics.

She paced from room to room, running her fingers over dust-free surfaces. The itching made her agitated. The blood from her scratching was seeping through her sleeves in patches, ruining her shirt. She would not have any peace from the rash if she did not check on her ex-husband. Somehow, his condition, the fox, and the extra paperwork after the murders were connected to the eczema. Such rashes were thought to be stress related.

She drove to his apartment. Using a second key she made when she rented it, she opened the door. The sight that greeted her was what she expected. Disarray, untidiness. Beer cans heaped on furniture. Dishes piled in the sink. A stale smell. Dale was stretched out on the bed. His eyes were closed. He was not dead. She saw his chest moving.

The itching was terrible. She pushed up her sleeves and dug her fingernails into the rash. Blood ran down her arms.

"Dale."

Unexpectedly, she sobbed his name.

His eyes opened half-way. He looks at her fuzzily, as if he had trouble placing her.

"You?"

"Dale." She continued to weep. "Please. Give me an Oxy."

27. THE COOK

Whenever Cosy Spirit shoes went on sale, the Cook rushed to the mall anchor store that carried them. They were one of the few comfortable flats that came in an extra-wide size. Her feet were broad. Bunions had developed, forcing her large toes to slam into the next ones, causing a pile up that looked like a bunch of crooked teeth. Fortunately, she knew her size and did not have to go through the embarrassment of struggling to shove on a new pair in the store.

She was surrounded by slimmer customers who slid their daintier feet into pointy high heels without a problem. The Cook was aware of how she must look to the well-groomed, attractive women who frequented the store, dressed as if they were about to attend an afternoon event with their wealthy husbands. If they noticed her at all, they saw an overweight middle-age woman in baggy sweatpants limping her way through the aisles.

"Too bad," she thought, "Poor people have as much right to be here as rich people."

Now that she was unable to work in the kitchen of the nursing home, because of the PTSD after the murders, she had to economize. She moved to an older trailer park. Her severance check was not enough for a decent place. She was lucky to have put enough aside for the Cosy Spirit shoes that made it possible for her to walk without too much pain.

The pleasant smell of leather pervaded the department. Stylish shoes were displayed on pedestals, like art objects. She picked up one of them and turned it over to see the price. Two hundred dollars. Two hundred dollars? For a pair of shoes? She was appalled and amazed. She guessed that someone in the undeveloped part of the world was paid the equivalent of two dollars to craft them. Shaking her head in disgust, she decided to buy the Cosy Spirits and leave the store.

It was then that she hear the whimper. It came from the next aisle. The Cook peeked around the corner. There was a tiny girl, maybe two years old. She was wearing a pale pink dress, white tights, and white patent leather shoes. Her thumb was in her mouth. As the Cook approached, she stared at her with large dilated eyes. It reminded the Cook of the big-eyed children and puppies painted on black velvet her mother had hanging through the house she owned when she was still alive. Her mother favored these idealized beings over any real puppies and children, and certainly more than she ever had her only daughter.

"Where's your mommy?" The child continued to stare. The Cook glanced around. Surely some woman was in a panic, calling for her child, who wandered away. Maybe the mother or maybe a nanny. But she did not hear or see anyone looking for the child.

"Let's go find your mommy, shall we?" She took the girl's tiny hand in hers.

Obediently, the child walked without resistance, as they made their way to the cashier. The Cook worried the mother might think she was stealing the child, so she quickly guided her around the counter.

"This child appears to be lost."

"Aw." The cashier squatted down in front of the girl. "You come with me. We'll find your mommy for you."

Picking up the child and forgetting to thank the Cook, the cashier walked away with her. The Cook had not yet paid for the shoes. She had to wait until the cashier returned.

With idle time on her hands, she thought she would look around. Next to the shoe department was an area of fancy dresses. Most were heavily sequined, the kind performers might wear on stage. The prices were astonishing, often in the thousands. In the middle of the department was a small stage containing two headless mannequins, one seated and one standing. The seated one wore a gold lame dress that opened on the side, revealing her slender crossed legs. The standing one had on a silvery dress made of the same flowing material, coursing down to her ankles. Both held out their arms with their elongated fingers outstretched, as if they were singing.

She was reminded of an art museum. So many gorgeous colors and fabrics. Soft music was playing in the background. A faint, agreeable perfume scent was in the air. A rosy glow lit the area. She was mesmerized, not daring to touch anything other than the price tags.

She was startled to hear a woman's voice over a hidden loud speaker system.

"There is a lost child waiting in the customer service department."

The voice was soothing, as if a hostess were saying dinner was served or an airline stewardess was asking for one's choice of beverage. The Cook imagined the mother, who was probably immersed in shopping, hearing the voice and suddenly realizing the lost child must be hers, then hurrying to reclaim her.

Feeling more at ease, she decided to return to the shoe department where the cashier was surely present again. Although she thought she walked back the way she came, she found herself not in the shoe department, but in a resort-wear section. Once more, she found herself spell-bound by the colors and, in this instance, bright floral designs. She noticed there were bikinis in all sizes, even her size—extra-large. She wondered why a woman as large as she was would expose her rolls of fat and hanging flesh to anyone. There was also XXS, or extra extra small, meaning some very underweight women were willing to show off their skeletal torsos.

"There is a lost child waiting in the customer service area."

That was the second announcement. Either another child had been lost or the mother of the first one had not claimed her. The Cook felt obligated to find out what happened to the little girl she had discovered. But first she should pay for the Cosy Spirits. Only they were not in her hands anymore. She must have lain them down somewhere. After she went to Customer Service, she would return to the shoe department to pick up another pair.

Customer Service was probably on the first floor. She could see the up escalator. The down one must be close by it. While searching, she found herself among a substantial number of fur coats. They were jammed together on racks, giving the impression of lush fur-lined walls. There were minks—did anyone still wear mink? Also leopard, something shiny and black, and a yellow-white that looked like polar bear. The Cook was shocked. Were such coats even legal? She dared not look at the prices.

Finally, she found a saleswoman who told her that Customer Service was on the second floor and pointed the way to the down escalator. The Cook tried to remember if she were on the third floor or the fourth floor. She decided to get off one floor down.

When she did, she saw that the entire floor was devoted to linens and household goods. Weren't these on the top floor in most such stores? Had she taken the up escalator by mistake? She looked around for some sign indicating which floor she was on, but saw none.

She was very tired. And her feet were swollen and hurting even in her old Cosy Spirits. She could not be on her feet this long without pain. Her energy was waning. Limping through the aisles, she looked in vain for a chair. Meanwhile, she passed displays of linens on sale that cost more than her entire severance check.

"There is a lost child waiting in the Customer Service Department."

Why didn't the mother claim her child? Perhaps she was in a fitting room and could not hear the announcement. That gave her an idea. If she could find a fitting room, she could sit down, maybe even take her shoes off for a few minutes and massage her feet. There would not be fitting rooms in Housewares. She had to go to another floor.

Back on the escalator, this time she found herself descending into the Men's Department, which, like Housewares, took up an entire floor. There were fitting rooms there for men only. Spotting a check-out counter, she approached the cashier and asked where the nearest restroom might be. She could sit there, if nowhere else. He directed her back up to Housewares. Fortunately, the up escalator was in sight.

Finally, she found the women's restroom. Exhausted, she went into a stall, closed the door, and wearily sat down. She must have dozed off, for how long she could not tell.

She was awakened by the voice of what sounded like the same woman who made the lost child announcements.

"The store will be closing in twenty minutes. Thank you for shopping with us."

The Cook jolted up. She had twenty minutes to find the shoe department and purchase the Cosy Spirits. If she missed the sale, she might have to wait a whole year for another chance, and the old pair she had on was deteriorating. She would have to give up finding out about the child, who was no doubt either in the hands of a parent or the police by now, and quickly find the shoes.

Retracing her steps as best she could, she found the down escalator. She noted in passing that there were lines at the check-out counters. Once again, when she stepped onto the escalator, she did not know which floor she was on or where to get off. Where were the directories? Why weren't they located at the escalator exits?

Elegant-looking customers walk briskly and purposefully, as if the store were as familiar to them as their own homes. No one appeared to be confused. Many carried purchases in shopping bags decorated with the store logo. No one look her way. She was too intimidated to ask any of them for directions.

Another announcement:

"The store will be closing in ten minutes. Thank you for shopping with us."

With dismay, she understood that the chance of finding the shoe department in time was diminishing. Unless there was a store lay-out she could see on-line on her phone. But where was her purse? The strap was not hanging from her shoulder. In a panic, she realized it must still be where she hung it, on the door hook in the stall in the restroom. If no one had gone in there after her and taken it to Customer Service, or, worse yet, stolen it.

Running as best she could to the up escalator, she ascended to Housewares again. She could not recall the exact location of the restroom. Was it nearer the linens or the kitchenware items? The cashiers were all busy with the remaining customers. Another announcement came saying the store would close in five minutes.

Finally, she found the restroom. A staff person was inside, mopping.

"I left my purse here. Have you seen it?"

"Yes, Ma'am. I gave it to my supervisor. It should be in Customer Service."

"And where is that?"

"Second floor, Ma'am."

"Could you please take me?"

"Sorry, Ma'am. I'm not allowed to leave my post. But the elevator is just to the right. Get off at the second floor, Ma'am. Customer Service is across from there, on the other side of the floor."

Thanking the staff person, the Cook left and found the elevator. The second floor button was clearly marked. Slowly, the elevator went down, stopping on what seemed to be the second floor. Or was it?

It opened to a large area of perfume and make-up counters. Most anchor stores had these on the first floor, near the store entrances. Nevertheless, she rushed toward the opposite end, looking for a Customer Service sign. Instead, she saw the opening to the mall to which the anchor store was attached. A gate had descended, closing off the opening, as the announcer repeated:

"The store is closed. The store is closed. Thank you for shopping with us."

Knowing she would have to leave, she approached a woman in a fine linen suit.

"Could you please tell me how to get to the exit?"

"The nearest one is next to Petites, over there." The woman pointed. "Is that where you are parked?"

"I guess so," the Cook stammered.

She followed the woman's directions. She thought if she could get to her car, a mall security vehicle could help her get in and start it. If they believed it was her car, since her identification was in her purse. Perhaps if she described the contents of the glove compartment, they would know she was the owner. This was a long-shot. She was terrified of being locked in the store for the night. She was having trouble breathing. She had to go outside and catch her breath. If she got enough air in her lungs, she could figure out what to do next.

She exited the store through the door next to the Petite area just before a cashier came with keys to lock it. Outside, she leaned against the building and tried to control her breathing. Her hands shook, and she felt chilled. If only she had a sweater. It was already dark out. It had to be around nine, the store closing time.

Nothing looked familiar. Cars were leaving the lot, but many still remained. Hers was an older model silver Honda Civic. There were many silver Honda Civics, all looking alike, even among the few vehicles remaining in the lot.

She began walking up and down aisles. If she had her phone, she could have used GPS to locate her car. Without it, she could only walk through the vast lot on this side of the store, and then through the lots on the other two sides. Without a purse or shopping bag, wearing perspiration-stained sweat clothes, with body odor she could detect herself, and with a limp that was becoming more pronounced, she had the appearance of a vagrant.

Nevertheless, what could she do but keep hunting for her car? As the overhead lights dimmed, she trudged through the emptying parking lot, stretching out on all sides like a vast concrete desert with no oasis in sight.

28. THE GROUNDSKEEPER

There were two things that tormented the Groundskeeper: his sister, Dora, had been raped at gunpoint by his ex-friend, Buddy, who was serving a long sentence for it in the Federal Corrections Facility in Terre Haute, Indiana. And his friend at work, the Maintenance Man, Sid, had gone crazy and shot ten residents before a cop killed him. The Groundskeeper imagined that, in some strange way, what happened to his sister and the residents were his fault.

Like, if he had not fucked Buddy's girlfriend a while back, Buddy would not have raped Dora. And if he had told his boss that Sid was acting weird, like he was high or something, the murders would not have happened.

These thoughts made him want to slam himself against the wall. He wanted to hear the loud crack of his head thwacking, like it used to when one of his mom's old boyfriends got rowdy. That's what she would call it—"rowdy."

"Now don't you get rowdy with him, Patrick. He's just a boy," she would say.

The Groundskeeper moved back to his mom's house after moving back home from Wichita, where he briefly lived. It had not worked out. He had not seen Dora yet. Since her time in the psych hospital, she stayed in her room. The door was shut tight. When the Groundskeeper put his ear to the door, he did not hear anything. His mind seemed to fill in the silence with Dora's voice.

"Why did you let this happen to me? Why?"

The Groundskeeper did not know what to say. He had been out of town at the time of the rape. But that did not seem like a good excuse. He should have killed Buddy. He should have killed Sid. Now it was too late. Buddy was in prison. Ten old people were dead. Sid was dead. And Dora was as good as in solitary, in their own house.

The Groundskeeper's old job at the nursing home was waiting for him. His boss kept calling, asking if he was ready to return to work mowing the lawn, watering, and weeding. But he didn't have the energy yet. Instead, he watched cartoons on TV and helped his mother carry groceries in from the car.

She was single at the moment. That put her in a bad mood. She was also fuming about what had happened to Dora.

"I hope Buddy is raped in the ass every day inside. That's what he deserves. I hope some big black gang holds him down and take turns. I hope they rip his asshole apart."

That night, the Groundskeeper took five dollars from his mother's purse. She must have just cashed her maintenance check from her last divorce. He left the rest. He only wanted enough to go to a bar and get a beer. It was a long walk, but he did not take enough for bus fare. That was okay. It was nothing compared to what happened to Dora.

It was still early when he got there. The bar was almost empty. The Groundskeeper ordered the beer. He would have to make it last. Further along the bar, a woman who looked like an old whore was drinking whiskey. She was probably fifteen years older than he was. She smiled at him. He was not really interested, but there was no one else to talk to. He moved to the seat next to her.

"Hey," he said.

"You look sweet. What's ya name?" Her hair was a flat black from the kind of cheap home dye kit his mother used when she was hunting for a new guy. Her eyes were framed by thick black false upper and lower lashes.

He told her his name was Buddy. He did not want to give her his real name.

"What'ya drinking, Buddy? Can I buy ya another?"

The Groundskeeper did not object. This is what he had been hoping for. Someone to buy him more beer.

"You look young enough to be my son. Can I call ya son?"

"Whatever." For some reason, he did not mind. She moved her chair closer and put a hand on his leg. He did not mind that either.

"I'm broke." He did not want her to give a false impression.

"That's okay. I'll take care of ya, son."

For the next two hours, they sat together as the bar slowly filled. A combo warmed up on the little stage. The Groundskeeper wound up telling the old whore about Sid. She put a compassionate arm around him. He leaned into her. When the combo played a slow number, they rose to dance. He clung to her and swayed to the music. They remained in a clutch when the tempo picked up, even though others were frenzied around them. Then they returned to the bar. She matched him shot for shot. The music was too loud for talking.

She put her lips to his ear. Maybe she was saying she hoped Buddy would be raped in the ass every day in prison. She hoped some big black gang would hold him down and take turns. She hoped they would rip his asshole apart.

The bar was a popular one because of the live music. It was at capacity by now. There was hardly room to move. Yet, over where the booths were, there was some kind of action. The Groundskeeper saw people jammed into a rough circle. The crowd was egging someone on. They were chanting, "Dance. Dance." Someone or something was banging on the floor, causing the room to shake. Suddenly, the crowd shrieked, then quieted. The Groundskeeper stood on tip toe. Someone yelled "Stand back! Give him air!" As the circle widened, he had glimpses of a large man lying on the floor, on his back. Clearly, he was injured. The bartenders ran over. One of them squatted down, over the injured person.

The old whore and others around them asked each other what happened? Was someone hurt? Had someone fallen? Did anyone call 911? The house lights came on. The combo stopped playing. The musicians were craning their necks to see what was going on.

Pretty soon, two EMTS pushed through the crowd. A short time later, the injured man was removed by stretcher. A siren grew fainter as an ambulance rushed away. The lead singer bent to the mic and asked everyone to pray for the injured man. Then he asked if there were any requests. People yelled out their preferences. The musicians began playing. The house lights dimmed. Everyone returned to drinking and dancing.

The whore tugged at the Groundskeeper. She wanted to dance. He pushed her away. It was not right. Someone had been hurt. Dora had been hurt. No one should be dancing or having fun. He had to find out who hurt Dora. He remembered. It was Buddy. Buddy hurt Dora. An ambulance had come to take her to the hospital. He had to find Buddy and rip his asshole apart. Over where the booths were, he saw someone who looked like Buddy from the back. He raced across the room, shoving people aside, and jumped onto Buddy's back. Both of them went down. He landed a punch in Buddy's face. Blood sprang from his nose.

Then he felt himself being lifted upward. He flailed. Three men who must have been Buddy's friends grabbed him. They slammed him into the wall. He heard the sound of his head thwacking. They slammed him again, harder. One of them got him in a neck hold while the other two lay into him. The crowd was chanting "Fight! Fight!." The security guy appeared. He threw Buddy's friends off of the Groundskeeper.

In the background, he heard the old whore saying "Now don't ya get rowdy with him." Or something like that.

The security guy was telling him to leave the bar. The old whore took him by the arm and led him toward the exit. Buddy's friends were already out there, but a patrol car was parked in front, so they walked away. The old whore pulled the Groundskeeper in the opposite direction.

Somehow, he was on a couch. The old whore was washing the cuts on his face with one hand and holding an ice pack on his eye with the other. He did not know where he was or how he got there. He sat up.

"Easy now, son. Let Mama help ya."

He lay back down. He was very sleepy. He shut his eyes.

Dora was bending over him with a wash cloth and an ice pack.

"Why did you let this happen to me? Why?"

"I was in Wichita. I didn't know."

"It's your fault I was hurt. Don't say you didn't know. He was Mama's boyfriend, and you didn't stop him. Now you have to be punished. He'll punish you. Just don't tell anyone." Her voice was high pitched, like a child's.

The Groundskeeper's eyes sprang open. It was daylight. He was still on the couch. The old whore was asleep in a chair beside him. He could see the place was a one-room mess. Probably, the couch folded out into a bed. A kitchen area spread across one wall. Dishes overflowed the sink. Piles of clothes and junk covered surfaces in the rest of the room. There was a sour smell. He did not care. He had a headache. He closed his eyes. He did not want to move.

He fell asleep again. This time he had a nightmare. Someone much bigger than him was about to beat him. Whoever it was had a stick or a thick dowel in his hand to beat him with. He could not see the person's face. The hand with the dowel was raised to strike. He jerked awake. Twice more he fell asleep and saw a hand with a dowel raised to begin beating him. But each time he awoke before the blow landed.

The last time he awoke after the third dream fragment, he already started to forget what it had been about. He knew he had dreamed. There was an object in the dream he could not make out. What was it? He was in pain as if he had been beaten. He remembered. He had been beaten in the bar the night before. By the friends of Buddy.

They had stopped him from killing Buddy or someone who looked like him, but he failed to stop Buddy from hurting Dora.

"You haven't been punished enough. You didn't stop him." It was Dora talking to him in his head.

Yet Dora was not there. She was back in her room with the door shut. The old whore was there, still asleep. Quietly, he stood up and made his way to the door. Outside, the sun hammered at his scalp. One of his eyes was swollen shut. It hurt to walk. He limped up the street. Despite looking in every pocket, he found no money for the bus. He would have to get home on foot.

His punisher was waiting there. Because he did not stop Sid. And because he did not protect his sister. Or maybe it was because he did. He tried to. He said he would tell if it did not stop. Didn't he? The punisher was waiting for him. The punisher was holding the dowel, preparing to inflict the punishment. It would be long and hard.

The Groundskeeper walked as fast as he could. It would be worse if he kept the rowdy one waiting.

VII. THE NEXT TIME

29. THE COPYCAT

It's lit!

This guy shot up a nursing home, killing zombies. I'm weak! Hondo P, he must have been salty to do something so straight fire, except not in a school.

The boy was in his room, watching the action on his phone. His eyes blazed with excitement. Lying on his stomach on his bed, he stroked his newly shaved head while watching reporters interview whomever they could corral near the cordoned off nursing home. Relatives of victims were beginning to make their way, numbly or hysterically—the hysterical ones were the *Gucciest,* he thought—to the building.

His mom hated his shaved head.

"Your beautiful golden curls! How could you!" She banged a pot down on the gas stove to make her point before snapping the range knob to high. Her own hair was a thin, dull brown.

You can just sip tea. Shaved heads are savage.

The reporter said the shooter had been killed by a police officer. There was no indication of a second shooter. Nevertheless, caution was being urged. People in the neighborhood—his neighborhood—should remain in their homes. Family members of the surviving residents were cleared to enter the facility to calm their parents or spouses.

Savage. The shooter let himself be shot. No prison for him. That's lit boots.

The boy imagined the thoughts that went through the shooter's head. How he was going to waste everyone he could because they were just old people who should be dead anyway. There should not be nursing homes. Anyone that ancient should be offed instead of taking up space on earth.

Like, there's not even enough for the rest of us, the ones who are still woke.

His Papaw, for instance, who had Parkinson's or something. He did not even move or talk, lying frozen in his bed throughout the boy's middle school years. In the same nursing home in the news now. How the boy hated the Sunday visits to that piss-stinking place. His mother dragged him there with threats to take his phone away if he did not go. What for? His Papaw did not recognize him. And his mother spent every day there anyway. Like, she was never home.

Now that Papaw was dead and his mother was around more, she thought she had the right to tell him not to shave his head. He was fifteen. He could do what he wanted.

No one is going to be the boss of me anymore.

At least his father let the boy alone. He taught in the college, sociology or something. He was what his mother called an "absent-minded professor." *Whatever.* All he talked about was college stuff, how he was treated unfair, not given what he deserved like a good office or a promotion. *So salty.* He did not notice the boy unless the boy irritated him with his loud music or a need for a ride. Maybe he forgot he had a wife and kids, even though they were right in front of his unfocused eyes at the dinner table. He shoveled the food in, not caring whether he was eating meatloaf or chicken, then went back to his office on campus. That is, if he bothered to come home to eat at all instead of grabbing a bite at the college cafeteria.

Not that he could imagine talking to his father about possibly being *avocado.* He was not sure. He liked girls and all, but was turned on by older *swole* guys, like his PE teacher, Mr. Burk. A couple weeks before, he hunted in the basement for his Pearl Roadshow Beginner's Drum set, unused since he did not have enough interest to keep practicing. There it was, in the corner, covered with a white sheet. He took the drumsticks back to his room and stuck one up his ass while picturing his teacher. It was *GOAT,* sort of. He secretly threw away his BVDs in the outside garbage bin because of the blood. But did it prove anything?

Like his father would want to know.

The one he really hated was his sister, who was a year older. Unless he loved her. She had a *dank bod.* He tried not to look when she walked around the house in a bra and panties.

"For God's sake, get dressed, will you?" His mother screamed, eyeballing his sister with a disgusted expression.

"Leave me alone, already." She screamed back.

There would be a roaring commotion. The boy escaped to his room, closed his door tight, and stuck on his noise-cancellers. He lay on his bed, staring at the stains on the ceiling from an upstairs water leakage. They looked like angry faces. He made out the eyebrows slanting furiously toward the noses and the turned down mouths.

His mind drifted to the PE teacher, Mr. Burk. The boy was way too *snack,* with his skinny-ass frame, child muscles, and small dick, for Mr. Burk. No way would the teacher think him *thicc,* if he thought of him at all. If he imagined kissing Mr. Burk or touching him, the angry-looking stains stared down mercilessly.

But if he tried to imagine kissing a girl instead, he would be jolted into realizing it was his sister. She was the only girl he had ever seen half-dressed, except in the movies. And once or twice, he saw her coming out of the house's single full bathroom undressed. She did not seem to care if he looked. He was as invisible to her as he was to their father, just another piece of furniture, like a chair or desk. Why care if a chair saw you naked?

On his phone screen, the reporter announced the identity of the nursing home shooter: Sidney Stone. He had been the Maintenance Man at the facility, and the location of his death was in the back yard of the building. The ten residents he shot had been in the Hospice section, also in the rear. They were pronounced dead by the Coroner. No names of the victims would be released until the relatives were informed.

Sidney Stone. *Maybe a swole guy like Mr. Burk.*

He daydreamed that Sidney Stone, who he thought of as looking like Mr. Burk, had texted him before the shooting.

Yesterday 8:47 p.m.: I've especially chosen you to join me on my mission. Meet me in the nursing home parking lot. We'll have us some fun.

Secretly, he would have left his home. A crisp breeze would have raised goosebumps on his bare arms. He would have jogged to the parking lot just as Sidney Stone pulled into a space. Because of the darkness, it would have been hard to see him in his black outfit and ski mask. His gun would have glinted, a signal to the boy to approach. Not a word would have been needed. Sidney Stone would point the way, making sure the boy was following.

Once in the building, they would have made their way stealthily to the rear section. Sidney Stone would have led the boy into the first room and shown him how to shoot an old person. Then he would have handed the gun to the boy and supervised while the boy shot the other nine. When the job was done, Sidney Stone would have nodded at the boy with approval. Then he would have put his hand on the boy's shoulder. Together, they would have walked out the back door to await their fate.

There was a bulletin. The body of Mary Stone had been discovered, dead from a bullet in her head. Sidney Stone murdered his mother before his shooting rampage. Momentarily, this confused the boy. Killing your mother—was that a test? Or was it *extra?* Did Sidney Stone want him to kill his mother?

The boy was a loner. He had no friends. The kids at school bullied him for being so skinny and girlish. He was almost pretty, especially when his golden curls circled his delicate face. He was teased for seeming to be straight and not coming out. He was teased for seeming to be gay, yet refusing to join the LBGTQ *squad*. He had no one to ask about what he imagined Sidney Stone might want of him.

But he was *thirsty* for whatever Sidney Stone might have given him, what Mr. Burk could still give him.

In his mind, he spoke to Sidney Stone.

"What should I do?" They would both be in his bedroom, lying together in his bed on their backs. The ceiling stains watched.

"Prepare yourself. Keep your head shaved."

"What else?"

"Only black clothing."

"Anything else?"

"Get a firearm."

"And then?"

"You will know."

Papaw had a gun collection that was still in Mamaw's house, locked in a gun cabinet. The boy knew where the key was kept, in a cigar box on

Papaw's dresser. Anytime, he could get it. As invisible as he was, there was no one to stop him.

His door opened a crack. It was his sister, fresh from her fight with their mother.

"Hey, idiot. What are you doing in there? Something gay?"

Now she was looking for a fight with him. Their mother had not been enough for her, apparently.

"Shut the fuck up. Go *smash* someone and leave me alone."

"Aw, did someone *curve* you? Is that why you're always in a bad mood?

"Close the fucking door."

"Okay. I was just trying to be friendly." The door shut.

The stains on the ceiling had a new expression, maybe from more water leaking. The eyebrows had straightened, and a corner of the mouths had twisted upward. They looked like they were jeering. Were they mocking him?

The thought came to him that they were all mocking him—his sister, the kids at school, even Mr. Burk. He'd show them! He knew how to use Papaw's guns. He knew where the school was.

But first, he would use the drum sticks. This time, he would imagine Sidney Stone shoving both way up his ass, forcefully. It would be *savage.*

30. THE OBSESSED

My eternal love forever began at a poetry slam in high school. Shyly, you approached the stage at one end of the old school gym, the veneered hardwood floor creaking beneath your feet. Some folding chairs had been set up for the few students expected to attend. At the other end, a couple of boys were practicing shots at the basketball hoop. A teacher rose from her chair on stage and called your name.

"Patrick McGee will be reading 'Eternal Love.' Patrick?"

The teacher sat down, and you took the center-stage position. You pushed your hair away from your eyes and recited without reading, looking upward toward the florescent-lighted ceiling.

"Without clock or compass

Is my love for you."

Hearing those words was a jolt, as if I had been slapped hard. I actually put my hand to my stinging cheek. In that moment, I began a deep love for you. As your words implied, my love was beyond time and space. It pre-existed both of us and would endure after our deaths. This was a truth I recognized right away. It was not a discovery. It was a re-discovery of something I always knew but never understood.

That was the first time I saw you or heard your name on this earthly plane. You, like others, probably already noticed me before hurriedly averting your eyes. Unless it was to laugh at me and call me by my odious nick-name, "The Gimp." Or to stick a foot out to trip me and make me fall, the more humiliating the better, as when my shirt rode up, exposing my pale fatty stomach.

On this earthly plane, I limped badly because of scoliosis and my one leg being shorter than the other.

"Would you put on your god-damned leg-brace," my mother yelled.

I hated wearing it. It was a cheap kind that rubbed my skin raw. And it drew even more negative attention my way. Each school day, I took it off in a bathroom stall and left it in my locker.

That was thirty years ago. Today, we are both forty-five. Over time, my love for you has only grown. I never married or had a lover. I never had a date. No one ever kissed me. Yet, I can imagine your naked body, with lush black hair covering your limbs, chest, and back, like the pelt of a sleek black cat. Although I have never seen a male member, I picture your manliness with the desire of woman-in-love. Even though in middle age you have gained weight and lost hair, I still see you as the beautiful boy reading his poem on a high school stage.

You are what has kept me going through years of cruel surgeries, chronic pain, and isolation. Disability checks are my only source of income. It makes no difference. My needs are simple. I live with my aging mother and still sleep in my childhood bed. I have a few items of clothing, a few books, a laptop, a small TV. They suffice because I have you, dear Patrick. Not on this earthly plane, but in eternity, I know you are mine.

I have kept track of you through the years. You went to a university and earned an MFA in creative writing. You teach English in the same high school we both attended. You published two books of poetry (which I own and have memorized). You are married to a woman named Cindy (no matter!) and have two children. That is all very temporary. We have the infinite ahead of us. Whether or not you ever come to love me, my love is strong enough to bind us together forever.

Here is an example of my love. Last week, I saw you through the window of a coffee-shop. I entered without looking your way, placed an order, then took a seat in the back where I watched you. When you left, I moved to your table before it could be bussed. There lay some treasures. A wadded paper napkin I shoved into my pocketbook. The fork you used to eat your snack and the spoon for your coffee. Both of these I put in my mouth and licked. A bonus was a small amount of coffee puddled in the bottom of your mug. I finished it, hoping I was ingesting a tiny amount of your saliva—of you. Similarly, I placed the bits of your leftover cake on my tongue. I was happy for the rest of the day, knowing some small bits of you were within me.

My joy may have been the cause of the onset of the fever I have had for the past few days. I am very sensitive, and any overstimulation can weaken my immune system. My wearied mother had to drive me to the chilly emergency room. It irritated her because of the no smoking policy in the hospital. So many hours without a cigarette there.

I must have been delirious because I could distinctly hear your voice;
Without clock or compass
Is my love for you.

In my fevered state, I first imagined that you were saying those words to me. But then, I had a vision. In it you were saying those words, not to me as I fervently wished, but to your young daughter. She would be fourteen or fifteen now, and a student at our old high school. I had seen her many times while sitting in my parked car across the street from the school, hoping to catch a glimpse of you. You drove into the staff parking lot in the morning. Often, your daughter rode with you. Sometimes, you placed a hand on her shoulder while you both walked to the entrance. It made my own shoulder ache.

While I waited for you to come out of the school at the end of the day, I saw her occasionally in the school yard. She was a popular girl with many friends. With her long straight back and athlete's build, she played volley ball and was on the girl's basketball team. I watched you watch her at practices.

Never had I reacted to her one way or another. But in the emergency room, before being admitted, I ground my teeth with loathing. Just as my love for you had been instantaneous years ago, my hatred for your daughter stunned me with its terrible sudden force. Through the night in my hospital bed, I twisted the sheets and alarmed the staff with my rising blood pressure. The call bell from the vital signs machine kept going off. It was an omen. It meant your daughter was intolerable. She was the one making me ill.

Now I have been discharged on three antibiotics. I am still required to take medication for my other conditions and for the side-effects from the medications: weight gain, constipation, suicidal thoughts. Often, I wish I could die to be out of my misery and with you instead.

But first, I must do something about your daughter. Not long ago, several people were shot in a nursing home in our town. It reminds me of

Sandy Hook and Parkland. I now understand mass shooters, especially school shooters. One or more of the students they killed may have had something that really belonged to the shooter. It might not have been apparent on this earthly plane. You could tell by the reactions of the parents and friends who were shown weeping on TV that the murdered children had been good-looking, popular, loved. No one asked if the love had been stolen from someone who may have been damaged or unattractive.

This has to be corrected. A plan is forming in my mind.

Fortunately, even though he died ten years ago, my mother never disposed of my father's gun collection. I am used to rifles from accompanying him during hunting season. But I never tried the pride of his collection: pistols fitted with Glock magazines. I will take one from the gun cabinet and familiarize myself with it. I may soon need it.

I am now in the habit of parking across the street from the school with one or more of the loaded pistols. When the right time comes, I will end this long wait. I will punish the daughter of my beloved. He will forgive me, knowing that chastising her was necessary. Together, we will leave this earthly plane and begin our time as one, "without clock or compass."

ABOUT THE AUTHOR

Carolyn Geduld is a mental health professional in Bloomington, Indiana.
Her fiction has appeared in numerous literary journals and anthologies.

NOTE FROM THE AUTHOR

Word-of-mouth is crucial for any author to succeed. If you enjoyed *Take Me Out the Back*, please leave a review online—anywhere you are able. Even if it's just a sentence or two. It would make all the difference and would be very much appreciated.

Thanks!
Carolyn

Thank you so much for reading one of our **Crime Fiction** novels.
If you enjoyed the experience, please check out our recommended
title for your next great read!

Caught in a Web by Joseph Lewis

"This important, nail-biting crime thriller about MS-13 sets the
bar very high. One of the year's best thrillers."
–BEST THRILLERS